Lee Read is a qualified bricklayer working as a building control surveyor. He holds a BSc (Hons) in Building Engineering and a PhD in the Built Environment. Alongside his surveying job, on a part-time basis, Lee has worked as a funding assessor for the E.U., an occasional university lecturer, and until 2023, he was a corporal in the RAF Police. Lee is a Fellow of the CABE, a Fellow of the ICWCI and a Fellow of the ILM. He has four adult sons and twin grandsons. He lives on a fruit farm where he produces bottled fruit juices.

Dedicated to my mother, Dawn Read

Lee Read

BEYOND THE TIME FRAME

Austin Macauley Publishers™
LONDON • CAMBRIDGE • NEW YORK • SHARJAH

Copyright © Lee Read 2024

The right of Lee Read to be identified as author of this work has been asserted by the author in accordance with sections 77 and 78 of the Copyright, Designs and Patents Act 1988.

All rights reserved. No part of this publication may be reproduced, stored in a retrieval system, or transmitted in any form or by any means, electronic, mechanical, photocopying, recording, or otherwise, without the prior permission of the publishers.

Any person who commits any unauthorised act in relation to this publication may be liable to criminal prosecution and civil claims for damages.

This is a work of fiction. Names, characters, businesses, places, events, locales, and incidents are either the products of the author's imagination or used in a fictitious manner. Any resemblance to actual persons, living or dead, or actual events is purely coincidental.

A CIP catalogue record for this title is available from the British Library.

ISBN 9781035864218 (Paperback)
ISBN 9781035864225 (ePub e-book)

www.austinmacauley.com

First Published 2024
Austin Macauley Publishers Ltd®
1 Canada Square
Canary Wharf
London
E14 5AA

I would like to thank Steven L Gibbs, a man who claims to have actually travelled back in time, for sending me the plans on how to construct my own time portal.

Table of Contents

Chapter 1: Malcolm	11
Chapter 2: A Step into the Past	18
Chapter 3: Reality After All	33
Chapter 4: The Sting	45
Chapter 5: Things Go from Bad to Worse	50
Chapter 6: The Enemy Within	55
Chapter 7: A New Life Beckons	63
Chapter 8: The First Mistake	73
Chapter 9: Tying up Loose Ends	80
Chapter 10: A Meeting of Minds	89
Chapter 11: A Case of Mistaken Identity	101
Chapter 12: Roman Makes a Decision	115
Chapter 13: Roman Alerted	126
Chapter 14: Roman Reunited	131
Chapter 15: A Race Against Time	142
Chapter 16: Mick Takes Control	156
Chapter 17: Mick Comes Clean	165
Chapter 18: Randolph	176
Chapter 19: A Fish out of Water	183
Chapter 20: Dream Big, Dream Bigger	194
Chapter 21: George Climbs the Ladder	202
Chapter 22: All's Well That Ends Well	217

Chapter 1
Malcolm

Malcolm lived in a flat. It was a small flat, but it was all that he could afford since he had split up with his wife. She had kept the council house, and Malcolm agreed to move out on condition that his eleven-year-old son came to stay with him at the weekends. Roman was Malcolm's only child. The flat had one bedroom, one bathroom, a kitchen, a dining area and lounge, all in the other room. The settee in the lounge doubled up as his bed when his son Roman came to stay at the weekends, as his own bed was given over to his son to sleep in. The flat was on the ground floor of a run-down, four-story housing complex in a lively area of Oxford City. The front door opened onto a communal corridor, which served seven other flats on that floor. Malcolm didn't know his neighbours and preferred to keep it that way. Some of his neighbours were rowdy and loud, especially when they came back from a night out drinking, and Malcolm was secretly scared of the bigger, noisier men.

Malcolm was a single, unassuming man of average build and height. He was short-sighted and wore spectacles for most of the things that he did. He was openly rubbish at most things physical but was good with electronic items. He worked for himself as a computer and mobile phone repairman. The business wasn't great, but it paid the rent on his flat, and the monthly social security benefit topped up his wages and paid for his weekly shopping and utility bills. Malcolm didn't have to pay maintenance for his son, as he and his ex-wife split the cost of Roman's upbringing as and when something new was needed, and he didn't have to contribute to his ex-wife's finances, as her new man was taking care of that. Malcolm was forty years old, and he had lived with his parents in Banbury, Oxfordshire, until he was twenty-eight.

He had met Roman's mother then, moved out of his parents' house and in with his girlfriend, and fathered a child, all in the space of one year. He got married the following year and lived his unassuming life until a few months previous, when out of the blue, he was told by his wife that their marriage was over and that he would have to move out. Although this came as a shock, he didn't protest. Malcolm was all for the quiet life, and his wife could become aggressive or physical if he argued with her. He simply found alternative accommodation that was within his budget, packed his belongings, and moved out.

It was a Sunday afternoon, and Malcolm had been on a webcam call with a customer whose electronic tablet had malfunctioned. Chatting via the web cam, computer to computer, meant that he could diagnose the problem visually, and the person probably wouldn't need to bring the tablet over to him. He could still be charged for his time, though. He had placed his web camera on top of his computer monitor, pointing it at his own face, in order for the recipient to be able to actually see the person that they were talking to. The outcome was successful, and he terminated the conversation. He was about to shut down his computer when someone or something banged on his front door. He immediately jumped up from his chair, walked over, and pulled the door open.

A lady was there with her back to him, talking to the man who lived opposite. Malcolm had seen her on a few occasions going into the flat opposite his. He knew the woman's name was Susan, but that was all he knew about her. She was tall and slim and aged around thirty. Malcolm thought that she was nice-looking—very nice-looking. She could have been a model, for all he knew. She did swear a lot, though, and was often quite loud. He had heard her shouting in the hallway before, and on a couple of occasions, he had heard her singing loudly as she entered the communal corridor from a boozy night out. She wore rather too much make-up, though, according to Malcolm, and rather too little clothing sometimes. Still, she had a figure for it, so why not? He assumed that the man and woman were partners, as he had seen them kissing at the man's door on a few occasions when the lady left.

Upon opening his own door after the loud bang, he caught the last part of the conversation between the two of them. They had obviously been arguing.

"I think we should leave it for a bit," said Susan. "I think Tony's getting suspicious. I know that he's been through my phone, so don't message me for a while. I will ring you when it's all died down. I think that Clem has been doing some stirring," added Susan thoughtfully. "He does have friends that live in this block."

The man shut his front door, and Susan turned to walk away. She stopped when she noticed Malcolm standing in his open doorway.

"Did you catch all that?" she said sarcastically, stepping closer to Malcolm. "You like listening in on other people's conversations. You should watch yourself. There are people I know that would cut your ears off as soon as they looked at you."

"I'm sorry," said Malcolm. "I heard a bang on my door and opened it," He pointed to a dented cola can on the hallway floor. It had obviously been thrown at his door.

"Oh that," said Susan. "I threw at him." She nodded her head towards the closed, flat doorway that she had just exited. "He dodged it, though. Typical man. Never where you want them to be when you want them to be."

Unbeknownst to Susan, she had been followed. Clem, Tony's henchman and acting under orders from Tony, had followed her. He arrived in the corridor just as one flat entrance door closed and the other one opened. By seconds, he had missed the conversation between Susan and her lover but had arrived to watch the conversation between Susan and Malcolm. He was too far away to hear the words, but to Clem, it looked like some sort of lovers' tiff. He avoided being seen and phoned his boss.

Clement, or Clem as he was known, was a stocky black man in his late thirties. He was British, of Jamaican descent. He had lived most of his life in poorer parts of the capital but moved to Oxfordshire after an altercation with a member of a London gang. He was usually well dressed and always wore a trilby hat with three or four cigarettes stuck into the elasticated headband. He was widely known as Tony's henchman around the area, and he liked the respect that people gave him for that. He was also well liked by the criminal fraternity. He had been a singer in a ska band when he was younger and would still occasionally jump on stage to stomp around or blast out a song at a pub gig.

The woman turned and walked away, and Malcolm went back inside his flat. He didn't like confrontation and made a mental note not to be in the corridor at the same time as that woman again. He looked down at his hands. They were shaking slightly. He decided that he needed a strong cup of tea or coffee if he was out of teabags, as this would calm his nerves. Whilst waiting for the kettle to boil, there was a knock on his door. He went back to his flat entrance door and hesitated. It might be that woman again. He opened the door slightly to peer out, and two men pushed past him and closed the door behind them.

"So, you're the weasel that's been seeing my wife," said a big tattooed, bald, headed man.

"I knew there was someone else," he paused for a couple of seconds and then said.

"I'm Tony, and this is Clem," he said, nodding towards his henchman.

"I don't need to know your name. You're just a man who got involved with the wrong person's wife."

With that, he grabbed the front of Malcolm's shirt and shoved him against the wall. Malcolm protested, and Tony punched him in the face. Malcolm fell backwards and into the table that doubled as his computer desk, knocking the computer monitor onto the floor. The webcam was left dangling from its USB cable but was still filming.

Malcolm slowly started to get up, clearly dazed. Clem helped him to his feet and then pinned Malcolm's arms to his sides by giving him a bearhug from behind. Tony punched him in the stomach, and Malcolm sagged to his knees. Clem pulled him upright again, and Tony punched Malcolm in the face again. Malcolm fell backwards again, this time hitting the back of his head on the corner of the dining table. He lay motionless on the floor. When Tony saw the unconscious Malcolm was not moving and a small puddle of blood was forming on the floor around Malcolm's head, he and Clem walked out of the flat entrance door. They had given out enough beatings to know that this one would have a serious ending.

Tony Babbage, or "baboon," as some people called him, was a large man. He was thirty years old and had been involved with crime since his school days. He had been educated at a modern senior secondary school where he had a reputation as a bully and a fighter. At school, he tried to blackmail two married teachers who he wrongly thought were having an affair. This culminated in Tony's suspension from school. On his return to school, he tried to set up a protection racket where he offered to insure the school against fire damage for a weekly fee. The headmaster had called the police, and although Tony was not charged with an offence, he was expelled from the school. Upon leaving school early, he worked his way up the crime ladder in his local area through vehicle theft and fencing stolen goods.

He now controlled the drug distribution in his own patch of Oxfordshire. He was doing well on the profits. So much so that he lived in an affluent area, in a large, detached house, that he was extending. He had a Range Rover that was his pride and joy, but usually Clem drove him around in it, as officially Clem was employed as his driver.

Tony had a penchant for rare coins. He had stolen a lot during his younger years but would now buy coins, legitimately and stolen, if the price was right. He saw his coin collection as an investment for his future. He was proud of his collection and got a great deal of satisfaction from it. A lot of men played golf to relax. Tony's idea of relaxation was walking around a field for a few hours on a Sunday with his metal detector and trowel.

With Malcolm's death, Roman was brought up by his mother, Ruth, and her new partner, George Woodford. Ruth was a small lady with a big temper. She had lived around Oxford for most of her life, but she had been born and spent her first five years in Essex. She hoped to one day win the lottery and move back there. She worked as a barmaid at the local pub on most nights, and this is where she met George. For additional wages, she also worked as a school dinner lady during the day. She had dated and then married Malcolm in the hope of working her way up life's social ladder, but Malcolm was content with life, and with his limited ambitions, he didn't want to rock the boat and upset people or cause problems. With the birth of Roman, Ruth felt trapped in a loveless marriage.

She had grown to resent Malcolm over time because of his lack of desire and determination to achieve success. She thought of him as a weak man who was happy renting their council house, whilst her friends were buying theirs. Her friends drove around in decent cars, held barbecues in their back gardens, and holidayed abroad every year. Malcolm didn't. Although she, Roman, and Malcolm did holiday occasionally in England on the East Coast.

Malcolm's death was ruled an accident, as there were no witnesses to the contrary. The man from the flat opposite told the police that he hadn't seen anybody in the hallway at the estimated time of death, and he surely would have, as his own flat door had been open for most of that day because he was painting his front door frame. With Malcom's computer lying on the floor but no sign of a break-in and no money or anything stolen from his wallet or flat, it was deemed likely by the police that Malcolm had simply tripped, dropped the computer, and banged his head on the corner of the kitchen table, causing the haemorrhage that killed him. One of Tony's friends, Morgan, had also given both Tony and Clem alibis for the afternoon, just in case a police enquiry led back to both men.

Malcolm's computer and laptop had been boxed up and given to Malcom's parents after his funeral, along with his other possessions that Roman didn't have room for at home. Roman kept Malcolm's phone repair kit, though, as repairing his school friends phones was something of a hobby for him, and it brought in the occasional amount of money that always came in useful.

To the outside world, Roman was a mild-mannered boy. He was a tall lad for his age, and at just eleven years old, he was taller than his father. He had ginger hair and an athletic build. He went to school regularly and worked hard whilst there. He excelled in computer studies and mathematics and was a good long-distance runner and short distance sprinter. He had a few friends at school but rarely went out after school to play, so these friends tended to be more acquaintances than bosom buddies.

At home after school, he tended to eat his dinner at the kitchen table and then retire to his room for the rest of the night. His mother's boyfriend, George, would often remark that any boy who didn't go out but preferred to sit in his room on the computer was more than a little strange. Even a stranger to George was someone who attended school regularly, studied hard, and completed his homework on time. George had done the opposite of this when he was at school, and it hadn't done him any harm, as he would often remark. George would also pressure Roman into borrowing money from Roman's grandmother, under the pretence that it was for Roman's clothing, toiletries, or school accessories. In reality, George needed it so that he could go out drinking with his mates or place bets on the horses.

At the weekends, Roman would walk or catch the bus to his grandparents' house, around five miles away from his own. Roman's grandparents, Mabel and Francis, were Malcolm's parents and had been married a few days before the end of the Second World War. Mabel was the only child of a local baker and had spent most of her early life working in the bakery. She was and always had been short and fat, whilst Francis was tall and thin. With Malcom being their only child, his death had hit them extremely hard.

The grandmother was the mentally stronger of the two, and she tried to hide her sadness from Roman when he came over. Granddad, a retired physics schoolteacher and an opinionated man with a strong sense of right and wrong, was consumed and often overcome by grief though, and so would retreat into himself and shut himself away in his garden shed so that he didn't have to face anyone. In his shed, he would tinker with old clocks and broken machinery, inventing new hybrid machines that would never see the light of day.

Roman had been in the shed on numerous occasions and had been fascinated by the new machines, even if he didn't quite understand what they were. In his latest project, Francis was working on something that required a series of diodes, flux capacitors, oscillators, reflectors, Tesla coils, and lots of copper wire, along with a couple of elliptical booms containing radiant energy. This was to bend space-time, apparently. The use of each item was explained to Roman, but it didn't make sense to him. *Small pieces of coal were also needed, which seemed a bit random,* thought Roman, for a magnetic/electrical machine.

Around six months after his son's funeral, Francis disappeared. Not just disappeared for a few hours or even days, but totally disappeared, seemingly off the face of this earth. He left his cash, credit cards, and wallet behind, along with his watch, change of clothing, and spectacles. Police and a few local villagers had initiated a search of the local area for him, but no body or clues to Francis's disappearance were ever found. It was a complete mystery to everyone, but secretly, people were saying that he had probably killed himself because he was unable to handle the grief of his son's death.

They said that his body would more than likely be discovered at some future point in time, lying in a ditch or hedgerow somewhere, or swinging from a tree branch. Over the proceeding months, Roman's grandmother began to think this too. Her only comfort during the week was her dog Buster, a small, lazy, overweight, wire-haired terrier who wasn't the best trained dog in the world, whilst her comfort at the weekend was that Roman would come to visit her, and with this grandmother-grandson interaction, Mabel visibly perked up over time.

Chapter 2
A Step into the Past

It was the start of the school summer holidays, and Roman was staying with his grandmother for a few weeks. He had recently celebrated his twelfth birthday and was preparing himself mentally for the new year at school. The school had been sympathetic about the death of his father and had offered him the chance to home study whilst he dealt with his grief. He declined the offer, though. Roman's mother's boyfriend, George, was unemployed, so he was at home most of the time. The thought of spending the day with George whilst his mother was at work was just too much for Roman. The pair hardly spoke anyway, and when they did, it was usually initiated by the boyfriend, and most of his conversation revolved around why Roman hadn't got a girlfriend, why he hadn't got a part-time job, or why he wasn't part of a gang.

George Woodford was a printer. He had his own printing business that was on the verge of bankruptcy. The business had been left to him by his father, and his father had left it to *his* father, also named George Woodford. George Junior had been named after his grandfather. During the Second World War, George's grandfather had been caught printing forged ration books and had been given the choice by an Oxford police detective to be arrested, convicted, and subsequently go to prison for five years or become an informer for the detective, informing on the local gangsters. George opted for the latter and became an informant under the alias Winston Brown. When George phoned the detective with information, he would say that it was Winston Brown calling and be put straight through.

This dual role was never discovered by the criminal fraternity, and George Junior never knew that his grandfather had been secretly informing the police. George was proud of his grandfather and told everyone who would listen about the exploits of his grandfather's criminal activity during the war.

George Junior's father, Robert, also had tenuous links to organised crime. In the nineteen-eighties, he supplemented his legitimate income by printing forged vehicle logbooks and selling them on to a gang of car thieves. He was caught in a sting operation, though, and convicted. He served two years out of a four-year sentence. George Junior was once again proud, this time of his father. With a father who had done prison time, George felt that *he* was getting closer to the local crime gang's inner circle. Unbeknownst to George, the prison had nearly broken his father, and although he put on a brave face when George Junior visited him, it was all an act. He would often cry himself to sleep in his cell at night, and because of the weakness he showed around the other inmates, he would often be bullied into giving away his possessions whilst in there.

When he was released, he became reclusive, and his printing shop remained legitimate until he retired through ill health. Upon his retirement, he had given over the thriving business contained within the two small brick-built workshops to his son.

George took over the business with anticipation, but this started to wane when he realised just how much effort had to be expended to keep the business afloat. George saw himself more as a foreman-type person who could order his employees to do the real grafting. Unfortunately, for him, he never had any employees. Nobody, in fact, that he could share the workload with, that would be happy to work for considerably less than the minimum wage or for free. After meeting and then moving in with Roman's mother, Ruth, he spent even less time at the printing shop.

Over time, George had become violent towards Ruth and abusive towards Roman. George fancied himself as being connected to the local crime gangs, though in reality he was just a "hanger on." Someone who would run errands for gang members, buy drugs from them, and occasionally buy them drinks if he saw them out on the town. They didn't respect him, though. He was of no use to them. It was suspect whether George would inform on them if he was caught being involved in anything illegal and threatened with a conviction, and so they never involved him or talked about anything big if he was around. They also thought that he was always on the scrounge for something knocked off and going cheap, or cannabis or cocaine going free. The gangs also knew that George's printing business was going down the pan, so they refused to let him build up a drug debt.

Roman's grandmother lived in a small, detached stone cottage with a large rear garden, which was becoming more unkept as the years rolled on. His granddad's wooden shed was at the bottom of the garden, which had been locked at the time of his grandfather's disappearance but had been forced open by police whilst they were looking for clues to his whereabouts. The shed seemed boring to Roman now, without his grandfather's explanations, descriptions, and vocal input. There were still lots of weird and wonderful inventions and parts of unfinished machinery in there, but nothing that looked complete and, as such, couldn't be started up. There was nothing in there that would hold Roman's interest for more than a few seconds, and so he stopped going in there.

On the left-hand side of the garden, the grounds opened up to a small spinney. The spinney belonged to the house. It consisted of half an acre of trees, bushes, and brambles, which Roman had explored on numerous occasions throughout his lifetime but had grown boring as he grew older. Exiting the spinney would bring you into a large field, which was dominated by a large three-story, derelict brick building, approximately one quarter of a mile away from Roman's grandparents' house, which itself was surrounded by a high steel fence. This building was known locally as the old workhouse. Parts of it date to the late seventeenth century, whilst the main bulk of the building was over two hundred years old. The structure had been earmarked for demolition for several years because it was deemed unsafe.

Romans' granddad had told Roman that at one stage the cottage that they lived in was part of this parish workhouse, and it was where the grounds warden lived until the workhouse closed down around a hundred years ago. He told Roman that the cottage was probably built in the late seventeenth century. Over the preceding years, the grounds of the workhouse and its adjacent woodland were used as a training ground for the home guard during the Second World War and some years after this, the smaller building at the extreme right-hand side of the main workhouse building was once used by a mechanic to service and repair cars and vans. The mechanic left the site for bigger and better things, though, when he realised that there was only so much work that needed to be done on vehicles owned by such a small village population.

A few years later, someone had been caught by the police growing cannabis in the workhouse basement, and they had closed his criminal operation down. The man was jailed under the 'Misuse of Drugs Act' for possession with intent to supply and a separate offence of production, cultivation, or manufacture of controlled drugs.

The workhouse had been an orphanage in the early 1800s but it had been a group home devoted to the care of children who couldn't be cared for by their biological families for at least one hundred years before this. Both the orphanage and the workhouse had historical records going back to the 1800s, highlighting just how cruel the conditions were to the inhabitants. These old records and reports were discovered some years ago in someone's loft, and they were given to a local museum, where some were put on public display. The records did not show the owners in a good light.

Some historical newspaper articles from the mid to late 1800s had also been photographed and archived in a local area historical database. A few people from the surrounding villages and towns could trace their family tree relatives to either the orphanage, inmates, or staff at the workhouse.

The workhouse had been getting more and more derelict as the years went by. It had been earmarked for demolition to make way for houses, but a local opposition group had formed a committee to try and block the demolition application on the grounds that the building should be declared a listed building and renovated for flats, as opposed to being knocked down entirely. This meant that all planning decisions were in limbo.

Roman's grandmother explained to Roman over dinner one weekend that Roman's great-grandfather had been the grounds warden for a long time and that it was he who had brought the cottage that they lived in from the workhouse estate when the workhouse had closed. She went on to say that sometimes weird things supposedly happen around the workhouse. It was rumoured to be haunted, and there was supposed to be treasure buried there. This whole area was apparently sitting on a magnetic ley line and this made the area attractive to hippies and druids around the summer and winter solstices.

The grandmother carried on. "If the old orphanage wasn't fenced off so securely, I would say that Francis probably wandered over and fell into the workhouse pond and drowned. The water is quite deep, apparently."

"Why is there a pond so close to the building walls?" asked Roman.

"It was unintentional. Some people say that there is an old cemetery under the pond where some of the orphans were buried. Someone was digging a new underground basement area through the limestone, and they hit a natural spring. They couldn't plug it, and the ground filled up with water. That's why one side of the pond is contained by the workhouse wall."

"I mean, who would intentionally have a pond built using the outer wall of an occupied building to contain the water? You'd have to be mad to come up with that idea. The water stopped rising when it found its own level, and any overflowing water was directed to an old stream further down the field. The stream has long since gone dry, so I think the spring must have stopped gushing out, or it is now reduced to a trickle. This is all hearsay, but it is what your grandfather was told."

It was the middle of the afternoon, and Roman was sitting around his grandmother's house. He had eaten dinner and had just watched a Robin Hood film on television. It was an old 1930s film starring Errol Flynn, and he couldn't get the theme tune about Robin stealing from the rich and giving to the poor out of his head. He was getting bored, though. Mabel was asleep in her armchair. He decided to take Buster out for a walk in the garden and around the spinney. Buster didn't like walks in any shape or guise but reluctantly accompanied Roman around the garden and into the spinney. The spinney consisted of a couple of oak trees taking pride of place amongst some ash, elm, and yew trees.

Brambles were everywhere, which was good in the autumn for picking blackberries. The spinney perimeter was bordered by thick, unkempt hawthorn hedging, which was also interspersed with brambles. The spinney floor was a carpet of nettles and bluebells, all vying for space and light. The spinney was home to countless rabbits and squirrels, and the occasional badger and fox.

As a young boy, Roman enjoyed exploring the spinney with his granddad. It was exciting hunting for lions and tigers together. His granddad was excellent at tracking both animals. He would inspect some disturbed foliage and sniff the air. He would then remark that a lion had passed through this area less than an hour before. Roman was both excited and impressed. However, as he got older, he realised that the whole wild animal thing had been made up, and the spinney then lost its sparkle. Nowadays, it is just boring. Roman had brought a tennis ball with him for the dog to fetch when he threw it, but the dog quickly got tired and got bored and, in the end, refused to bring the ball back. Roman threw the ball for the final time in the hope that Buster would have a change of heart, but the dog just sat down and then laid down for a rest, leaving Roman to retrieve the ball himself.

The ball had landed near the spinney perimeter, just in front of a thorny bramble hedge. As Roman bent down to pick up the ball, he noticed a small opening through the base of the hedge, created by a crude wooden frame. The frame was approximately two feet in height and width, and both sides and the top were surrounded by tightly coiled copper wire. The wire had obviously been there for some time, as it had mostly turned green. Green-coiled wire could also be seen protruding through the soil. The whole wooden frame was surrounded on all four sides by thin copper wire.

Stepping back, Roman could see that contained in the hedge and mostly overgrown was another larger wooden frame. This frame surrounded the smaller frame. This frame was made of substantially thicker posts. Two for the sides and a heavier one loosely balanced on the top. This frame was also wrapped in tightly coiled copper wire. The wiring looked very neat. It was also mostly green, but the spacing was very tidy, with no overlapping of the coils. Attached to the frame were some of the objects that Roman had seen in his grandfather's shed. He couldn't remember their uses or the names of each item, but he had definitely seen them before.

Under an upturned plastic dustbin on the side of the frame was a car battery. It was a big, heavy-looking battery, probably from a lorry, or other large vehicle. One terminal had a length of copper wire connected to it, whilst the other side had nothing connected to it. A length of copper wire with a looped end hovered close to the terminal but had obviously become disconnected sometime in the past. Probably when the police were conducting a search of the garden looking for clues to the whereabouts of Roman's grandfather. Roman connected the looped wire to the free terminal, curious to see if anything happened. Nothing happened though.

Buster had ambled up to Roman and was sniffing around the hole created by the smaller frame. It peered through a couple of times and then slowly walked through the small copper coiled wooden frame. Roman waited a few minutes for the dog to return, and because the dog didn't respond, he got down on his knees to look through, the frame. There was no sign of the dog. The hedge was too thorny to get through and so he decided to crawl through the same wooden opening as the dog. It was a struggle because of the frame's small dimensions, but by half crawling and half wriggling, he got through to the field on the other side. He stood up. The field looked different from how he remembered it.

He hadn't been in the field for a couple of years, but the last time he was there, it had been one large open field. It was now a series of smaller fields, separated by hedges. There was also a cottage in the distance with smoke coming out of the chimney, which he couldn't remember seeing before.

Buster appeared and trotted over to him, then stretched out on the ground for a rest. Roman decided to go for a walk now that he was in the field. He called Buster, but the dog ignored him. He decided to leave the dog where it was and head over to the old workhouse alone. As he got closer, he realised that something was different. It looked like a *new* building. There was no perimeter security fencing, the windows were intact, not boarded up with steel sheeting, and the paintwork on the iron gates was fresh.

There was a stable block at the far end of the building, but the biggest surprise was that there was no pond adjacent to the side wall of the building on this nearby side. The gates were open, and Roman thought about walking through. He hesitated, took a few steps, stopped, thought about it again, and then walked through the gates. He couldn't see anybody around, so he walked over to a side entrance door.

He was curious as to what the interior would look like. The building he remembered was spray-painted with graffiti on the outside and pretty much wrecked inside. In his mind, he made a mental note that if he had to flee the scene, entering the building through the side door, as opposed to the grander main doors further down, would give him less distance to run back to his grandmother's spinney if he was chased.

Roman walked through the unlocked side door. The workhouse (or orphanage) was obviously in use, but nobody was around. He stopped to think about the situation he was in. Either this was all a dream, or he had stepped back in time. The wooden frame he crawled through was obviously a doorway into the past—a time portal, if you like. He attempted to rationalise this conclusion in his mind. His granddad had been experimenting with bending time and had obviously constructed something that worked, building it in his garden. Perhaps his grandfather had gone through himself and was waiting in this time zone, whatever year this was.

Was this eighteen or nineteen hundred? It may even be seventeen hundred. Did they have workhouses in the seventeen hundreds? His thoughts turned to his grandfather again. He may have been trapped at the time and would need help returning to his own. Maybe he had become the new leader of these people. Roman had seen a film once where the inhabitants of a jungle tribe curtailed a knowledgeable man and made him their leader. It hadn't ended well for this man, though, as the tribe had executed him. Roman decided to go along with the time portal idea until he was either proved wrong or woke up from a sleep.

He looked around the walls of the room and saw a wooden sign with the word 'orphanage' painted on it. The sign was decorated around its borders with painted red, blue, and yellow flowers. This room was obviously some sort of storeroom, and the door that he had just come through was most likely the tradesman's entrance.

Roman decided to investigate further. The orphanage was a large rectangular building spread over three floors. The outside walls were constructed of red bricks, with windows spaced uniformly on all the sides that he had seen. The building had numerous dormitory rooms and a large dining room with wooden benches and long tables taking up most of the floor space. There were some people, in the building judging by the occasional shouts and coughs, but Roman tried to avoid contact with anyone who was in there, at least for the time being. He walked past the kitchen and saw the cook in there, stirring something in a large pot that was swinging over an open fire.

She had her back to him, and so he quietly watched her for a few seconds before silently gliding past the open door. There was a basement that was accessible through another doorway. Roman opened the door but didn't venture down the steps. It was too dark. Going up the stairs to the first floor, he noticed that most of the rooms on this floor were used for sleeping accommodation, with one room at the end of the building probably a room for ill people, judging by the amount of coughing, moaning, and sneezing that he could hear from inside it. He ventured up the stairway, to the top floor. This floor had a few more dormitory rooms and some better furnished bedrooms, probably for the staff, reasoned Roman. The end room's door was ajar, and this looked like a study or an office. This room was occupied by two men, judging by the voices that Roman could hear.

Roman walked quietly over to the slightly opened door. There was an adjacent empty room with its door open. It was dark in this room, and Roman made a mental note to step into it if he heard anybody coming. The slightly open office door had a large keyhole, and so Roman stooped and peered through it. Two men were talking. One standing and the other sitting behind a desk. After a few seconds, it became obvious to Roman that the seated man was called 'Wilson' and the standing man was "Williams". Wilson was obviously in charge. Wilson was a tall, thin man in his early forties, but he looked like he was in his early fifties. He had a large nose with a thin moustache underneath that underlined the size of his nose. He talked with a nasal voice. His hair was going grey, and a bald patch was appearing on the top of his head. He spoke with an authoritative tone, which to Roman made him sound like a military officer type that Roman had seen on various war films on television.

In reality, Wilson was a vain man who, in conversation, would hint that he came from noble stock. He preferred to be called by his surname, and most people, including the orphanage staff, didn't know his Christian name. He was unmarried, although he did once come close to tying the knot. The proposed marriage had all gone pear-shaped, though, when a lie he had embroiled himself in came to light. He had told his fiancé and her father that he was a retired cavalry officer, but during the engagement party that his soon-to-be father-in-law threw for the couple, an actual serving cavalry officer friend of the father quizzed Wilson about his time in the military and discovered that Wilson's entire military history was a fabrication. The marriage was called off, and Wilson left the area in disgrace.

Williams was a large man with a big, square head. He was ten years younger than Wilson. Officially, he was employed as an orphanage groundskeeper but tended to be more of a personal assistant to Wilson. He admired Wilson, not least because of Wilson's university education and because of Wilson being the captain of the university fencing team, but also because Wilson could quote passages from the Bible and quotes from Shakespeare. In reality, Wilson had never held a fencing foil in his hand, nor had he been to university. He had a Bible in his top desk drawer and an old copy of Shakespeare's 'The Tempest' in the drawer below. He would memorise certain phrases from both books when he was sitting in his office alone and then guide future conversations so that he could incorporate the learned quotes and phrases into the conversation.

During walkabouts around the orphanage, Wilson would don his black mortarboard hat and gown. Although he had never graduated, he had once met a university dean at a formal gathering and was immediately impressed by how much respect the dean commanded in his mortarboard cap and gown. Wilson was there and then decided to emulate him.

Roman watched as Wilson took a small leather purse out of a cupboard in the oak wall panelling. He gave Williams a single gold coin and then pulled the purse drawstring tight before replacing it back in the cavity where it had just come from. The cupboard door was disguised to look like one of the surrounding oak panels, and when shut, it was almost impossible to distinguish this door from the surrounding oak panels.

"We need more kids," said Wilson. "Tell Strachen to go further afield and bring us more. We need more children, but without the expense of spending any more money on food or clothes."

Wilson pointed the finger at Williams. "If he must buy them, then so be it. But it's copper and silver at a push only, and no sick kids this time."

"I'll see what I can do," said Williams. "Strachen said if he can get a waggon, in and out of London without being stopped, he's got contacts down there that will help him."

"Good. I'll leave it in your capable hands. We've got the church and the nobility coming round next month, and I want them to see a full house, and I want a full purse for their upkeep."

"Anyway, talk me through the punishment book," said Wilson, changing the subject and visibly perking up.

"Reading from the punishment ledger, there are seven boys and one girl." Williams replied.

"What did the girl do?"

"Refused to collect firewood," came the reply.

"Mitigation?"

"She said that it was raining," replied Williams.

"The boys?" said Wilson.

"Two cases of insubordination to a dorm master, one case of being late to lessons, one case of truancy, two cases of refusing to work, and one for stealing food."

"Enlighten me on the food theft circumstances," said Wilson.

"Half a loaf of bread and a few ounces of salted brawn went missing from the kitchen." said Williams. "We were tipped off as to the offender's name by one of the older boys. Some breadcrumbs and a small amount of brawn were found in the boy's bed."

"Mitigation for the food theft," said Wilson.

"He denied the theft and said that he thought that one of the older boys had planted the food in his bed to incriminate him."

"I won't tolerate lying to authority," said Wilson. "He shall be punished twice, once for lying and once for the theft."

Wilson stood up and proceeded to warm up for the morning's excursions. He pushed the fingers of his right hand into a thin black leather glove. He then walked over to a wooden rack that held a long, thin cane, a long leather flat strap, and a smaller wooden truncheon. Wilson looked at the truncheon longingly. It had been given to him by a policeman. He rarely had the opportunity to use this on the children these days, and the strap hadn't been off the rack for a long time either. He took the cane out of the rack. Secretly, he wished that the children would occasionally commit crimes that were deemed more serious, so that he could let loose with the strap or truncheon.

Still, it was another outing for "Old Faithful." Wilson swished the cane around as if he was fencing with a rapier. He put his feet together, lowered himself down, and then stood back into an upright position again. He moved his head from side to side and then put his left arm behind his back whilst rotating his other wrist that was holding the cane.

"This is how I would warm up before a fencing match," he told Williams for the umpteenth time. He then straightened up and tucked the cane under his arm.

"Come, Williams!" he said. "Hand me my cap and gown, and we will head down to the punishment area."

This was Roman's cue to step backwards into the adjacent darkened room. He pressed his back against the wall behind the open door and watched both men walk out of the office, viewing them through the gap between the door and doorframe. After waiting for a few minutes, he stepped out of his room, opened the unlocked office door, and went inside. The first thing he noticed was a wooden sign on the wall with the words 'Spare the rod and spoil the child' painted on it. Underneath, in smaller letters, it said "Proverbs 13:24." This was obviously a quote from the Bible, thought to be Roman. He moved around to the other side of the desk. There was a financial ledger in front of him.

The pages were opened at March 1861. He picked the ledger up from the desk, and a few loose pages fell out and dropped onto the floor. He bent down and picked them up, but instead of putting them back into the ledger, he folded them up and put them into his trouser pocket. They would come in useful when he got back home if nobody believed where he had been.

His eyes wandered around the room and stopped at the secret wood panel cupboard. He opened the door and took out the leather purse that Wilson had placed in there a few minutes before. It was quite heavy. Roman hesitated as he briefly wrestled with his conscience regarding stealing the purse. The men who were in this room were cruel and corrupt. This whole institution looked like it was run on cruelty and corruption. He would take the money and try to put things right. He turned around and headed to the door. In the doorway, a young girl appeared. He estimated her age at around ten years old. She had very pale skin.

"What are you doing?" said the girl, looking at the leather purse in Roman's hand.

"I'm stealing from the rich and giving to the poor," replied Roman.

"Just like Robin Hood," he said, thinking back to the movie he had watched earlier that day. He asked the girl who she was, and she replied that her name was Mary. She told him that she was ill with consumption and should really be confined to bed, but she liked to wander around the building when everyone had gone outside for the punishment beatings. She went on to tell him that the canings went on once a week, and the whole orphanage was made to watch as a deterrent to the other children.

"Doesn't anybody intervene?" asked Roman.

"No!" replied Mary. "Although around a year ago, an old man did. Nobody knew who he was, but it turned out that he was insane. A lunatic. He kept saying how he was from the future and how corporal punishment was not the answer. They carted him off to an asylum in the end."

Roman went silent for a moment, and the girl interjected.

"If you go downstairs to the laundry room on the ground floor, you can watch the canings from the window in there."

Roman said goodbye to the girl and made his way to the laundry room downstairs. It was hot in there and quite dark, as it only had one little window. As it happened, the window was open, and Roman could see and hear everything that was going on outside. There was a large crowd of boys, probably ranging in age from six to sixteen. They were standing in a semi-circle around a curved cast iron bench. A boy of around eight years old was bent over the bench. He was wearing grey shorts. Two older, larger boys held each of the younger boys' wrists from the opposite side of the bench to stop the boy from struggling free or running. Wilson, dressed in his cap and gown, was warming up by making large, exaggerated swishes through the air with his cane.

Just as he stepped forward, the fat female cook appeared. It was the one that Roman had seen earlier in the kitchen. She hurried over to Wilson as he was getting ready with the cane to land the first blow.

"Sir!" she said in a breathless tone. "We have an intruder."

She swallowed some air and carried on.

"I saw his reflection in my silver ladle. I followed him from the kitchen. He was probably going to rob me or steal one of the knives. A very shifty looking lad and fair gave me the creeps he did. Probably part of a gang. More than likely, it came up from London. I'm not sure if he was armed. He had a good wander around the building. He was looking in all the rooms. I think he's still on the top floor."

Upon hearing this, Roman decided it was time to head back home. He quietly made his way to the tradesman's door and debated how best to get back to the spinney at his grandmother's house. He would need to make a dash for it and keep going until he got there. The only drawback was that for the first fifty metres or so, he would be visible to everyone that had gathered for the beatings, and they might give chase. It was either that or to lie low until it was dark and then make his escape. The drawback of this, though, was that they might organise search parties to look for him, especially when the money was discovered to have been stolen. He decided to make a run for it. He checked that his laces were tied, luckily, he was wearing trainers. He took a couple of deep breaths and sprinted out of the doorway.

Wilson was the first person to spot him.

"Stop that boy," said Wilson to a couple of older boys. "Search him. Bring him to me."

He turned to Williams. "Fetch me the strap, Williams."

A group of the older boys gave chase.

"A sixpence to the boy that catches him," shouted Wilson after the running boys.

As the boys gave chase, Wilson contemplated his next move. The boy would have to be restrained when he was caught, as he looked quite tall and might get physical. He could let the older boys beat him for a few minutes, or he could set his dog on the boy, which might take the steam out of him. The trouble was that dogs didn't like Wilson, and most dogs, even his own dog, would just as soon go for *his* ankles as for anybody else's. However, once restrained, he would then strap the boy to within an inch of his life and then hand him over to the local constable. He might even say that the boy was armed with a knife and that he had disarmed him. That might make the papers, which would only improve his social standing within the community. Also, there might also be a reward for the boy's apprehension. This would top up his savings.

Wilson had no intention of staying as an orphanage governor for life. Things were changing. The powers that be were considering turning the orphanage into a workhouse to get some return on their charitable donations that kept the orphanage afloat. No, he wanted to go into politics. Preferably as an elected member of parliament. The money he had saved in his office was his election fund. This would act as his deposit and may possibly be used to grease a few palms. Once in parliament as a minister, his social standing would be raised, and he could move to the posh part of Oxford and mingle with the social elite. He even dreamt of becoming prime minister. The country was overdue for a change. Prime Minister Henry Temple was leading the country to the dogs. He was getting old and soft in his old age.

Just last month, three hundred and fifty convicts rioted and took over their prison at Chatham Dockyard. Temple government's response? A few lashes with the strap. If he were in power, he would have hanged the lot of them.

Buster was sitting near the gap at Roman's grandmother's spinney hedge, and Roman could see him. The dog hadn't moved the whole time that Roman had been away. He used the dog as a marker to identify the position of the portal doorway back to his grandmother's garden. He was running as fast as he could, but he was panicking, and his breathing was getting out of sync, making him tired, and he started to visibly slow down. He glanced behind, and saw that there were quite a few pursuers. Wilson's sixpence offer had stirred more boys to join in with the chase. A couple of the bigger boys were gaining on him. The last thing he wanted was to be caught with the purse of money that he had stolen.

Buster thought that Roman's running was part of the game, and so he dashed through the small wooden frame back into the grandmother's spinney. Roman made it to the hole but decided to ditch the purse in case the boys caught his legs and pulled him back before he could completely wriggle through.

There was a rabbit hole near his right hand, and so he pushed the purse into it and dove into the hole in the hedge. In his panicked state he became wedged into the frame, and the copper wires caught his jumper and snagged his trousers. He forced his way through. His jumper tore along one side, and his trousers ripped along one leg. He tried to stand up but was not completely through the frame, and so the snagged wires started to pull on the larger surrounding wooden frame. He had just managed to get through to his side of the hedge when the heavy top wooden post dislodged from the wavering structure and dropped onto his head. The shouting from the other side of the hedge immediately ceased, and everything went black.

Roman lay unconscious on the ground for a few minutes. He came round to find Buster licking his face. He felt the top of his head and tenderly touched the bump and the blood that was trickling from the cut. He slowly got up and turned to look at the wrecked wooden frames and tangled wires. At least nobody could follow him through now. He walked into the house and showed his bump to his grandmother. She insisted on calling a doctor. There was a retired doctor in the village who she knew well, and he agreed to pop round. She shushed Roman when he started talking about going back in time, putting the whole thing down to concussion. She helped him out of his torn trousers and jumper, putting the jumper into the bin and the trousers into a clothes basket to be repaired at a later date. She put Roman to bed whilst they waited for the doctor.

With both the doctor and his grandmother both insisting that the whole time-travel episode was a result of his concussion, Roman started to think that he had imagined it. The next day, he walked back to the destroyed mass of electrical components, wire, and wood. He pulled it all out of the way and wriggled through the gap in the hedge to the field on the other side. There was no rabbit hole where he thought that he had pushed in the leather purse; there was no cottage with a smoking chimney in the distance, and there was a modern tractor ploughing a field in the distance. Looking over at the workhouse, he could see the place was derelict, and the security fencing around it was still in place.

"Perhaps it had all been a dream." sighed Roman.

Chapter 3
Reality After All

It had been almost ten years since his father had died, and Roman was standing in a cold, wet cemetery, paying his last respects to his grandmother. There were only a handful of people there, but she didn't really mingle with people, and she had very few relatives still alive, reasoned Roman, so you couldn't really expect many more people to be at the funeral. He had left his grandmother's cottage and all of its contents in her will, and he had recently moved into it. To be fair to him, though, his relationship with his mum's boyfriend had broken down to such an extent that he practically lived at his grandmother's house anyway. At just twenty-one years old, and as a self-employed computer repairman, he was on the property ladder. Roman looked upon being left the house as a blessing, as he could never have afforded to buy the house, or rent any other house especially one with a large garden that came with it. His income would never stretch that far.

He had decided to wait until after the funeral before he started to get rid of the things left in the house that he didn't want, in respect of his grandmother's memory. He would start clearing the house first and sort out the garden and garden shed last. He had ordered a skip for the garden stuff. This was partly because at his last rummage around in the shed, he had dislodged a plastic bottle of hydrofluoric acid off a shelf, and it had fallen onto a leather chair below. The bottle cap had leaked, and immediately the acid had burned through the leather covering, ruining the chair completely. The chair would go into the skip, but Roman decided that he would water the acid down before he disposed of it. It would be too dangerous to put it in a bin or skip at its present strength.

There was also his granddad's old moped in the shed. It looked old. It was old and quite rare now, apparently. Roman had asked his neighbour to get it started. The neighbour duly obliged, and after a couple of hours, tinkering with it had started it up. He then offered to buy the moped from Roman when his wages went into his bank at the end of the month. Roman agreed to sell the moped to him at the end of the month.

Roman had decided to start clearing the top of the house and work his way down. He bagged up his grandparents' clothes to take to the charity shop and put some other stuff on a free ads' website, listed as free to collectors. Buster had died around five years ago, and so there was a lot of dog stuff that he had promised to another neighbour, who had recently purchased a puppy. He also found a cardboard box that had a couple of wigs in it, one black and one blonde. He chuckled to himself, thinking of his gran with black or blonde hair. She had gone grey relatively early in life, and he had only ever known her with grey hair.

There was a shotgun cabinet in the corner of one bedroom. It was bolted to the wall. Roman knew there was an old, deactivated, double-barrelled shotgun in there and that he would get rid of it when he came across the cabinet keys. The shotgun had originally belonged to his great-grandfather. He had bought it in the 1940s during the Second World War. He used it to shoot rabbits, pigeons, and pheasants to supplement the family's rations. When he died, Roman's granddad had it deactivated and put it on display on the living room wall. Over time, it eventually made its way into the gun cabinet in the bedroom.

Roman was bagging up stuff in the spare room when he came across some of his old clothes. These hadn't been seen or worn for years and were too small for him to wear again. He bagged up the shirts and jumpers and searched the pockets for money before he did the same with the trousers. A pair of trousers had a tear down almost the full length of one leg. He remembered this as the pair he had been wearing when the timber post had fallen onto his head. Obviously, his grandmother never got around to mending these trousers. He put his hand in the pockets to check for money and pulled out a sheet of folded paper. It was the finance ledger page, dated 1861.

Roman sat down. He couldn't believe it. This was proof that he had travelled through time. The whole orphanage episode was real. It meant that his grandfather really did build a time doorway. It also meant that his granddad had probably died in an asylum sometime in the late 1800s. He decided to do some online research. As it happened, his laptop was in bits. He took it apart to add extra memory but hadn't bothered to put it back together yet.

He decided that he couldn't wait the hour or so that it would take to complete the rebuild, and so he would conduct the research on a different one. He had seen an old home computer in a box in the back room. It was the one belonging to his late father, and if it still worked, he should still be able to access the internet with it.

With his father's computer and monitor set up, Roman started online historical record searches regarding the orphanage and workhouse. Neither told him much more than he already knew or had witnessed with his own eyes. It was when he was searching through the digitised archives of the local newspapers that he got his breakthrough. Technically, there were two breakthroughs. The first breakthrough came from a newspaper dated 1860. It told the story of an insane old man who had wandered into an orphanage and tried to attack a member of staff. The article claimed that the orphanage governor had restrained him and held him in a locked room until a doctor had arrived.

The doctor certified him insane and escorted him to the local asylum. The article suggested that the governor was a hero for defending the orphans against the violent madman. Nothing more was mentioned about the incident in that newspaper. A second article in a newspaper dated 1861 told the story of an armed intruder who had managed to gain access to the orphanage, intent on stealing. The article went on to say that the intruder had tried to attack the orphanage cook but had been chased away by the members of staff. However, they had lost him at the edge of some nearby woodland. The newspaper said that the boy had a London accent and was probably part of an organised gang. It was later discovered that the boy had forced open a wall safe and had stolen the entire year's orphanage budget.

As Roman was about to click out of the archive, one last headline caught his eye. It was dated 1876 and described how the governor of the local workhouse had passed away peacefully in his sleep. It said a large slate memorial stone had been commissioned to recognise Julian Wilson's tireless commitment to the orphanage and workhouse over the previous years. This memorial stone had been built into the basement wall as a lasting reminder of the man's dedication to his duties. A small portrait had also been commissioned, and this would hang in the workhouse hallway.

Roman immediately decided that he would buy or borrow a metal detector and go looking for the coins where he remembered pushing them into the rabbit hole, in the field next to where the wooden frame that he had crawled through had been. Obviously, his pursuers that day hadn't seen him do this, or the money would have been recovered that same day. Hopefully, nobody found the coins over the following years.

Now that he had the computer fired up, Roman decided to open his father's old files. He knew that his dad had an archive of old photos showing Roman's grandparents and parents. If he liked any of them, he would be able to print them off onto photo paper and put them into photo frames. There was one file that hadn't been labelled and seemed to be hanging in computer limbo. Roman clicked on the recording taken by the fallen webcam and watched Tony and Clem kill his father.

Roman watched the clip over and over. He was shocked. However, the webcam stopped recording after the first few blows when Malcolm fell backwards, knocking over the monitor and dislodging the webcam. The fatal punch and subsequent bang to the head were not shown in the clip. Even though the date on the screen was the same date that Malcolm had died, and Tony and Clem were clearly identifiable, Roman thought that it would be unlikely that there would be enough evidence to gain a conviction for murder. There wasn't a body to exhume; Malcolm had been cremated. The coroner ruled accidental death, and without the final portion of the recording showing the fatal blows, murder or manslaughter would never have been proven. Especially as the men would no doubt hire expensive lawyers for their defence.

"They will pay though," vowed Roman. "One way or another, they will pay."

The next day, Roman and his borrowed metal detector went out to look for the money he had stolen that day, one hundred and sixty years ago. He preferred to call it liberated money, as he still had a charitable use for it if he ever found it. In less than an hour, the metal detector started to beep. In his haste to get started with the detector, Roman had forgotten to bring a trowel or spade to dig with. He marked the spot with an upright stick and went back for a digging tool. On his return, he quickly found the money; it was in a pile in the ground. The leather pouch had rotted away, but the gold coins looked like they had just been minted, and the silver ones would come up the same with some careful cleaning.

Thinking over the legal ramifications of the find, technically they were on his property. Just. Over time, the spinney and hedges had grown outwards, and his garden boundary had moved outwards with them. He took the coins into his house then went back outside, and into his grandfather's shed. He was looking for any paperwork, descriptions, or instructions that his grandfather may have stored there that would help him build a time portal himself. He found an old biscuit tin and opened the lid. There were a lot of papers in there, different sizes and different colours, but on the top of the pile was a bundle of papers, stapled together, that read "Time Portal." Roman took out the papers and read the instructions on how to build one.

The instructions seemed simple enough. Maybe it's too simple to work. However, he was living proof that they did work. On the front page, the paper gave instructions that a copper cross must be fabricated out of copper pipe. The pipe ends, should be capped with copper stop ends and this should be buried approximately nine inches into the earth, below where the time portal was going to be erected. This was to harness the ground's natural electricity and set up the electromagnetic coil. The pipe arms should be aligned with the four points of the compass. The instructions went on to state that if the copper cross couldn't be buried, then it was to lie on top of the ground, still aligned with the compass points, and that the copper cross would create the first and second fields required out of a series of four.

The following page of the instruction manual went on to describe how to make the wooden portal doorway, which could be made more effective if the power supply to it was limited or weak, by making a smaller wooden portal door inside of it. The smaller the better for this doorway, according to the instructions, but at least big enough to crawl through. If the electric current feeding into the coils was strong, then the smaller wooden frame would not be necessary. The frames should be encased on all sides with tightly coiled copper wire (time coils), which should be connected to an electricity supply via two hyper dimensional resonators, which in turn were connected to two electromagnets. If switched on, this would create a third field. The fourth field would be actuated by aligning the door frame to an east/west position.

The last page of the instruction manual stated that the time portal would work best on the day or night of a full moon, when the moon's gravitational pull was at its strongest, and that entering the portal could only take you backwards in time, not forwards. It concluded with a short warning that only copper wire should be used, not steel, and definitely not aluminium. Aluminium might take the person entering the portal into a different realm, reality, or dimension from which there would be no way back. Underneath this warning were various calculations regarding the correct frequencies required by the two resonators. If the two frequencies were not aligned, then they would interfere with each other and cause parasitic oscillations, rendering the doorway useless.

The correct frequency was underlined in red ink, with a brief instruction written beneath it stating that if the exact frequency wasn't used but the portal frequency was very close to this, then the time portal may still work, but only for a few minutes. If the person stepping through did not step back again within three to five minutes, then time would have moved on, and they would be trapped in the past forever. In pencil underneath this was another sentence that said if one resonator failed, the portal would stop working completely.

If it failed whilst part of the body was between times, then the whole body would disappear into an unknown dimension that was unlikely to be part of this universe. The last sentence at the bottom of the page said to be cautious when jumping through time, as time runs at different speeds. One minute in our time could be one day in the past, although you could never know this whilst experiencing it.

Roman gasped. The diagram in the manual looked like the time portal that he had crawled through. He looked around the shed. The diagram in the instruction manual clearly identified each component part, which made it easier to visually identify the parts on the shelves in the shed. All the parts listed are in there. In theory, this meant that he could build his own time portal and go back in time again. He thought back to his physics classes at school. Einstein had said that only gravity could bend time. Did this mean that the time frame altered gravity? Roman didn't know. The portal obviously worked, but he couldn't be bothered to find out why it worked. It was just too complicated.

A couple of weeks after Roman's coin was found, he had tracked down Tony and was standing at Tony's front door. Tony was easy to track down. His reputation as a gangster was widely known to most people in the area, and many people had witnessed the drunken arguments between Tony and Susan in the local pubs and clubs. Nobody, not even bar security, intervened in these arguments or ejected the pair from the premises. Roman looked deliberately scruffy in his dirty jeans and a dirty shirt. His trainers were falling apart, and Roman's socks were visible through the splits on the sides of them. The door opened, and Tony stood there, filling the doorframe. He looked older and fatter than he had on the webcam recording.

"What do you want?" said Tony annoyed that he had had to get up from his office desk to answer the door. He had just started to nod off when the doorbell rang. Last night had been a long night. Tony and Sue were supposed to fly to Paris for a couple of days, but the plane had been delayed. They spent the additional hours drinking alcohol in the airport lounge and then arguing. Once on the plane, the argument continued. It culminated with Susan rolling up a magazine and jabbing Tony in the face with the end of it. She had cut Tony's bottom lip, and he had retaliated with the back of his hand. They had both been escorted off the plane before it took off.

"I'm Danny Tucker, and I hear you buy old coins," said Roman to Tony, holding out a silver coin.

Tony looked at the coin and then at the young man. A scruffy ginger headed man, not much more than a boy.

"You better come in for a minute," he said, leading the man to his study. They sat down on opposite sides of a desk. There were two bundles of money on his desk. Both were marked with a bank band, stating five thousand pounds for each bundle.

"Show me the coin," said Tony. It was more of an order than a request.

Roman handed over the coin and Tony studied it. It was old and it was rare, no two ways about that.

"Nicked, is it?" Tony said suspiciously.

"Not at all; I found it," replied Roman.

"Okay, whatever you say. I'll give you fifty pounds for it." Without waiting for a reply, he slipped fifty pounds out of one of the bundles on the table and passed it to Roman. There was no way Roman would be leaving with the coin. It was worth at least five hundred pounds. Tony got up and ushered Roman back out of the front door.

"If you find any more like this, come to me first," said Tony.

Two weeks passed, and Roman was back at Tony's property. There was an extension being built in Tony's large rear garden. It was a detached extension to accommodate a swimming pool. When it was finished, it would match Tony's large, detached house in style, with a similar brick match and similar tiled roof. The home's front drive was now a storage site for building materials, diggers, dumpers, and a blue plastic portaloo. A group of men were standing in one corner of the drive, looking over a paper plan. Roman walked over to these builders. He had a briefcase in his hand.

"Are you the building inspector?" asked one of the builders, looking up from the plan.

"Yes," replied Roman. He had turned up at the property in the guise of an insurance man, but a building inspector would do just as well. He was sporting his grandmother's blonde wig, and he was wearing thick-framed glasses. He was dressed in a white shirt and blue tie and a pair of black trousers with polished black shoes.

"You're a bit early; I thought you were coming tomorrow." said a different builder. "The main steel's not in yet, but you can have a look at the pool reinforcing." The two men and Roman walked around to a large hole in the ground, obviously the pool excavation.

"It's a sixty-foot swimming pool, and he can't even swim," said the first builder sarcastically. "His missus wants it to host cocktails, swimming parties, and stuff."

There was a large steel beam on a forklift's forks a few feet away from the edge of the excavation.

"What size padstones do we need for that?" said the builder to the building inspector. "It's the steel for over the bi-fold doors."

"What size padstones do you normally use?" said Roman.

"Three courses of engineering, or blue bricks," came the reply.

"That will be fine," said Roman.

"What size rafters do you want us to use over the shower and changing area roof?" asked the builder again, looking at Roman.

"What size do you normally use?" came the reply.

"Well…six by twos, seven by twos, or something like that."

"Either way, it will be fine," said Roman.

Tony came out of his house's front door. Roman turned his back to him and began examining the large steel lintel that was on the forklift's forks. One of the builders walked over to Tony and relayed the news that he had just confirmed the rafter sizes from the building inspector. Roman started talking to the builder, who was still standing near himself, still keeping his back to Tony.

"Can you tell the homeowner that I need a copy of his building and contents insurance, please? I will need it today, it's council policy," said the inspector. "I'm going over to the far side of the excavation to check the ground conditions."

Both men started walking in opposite directions. Tony was also walking towards his car when the builder stopped him.

"The building inspector needs a copy of your building and contents insurance policy. Do you have building and contents insurance for your house?"

"What? Why? You mean for the extension?"

"No for your house, he said."

"Why? What's that got to do with my extension?"

"Council policy apparently—it's a new thing that's just come out, he told me to ask you."

"Yeah, I'm sure we've got it, I'll send it over to him," said Tony.

"He said he needs it today," said the builder.

"Sake," said Tony under his breath. "Sue…SUE…"

Sue appeared at the front door.

"Have we got house insurance?" said Tony.

"Err, yes…I think so," came the reply.

"The inspector needs it. Can you dig it out and give it to him?"

Tony turned to the builder and nodded towards the front door where Susan was standing. "She'll deal with it. I've got to go."

Tony got into the passenger seat of his car, and Clem drove him away. Tony had a meeting with a friend of his, Gino Turtelli, a drug dealer from Manchester. Gino and Tony had met in a youth prison some years previously and had remained friends ever since. Tony was sentenced to six months in youth custody after the idea that he had been put in motion had gone pear-shaped. At that time, Tony was doing a lot of house break-ins and had been the police's number one suspect for a long time. Tony knew that his luck wouldn't last forever, and it was only a matter of time before he was convicted.

So, to throw the police off his trail, he decided to break into the local mortuary, steal the fingers from a corpse and use these to leave fingerprints at the scene of the crimes he was committing. Unfortunately, for Tony, he was caught with a hacksaw by a security guard in the mortuary midway through removing the index finger of a dead body. In court, Tony protested his innocence by saying that he was in the mortuary to pay his last respects to a dead friend, who had promised Tony his finger. Tony's defence collapsed when he admitted that he didn't know the man's name.

Gino Turtelli, or 'The Turtle' as he was known, was the son of Italian migrants. He was small in stature, but he had a big ego. Some people remarked that he suffered from small man syndrome. Early in his crime career, some people referred to him as 'The Terrapin', whilst others referred to him as 'the turtle's head' or 'the missing link', in reference to his prominent forehead, hairy body, and ape-like posture. Gino was older than Tony and was born and bred in Manchester. He was recently divorced and was now dating a woman twenty years his junior. When he had originally asked his wife for a divorce, she became violent and hit Gino in the face with a wine bottle. After this, she calmed down for a few days, but in these few days, Gino was rushed to hospital, with symptoms of food poisoning after his wife had made him a salad lunch, accidentally using rhubarb leaves instead of lettuce. Twice.

Gino originally trained as a chef for the first couple of years after leaving school, but his apprenticeship didn't pay well, so he dropped out of college and turned to a life of crime. At the beginning of his crime career, Gino saw another drug dealer operating around Manchester as his rival. In warning his rival to stay away from Gino's area, Gino hit upon a plan that ultimately ended with a spell in hospital, and then a spell in youth custody for him. One night, Gino traced his rival to a house on Moss Side. He had taken a can of petrol out of the passenger-side floor of his own car and poured it over the roof and underneath his rival's car. From that car to his own car, he left a petrol trail that he was going to ignite by dropping a lit cigar out of his car window into the petrol stream when his rival exited the house that he was in.

Unfortunately, Gino had dropped the petrol can lid whilst throwing the petrol onto the car, and this had rolled away and was lost to him. Upon reaching his own car, Gino had placed the petrol can back into the passenger-side footwell whilst he waited for his rival to appear. Gino's plan was to wind down his window, smile and wave at his rival, and then drop his cigar onto the petrol trail. He would then drive off as the other car went up in flames.

Whilst waiting for his rival to exit the house, Gino decided to light a cigar whilst sitting in his car. The fumes from the small amount of petrol still left in the open petrol can in his car ignited in a flash of fire and heat, and although Gino wasn't seriously burnt, his eyelashes, eyebrows, and the front and top of his head hair disappeared. He managed to exit the car and flag down a passing car, and the driver took him to hospital. Gino was left with scarring on his face and head, and his hair never grew back properly. His receding hairline only extenuated his prominent forehead, and so as soon as he was released from prison, he made a couple of trips to Turkey and came back with ultra-white teeth and a floppy curtain hair transplant.

As Clem and Tony exited Tony's drive, Roman walked up to the front door. It was open, but the hallway was empty. Roman called into the hallway, and Susan appeared.

"Hi, I'm the building inspector. I'm here for a copy of your insurance policy," said Roman.

"You better come in then," said Sue as she walked off towards the study without looking back. Roman followed her.

The study had a display cabinet exhibiting a collection of rare British banknotes. Tony was proud of these, and everyone that came into his house got the history lecture of the origins and worth of his banknotes on display.

"These are impressive," said Roman, looking through the glass top of the display cabinet at each of the notes on display.

"Just keep your hands to yourself," said Sue. "They're Tony's pride and joy. Worth a fortune. He even showed them on the telly once, on that antiques programme."

Roman looked around the room, and his gaze settled on a shelf above the fireplace. There was a wooden object on display. It was an old policeman's truncheon. He had seen one like it before. Sue saw him looking.

"That belonged to Tony's great-grandfather. He was brought up in a workhouse, and he used to get beat up by it. It's an old copper truncheon. When Tony's great-grandfather eventually left the workhouse, he broke back in and stole it. Not before giving the workhouse governor a good beating with it, first though. It's a family heirloom. It's been handed down through the family ever since."

"It does look impressive. I wouldn't want to be on the receiving end of it," said Roman. "Oh, before I forget, I will need Tony's email address and his mobile number."

Sue spelt out Tony's email whilst Roman wrote it down. She then scrolled through her mobile phone to retrieve Tony's mobile number. She read it out loud and then suddenly stopped.

"Sorry, I'm not allowed to give out Tony's mobile number, you will have to have mine or use the landline number," she said.

"No worries, I'll put a line through it," said Roman. "What's the landline number?"

After rummaging through the desk drawer, Susan handed over the insurance documents.

"You can copy the details off them, or I can photocopy them for you."

"If you don't mind," said Roman, handing back the documents. "Can you also write Tony's date of birth on the top as well."

Susan photocopied the insurance documents, and Roman put them into his briefcase. He then walked to the front door. As Sue opened the door, Tony rushed in and ran past Roman and up the stairs. He didn't notice the building inspector leaving, as he was in too much of a rush.

"Forgot my cash card," he shouted from the stairs. A few seconds later, he shouted downstairs from the bedroom.

"Sue," No reply. "SUE."

"What?" came the reply.

"Have you put my trousers in the wash? My cash cards are in the pocket."

Roman was walking to the driveway gates but stopped at Tony's car. Clem was sitting in the driver's seat, listening to the radio."

"Can I give you a leaflet to give to Tony? I forgot to leave it with them in the house," said Roman.

"No problem!" came the reply.

Roman opened his briefcase and rummaged around in it. He took out two short, thirty-centimetres-long, steel tubes fixed together. "Can you hold these a minute?" he said to Clem, passing the tubes to Clem before Clem could reply.

Clem held the tubes and looked at them.

"What are they?" said Clem.

"I make model aircraft. It's part of the fuselage," replied Roman. "I've come out of the office without the leaflet, I'm afraid," said Roman, taking the tubes back off Clem. "I'll send it out to him."

Clem noticed that Roman was wearing gloves.

"You're hands cold or something?" he said, nodding towards Roman's gloved hands.

"All part of being a building inspector, I'm afraid," replied Roman. "They stop cement and concrete from getting on your hands. It's health and safety gone mad."

Roman walked to the gates at the same time as Tony stepped out of his front door. By the time the car containing Tony and Clem exited the driveway, Roman was nowhere to be seen.

Chapter 4
The Sting

Tony was standing with Clem in the construction area of his garden, at the site of his soon-to-be detached swimming pool. He surveyed his house and garden. He had achieved a lot in life. His mobile phone rang. He didn't recognise the number, but he answered the call anyway. As he listened to the voice on the other end of the phone, a big grin appeared across his face. The conversation ended, and Tony turned to Clem.

"They want me back on that antique programme. They had a cancellation at short notice and wanted me to replace the bloke that was going on. They want me to take my old banknote collection to be valued. They want me to meet them in the foyer of Carlton. They're going to film it today, and it goes out on the telly in four weeks' time. They are going to generously reimburse me for my time. I've got to be there for six thirty this evening. Clem, you pick me up at six and drop me off at the Carlton, and I'll phone you when filming's finished, and I need picking back up."

Roman was sitting in the Carlton Hotel's lobby. He was disguised in his grandmother's black wig and a pair of thick-framed glasses. He had a lanyard around his neck, identifying him as part of the television network. He was sitting in the lobby's comfy chairs, stretched out, and drinking a cup of coffee when Tony walked in.

"Hi!" said Roman, standing up and stretching out his hand for a handshake. "I'm Declan. We are running a bit behind, so we will be going straight to filming shortly. Did you bring your banknotes?"

Tony opened a plastic carrier bag to show a bundle of notes, each one in a clear plastic wallet, looped together by a rubber band.

Both men sat down. Declan looked vaguely familiar to Tony, but he couldn't recall where he had seen him before. He had probably met him on his previous TV appearance.

"I suggest that you put the notes into this security briefcase," said Declan. "You can never be too careful around here." he passed Tony the briefcase and Tony put the banknotes inside.

Declan took back the briefcase and compared its combination lock number to a number he had written down on an envelope that had been placed on the seat beside him. He passed Tony the briefcase combination paper, telling him that the number on the envelope was the number to open the briefcase.

"Right," said Declan. "Let's quickly run through the procedure," he put the briefcase on the floor, between his and Tony's seats.

"There is a celebrity antique valuer in the room. He will look through the notes and give you a valuation. After that, he will ask you some questions about why you are interested in collecting them, how long you've been a collector, and all that kind of stuff. Have a bit of banter with him, and feel free to ask him any questions that you may have."

Tony nodded. "Okay. When do we go up?"

"I'll just pop up and check," came the reply. "I suggest you freshen up, have a pee etc. Take your case with you," said Declan, handing him the security briefcase, "and I will be back down in two minutes and meet you here."

Both men stood up. Tony walked towards the toilets, and Declan walked towards the stairs. As soon as Tony was out of sight, Declan walked back to the lobby chairs where the two of them had been sitting and picked up another security briefcase, identical to the one that Tony was carrying, that had been hidden between their two chairs. Without looking back, he walked out of the main exit double doors and disappeared along the street. Tony came back to the lobby a few minutes later. He waited…and waited, and then tried to phone Declan on Declan's mobile phone. Declan's phone was turned off. After waiting a few more minutes, he walked over to the reception desk to inquire as to which room the film crew was in. The receptionist said that she wasn't aware of any film crew being in the building.

Tony argued that he was there for a television filming meeting in one of the rooms upstairs. Again, the receptionist looked blank. Feeling himself starting to go into a rage, Tony walked back to the chairs that he had been sitting in earlier and tried to phone Declan again. The phone was still turned off. He walked out of the double doors and into the street, looking for anyone that resembled a film crew or celebrity antiques dealer. He phoned Clem, who came to pick him up.

"How did it go?" said Clem cheerfully.

"It didn't go. It was a complete waste of time," came the reply. Tony was trying to unlock the briefcase.

"I don't believe it!" said Tony in a raised voice. "He's gone and given me the wrong combination; I can't get the bloody thing to open." He opened the car door and sat down in the passenger seat.

Thirty minutes later, Tony was at home, sitting at his dining table. He had a hammer. He was going to have to smash the locks off the briefcase with it. Ten minutes later, the case was opened. Inside was a collection of clear plastic wallets containing banknotes. Not his banknotes, though. These were banknotes of different denominations from a 'Monopoly' board game. Tony, realising that he had been scammed, angrily erupted and threw them onto the kitchen floor.

It was around a week later, and Tony had an appointment with his financial adviser. Miss Merryfield had taken over from his own long-standing adviser when Mr Wooldridge retired. Tony had never met Miss Merryfield before, but he had noticed that she was a 'Miss' not 'Mrs' and that she sounded jolly on the phone. To impress Miss Merryfield, Tony had decided to wear his leather jacket, and this was no ordinary leather jacket. It was his pride and joy. Apparently, it once belonged to the lead singer of the punk group "The Clash."

A lighting rigger working on stage in the late 1970s had stolen it from backstage and years later had given it to Tony as part payment on a drug debt. It was black in colour and frayed in all the right places. It was slightly tight on him now but looked the part if it wasn't zipped up. To save time for both Miss Merryfield and him, they had agreed to meet at Henshaw's coffee shop, which was within walking distance from the girl's office and a short drive from Tony's house. Clem would drop him off and pick him up afterwards. A few years ago, Tony would have been at the pub for a combined liquid lunch and meeting, but these days he was trying to project a different image, so he could normally be found drinking coffee al fresco outside of the local coffee shops.

An hour before the meeting was due to start, as regular as clockwork every day, Tony and Clem parked up at the bookies to bet on the horses or dogs and have a catch-up with their friends. They parked up Tony's Range Rover and walked through the bookie's entrance door. Roman appeared in Tony's car. He bent down to tie his shoelaces and pushed a potato into the car's exhaust pipe.

Thirty minutes later, Tony and Clem exited the bookies and went to drive off to the meeting. The car started and then stopped. Clem started it up again, but once again, it stopped. Clem tried a further three times, but each time it culminated in the same outcome. Clem popped the bonnet, and both men got out to look at the engine. Clem jiggled a few wires about, but nothing seemed loose.

Roman appeared on a motorbike. He was wearing a full-face helmet and never lifted the visor. He stopped beside the Range Rover.

"You guys got problems?" he asked, his facial features obscured by a tinted visor.

"It won't start," said Tony. "Well, it starts, but then cuts out."

"Where are you going?" said Roman.

"Henshaw's over the bridge," came the reply.

"Snap!" said Roman, passing Tony a motorcycle helmet.

"Jump on; I'll have you there in five minutes," Clem would stay with the car and wait for the recovery truck.

Tony put the helmet on and climbed onto the back of the motorcycle. At least with a helmet on, people shouldn't recognise him on the back of the motorbike. It wasn't even a proper motorbike. It was an old-type moped that Tony wouldn't normally be seen dead on. There was ample room for two people, and the rear passenger had the luxury of a padded back rest, which Tony thought looked like it was made from a cut-down ironing board. It was. With Tony seated comfortably on the back, Roman sped off.

After a few minutes, Tony's back began to feel warm.

This must be a heated backrest, he thought.

In actuality, it wasn't a heated backrest. The diluted hydrofluoric acid-soaked sponge was covered with a cotton towel that had been fixed to the backrest and leaked acid every time Tony leant back and compressed the sponge. The acid-soaked through the towel and onto Tony's leather jacket, slowly burning a sponge-shaped hole into the back of it.

They arrived at Henshaw's, and Roman stopped the bike. Tony climbed off, and as he was removing his crash helmet to give it back, Roman revved the bike's throttle and sped away, leaving Tony still holding the helmet. For a few seconds, Tony didn't notice the foam crash helmet liner superglued to his bald head. He had taken off the helmet, but the black foam liner was stuck to his head. When he did notice it, he went ballistic. He tried to pull off the foam and did manage to pull the majority of the foam off, but a thin layer, the part that came into contact with his skin, was hard to budge. He had to stop trying in the end, as each tug was also painfully removing parts of his scalp.

Tony walked over to Miss Merryfield and held out his hand for a handshake.

"Janet," said Miss Merryfield. "Tony," said Tony.

Tony was conscious of the black foam remnants glued to his head, but they were so small that he didn't think they were noticeable. He would give the motorbike bloke a hiding though if he ever saw him again. The trouble was, he hadn't seen his face, so he didn't know what he looked like. He would recognise that moped, though, if he saw it again.

Tony's first impression of Miss Merryfield was, "Wow! Fit!" She looked like his wife, Susan, twenty years ago. Janet's first impression of Tony was that he looked like the animated character "Crazy Frog," with his big belly and thin legs. She looked at his bald head. Had he tried to give the impression of having hair by glueing some black foam to his head? And what was with that jacket? It looked like he had tried to make it appear trendier by burning the back off with acid or something. She wondered if she could take a discreet photo on her phone and send it to the girls in her office.

Forty minutes later, the meeting concluded. Tony thought that the meeting had gone well. He had paid for the coffee and cake, making sure that Janet saw the contents of his wallet. The girl certainly had a sense of humour. She kept bursting out laughing for no reason and then apologising. He could also tell that she was impressed with his jacket by the way she kept looking at it. He had posed for a selfie with her, at her request, at the end of the meeting. Result. She was one to definitely work on in the future.

Chapter 5
Things Go from Bad to Worse

A week had passed since Tony's meeting with Miss Merryfield, and the foam was gone from his head, albeit leaving a few scabbed grazes. Sue came into the bedroom as Tony was getting dressed to tell him that someone wanted to speak to him on the landline. She didn't know who it was, but whoever it was had a very deep voice.

Tony picked up the receiver, and a deep voice told him to go to his front door because he had posted an envelope through Tony's letterbox. The voice then told Tony to watch the video on the memory stick contained within the envelope and that he would call again with his demands and instructions in an hour's time. Tony went to his door and picked up a grey envelope from the mat. Inside was indeed a memory stick and a self-addressed yellow envelope made out to "Reuben Kowalski." Tony picked up Susan's laptop and took it into his study, closing the door behind him. He plugged the memory stick into the USB port. There was a video file attached, which he opened.

It was a recording of the fight between him, Clem, and the man who had been seeing his wife all those years ago. The clip showed both Tony and Clem during the fight in the flat, with Tony beating Malcolm. Their faces were clearly visible, and their voices were clearly audible. The date and time were shown in the top left-hand corner of the screen. The recording stopped short of the fatal punch that led to the man's death.

Clem arrived at Tony's front door. Tony let him in, led him to the study, and then showed him the recording on the memory stick.

The telephone rang again. Tony put the call on the loudspeaker.

"I have the rest of the video showing the man's death, and I'm prepared to take it to the police. I want nine thousand, nine hundred and fifty pounds in notes. Go to the post-box on the corner of Winchester Drive at eleven o'clock this morning. I will be watching you through a telescope. Hold the money up and then put it into the self-addressed envelope I've posted through your front door, and post that into the letterbox. The envelope is first-class signed, so I will receive it tomorrow, and then you can have the memory stick. I will post it through your letterbox. Don't be late."

Tony looked at Clem.

"I don't recognise the voice," said Clem.

"Me neither."

"What's the address?" said Clem.

"Timpson Avenue," came the reply.

"Whose name is on the envelope?"

"Rueban Kowalski." said Tony. "He sounds foreign. He wants nine thousand, nine hundred and fifty pounds in cash. That's a weird number." By coincidence, Tony had that exact amount in his wall safe.

"He's going to want more. It's too cheap. He's going to keep coming back for more." said Clem.

"Well, he's made a big mistake trying to blackmail me. In fact, he's made two mistakes, giving me his name *and* address."

At eleven o'clock, Tony walked to the post-box. He took the two bundles of money out of his right pocket and the self-addressed envelope out of his left. He held both in the air, then put the money into the envelope and posted it through the letterbox slot. He then turned and walked away.

Two hours later, before the postman emptied the letterbox, Roman was at the post-box. He looked carefully at the front of the box and identified two carefully concealed, almost invisible fishing lines. He gently pulled on both until a nylon net appeared inside the mouth of the post-box. Roman pulled the net and the contents to the outside of the box. Three envelopes had been caught in the net. He took out Tony's letter and reposted the other two.

The following day, Clem was sitting in his car, waiting for signs of movement at number nine, Timpson Avenue. He had parked down the road so as not to be spotted by anyone at the property. He was getting bored. The house looked empty. As he sat there smoking a cigarette, he noticed a police car pulling up behind him, whilst at the same time one pulled up in front of him. Armed police jumped out of both cars and ordered him to exit his car and lie on the ground. He was told he was being arrested for unlawful possession of a firearm. Clem was stunned. He never owned a gun in his life, unlawful or lawful.

One policeman started searching Clem's car, and after looking under the driver's seat, the policeman pulled out a shotgun, with both barrels sawn off at approximately thirty centimetres. Despite his protestations of being innocent of any crime, Clem was arrested, handcuffed, and placed in the back seat of one of the police cars.

"You're fitting me up," he said to the driver of the police car. "I've never seen that gun in my life."

"We've had a tip off that you've been waving it around and threatening people with it," came the reply.

Clem, shut up. He had been arrested enough times to know that it was wiser to keep quiet whilst under caution. The following day, Clem was released on bail and went round to Tony's. He had telephoned his solicitor from the police station, and his solicitor had phoned Tony. Tony was keen to hear what had gone on.

"I think they're trying to fit me up," said Clem. "They found a sawn-off shotgun in my car, and it's got my prints on the barrel. I can't understand it; I've never seen it before in my life. They've taken it away for testing, and I'm on a delayed charge."

Tony agreed to put his own solicitor on the case. His solicitor was expensive, but he got the right results. Clem, duly reassured, headed back home.

As Clem was driving home, he had to stop at a red traffic light. As he did so, a cyclist wearing full cycling gear pulled up alongside Clem's passenger side and tapped on the side window. Clem pushed the button, and the electric window wound down.

"Your wheels are wobbling, mate," said the cyclist, pointing to the front driver's side tyre. "Your wheel nuts are loose."

Clem thanked the cyclist and opened his car door to look. Unable to determine if his wheel was falling off from his seated position, he stepped out of the car to check the wheel nuts. As he turned away from the man on the bicycle, the cyclist put his hand into the passenger-side window that Clem had just opened and lifted the trilby hat off the seat. He then mounted the pavement with his bike and proceeded to pedal furiously away. The car tyre was fine. Clem got back into the driver's seat and looked through the car's open side window. The cyclist was gone. He didn't realise that his hat had been stolen, though. The driver of the car behind Clem parped his horn to alert him that the traffic lights had changed to green, and Clem quickly drove off.

Tony was awakened at 3am by his dog barking. He had gotten out of bed to chastise the dog when he noticed flames and smoke through his bedroom window. It looked like the changing area of his detached swimming pool building was on fire. He grabbed his dressing gown and ran outside, shouting at Sue to wake up and call the fire brigade.

He got close to the pool building. It was well and truly on fire. He grabbed a plastic bucket from beside a water butt and filled it up. He threw it towards the fire, but it was too little, too late. The water hardly touched the flames, as he couldn't get close enough to throw it directly onto the fire because of the heat, forcing him from standing too close. There was nothing he could do but stand back and watch. The fire brigade arrived and took over. Within ten minutes, the fire was out, and what was left of the charred wooden structure was soaking wet. One of the firemen showed Tony a trilby hat with cigarettes in the headband.

"We managed to save this," said the fireman. "But we need to hang on to it in case it's needed for evidence."

"Evidence?" said Tony, looking puzzled.

"Yeah, it's arson, mate," he pointed to two partially melted petrol cans. "Petrol's been chucked everywhere."

"The hat's mine," said Tony, taking it from the fireman. "I must have left it out earlier."

Clem had been out drinking with some mates. These mates were not part of his or Tony's immediate circle, but they were part of another local gang, and Clem often bumped into them whilst doing business for Tony. They were all drunk, and they had all had a good time. The gang that Clem had been out with was obviously respected in their local area, as in the pubs that they had been to that night, with just a click of their fingers, additional rounds of drinks were brought over to their table. The criminals had the usual 'hangers on' surrounding them, and these sometimes paid for the beer, so it had been a cheap night. However, it was nights like these when Clem missed female company and wished that he never lived alone. His previous girlfriend had left him when she discovered what Clem really did for a living. He put his key into the front door, unlocked and opened it, and stepped inside. He switched on the kitchen light and saw Tony sitting at the kitchen table.

On the table in front of Tony were Clem's trilby hat and the yellow envelope addressed to Reuben Kowalski. The envelope was empty. Beside the envelope, was also one of Tony's antique banknotes in a plastic wallet.

"Reuban Kowalski, I presume," said Tony.

"Where's my money and where are my banknotes?"

Two men walked into the kitchen from the living room.

"You know Mick and Nick," said Tony as the two muscular men stepped into the room. Clem started to protest. He knew both Mick and Nick, and he knew why they were both here.

Mick and Nick were cousins. Both were thirty-three years old, and to a certain extent, both were similar in appearance and build. Both went to the gym every day, and both worked as enforcers for Tony. Mick was the more intelligent of the two and was usually the one to make verbal threats to people, whilst Nick was more physical. Mick was an athlete and good at all the physical sports that he partook in. One of his hobbies included reading books on facts and taking part in pub quizzes. He had a very good memory for reciting facts, especially sports-related facts, and was always the first person to be included in a pub quiz team.

With his sports knowledge of football, rugby, and boxing, he could hold his own both mentally and physically against most sports presenters, opponents, and professionals. Occasionally he would work in a bookmakers that Tony frequented, and sometimes he worked as a driver for Tony's criminal mates. He was a popular man, but he was known to have a vicious streak, and he was known through the underworld as being both loyal and ruthless.

"I trusted you, Clem. I really did," said Tony. "You got greedy, though. You can tell these two what you've done with my money." With that, he got up and walked out of the room, then out of the broken back door, leaving the three men alone.

Two days later, Tony was awakened by a phone call from the police. They wanted a meeting with him because of a suspicious insurance claim that Tony had just made. They said that Tony had phoned his insurance company to make a claim regarding the fire at his property the day after the fire. The insurance company had alerted the police when they realised that Tony had had a fire, just two days after amending his insurance policy to include arson and upping any insurance payout to double what it had been before. The payout was put on hold pending an investigation by the police into potential fraud.

Chapter 6
The Enemy Within

Tony was in the bookies. His friend and sometimes partner in crime, Morgan, walked in. Morgan owned a percentage of the bookmaking business. Morgan, or Morgan the organ, as a few lady friends called him, was a big man who spent a lot of time in the gym. He was thirty-four years old and highly respected throughout the underworld. He didn't particularly like Tony and secretly wanted to take over Tony's drug empire, but there was no overt animosity between the two men. Morgan had once had a promising career as an amateur boxer and was on the verge of going professional, but he had received a lifetime ban from the sport for attacking his opponent during a match.

His rival had been taunting him through the early rounds, and Morgan had attacked him with his knees, feet, and head and had been immediately disqualified. He had a few unlicensed boxing matches that he won, but he gave it all up for his criminal career. He was known as a violent man to the police, and if he was ever arrested, the police would do so as part of a group. Not that he was arrested much these days. He had a friend in the force who would tip him off if the police were planning anything against him. Morgan would pay this man money every few months to keep this friendship alive.

Morgan walked over to Tony.

"Is this the right room for an argument?" he said smiling, quoting Monty Python.

Tony looked at Morgan but said nothing.

"Tony," Morgan carried on, looking at Tony's face. "Why did you kill Clem?"

"He tried to burn my extension down," came the reply.

"You sure about that."

"Of course, I'm sure!" snapped Tony.

Morgan took his phone out of his pocket and showed Tony a video clip.

"He was out with us that night. All night. He was steaming. We were in the Earl. There was a group on. That's him jumping around on the stage."

Tony looked stunned for a moment and then said, "Well, he robbed me."

"I don't think it was him," replied Morgan.

"It was too neat." Nick said that all the evidence was on the kitchen table. "Clem never admitted it. Even Nick doesn't think he did it. I think someone set him up to split you two up. Someone's coming after you, and you've made their job a lot easier by getting rid of Clem. It's either a bent copper trying to make a name for himself or it's a rival. If it's a rival, we both need to watch our backs."

Tony nodded thoughtfully. It would make sense to try to isolate someone before going in for the kill.

Morgan looked at Tony. Tony was getting soft, a has-been. Nick had told Morgan that someone had burnt Tony's extension down, and Mick had told Morgan that someone had robbed Tony of ten grand and stolen his antique banknotes in a sting type of scam. Tony couldn't go to the police regarding the thefts, but he had told everyone to keep their eyes and ears open for anyone selling old banknotes. No doubt, whoever it was that was targeting Tony would carry on with his vendetta against him now that he was on a roll. Morgan decided to put a man on Tony to see if the perpetrator could be identified. Morgan recalled the time he had told Tony that Tony's wife was having an affair, hoping that Tony would kill or maim the bloke in question.

Morgan had received word that the man had been selling ecstasy tablets on Morgan's patch, and Morgan wanted a warning sent out. Clem had bungled it, though, by identifying the wrong person, and Tony and Clem had killed the wrong man. Morgan and his friend Eddie then had to go round a few days later and finish the job properly. They never killed the man, but they gave him a severe beating and slashed his face with a knife. The man spent nearly a week in hospital, before he was discharged. He then moved away from the area.

It was a constant battle to prevent other dealers from selling on his and Tony's patches and undercutting their prices. A few years earlier, a young, enterprising individual had gained access to a derelict workhouse basement and somehow managed to turn the electricity on. He had managed to bypass the existing fuse boxes and regulators and hook up an electric feed directly to the incoming power source.

The cable had no way of being shut off once it went live, though. The man had set up a very productive cannabis factory in the basement and was selling it on Tony's turf. When word filtered through to Tony, he got Clem to follow the man. The man had led Clem to the workhouse, and Tony made an anonymous phone call to the police, and the basement was raided. All the cannabis plants and growing equipment were seized and destroyed by the police, and the dealer went to prison.

It was a few days later, and Morgan had been doing his own investigation into the stuff that had happened to Tony. He concluded that there was more to Tony's misfortune than met the eye. Tony had been conveniently stitched up, and it wasn't by him or anyone he knew. Tony thought that Clem was behind all his troubles, but Morgan had known Clem for several years, and that just didn't add up. Was someone else trying to muscle into their territories? Morgan's sometimes partner, Eddie Monkton, or Monkfish, as he was known, was in the scrap metal business. He and his brother had started their life of crime by trading in stolen scrap metal. They often laundered both Morgan's and Tony's drug profits for a fee. Over time, their business had grown to such an extent that it was on the cusp of becoming legitimate.

Morgan knew that the brothers had differing opinions about this. Perhaps one of them was thinking of moving into the drug business on Tony's patch. Eddie also branched out into the recycling business in other ways. He had started to deal with shredded recycled plastic as well. This hadn't gone down well with another recycling outfit a few miles away, and a feud had started between them. Eddie wasn't too bothered about this, though. He had friends. Morgan and Tony could supply muscle if he needed it, and he could also muster a crew together if violence was required. All of these men were up for a fight.

Roman had gone to visit his mother. He thought that George would be down the pub, so they could sit and talk in a relaxed atmosphere. Roman wanted his mother to either throw George out of the house or leave him and come and live with him at his cottage. He had asked her on numerous occasions, but each time she declined, stating that she didn't know what George would be capable of if she did either. If she went to the police to have George prosecuted for the many beatings, he had given her or applied for an injunction against him, his friends would find her, or even worse, Roman, and god knows what they would do. Roman sat her down at the table. Unbeknownst to him, George was only half asleep on the settee in the other room.

"Dad was murdered," declared Roman. "I found a video clip on his old computer where his webcam had filmed it all."

"Murdered by who?" said his mother in an incredulous tone. "Who would want to kill your father?"

It was a man called Tony Babbage and his friend Clem. "I think they thought that Dad was having an affair with Tony's wife. Tony's a gangster."

George sat up noisily in the other room. Roman quickly pushed an envelope over to his mum.

"This is for you, keep it away from George," he said in a low voice. George walked into the kitchen, too late to see Ruth drop the envelope onto her lap.

"I'm nipping out to the bookies," said George.

"I might go to the pub afterwards so don't do me any dinner. I'll see how hungry I am when I get back," he shot a look at Roman.

"Try not to be here when I get back," he said, as he walked out of the house.

When he had gone, Roman told his mother about the money in the envelope. It was stolen from Tony, but it couldn't be traced. There were five thousand pounds in there. He had split the other five thousand between ten charities. He didn't mention the old banknotes or the fire in Tony's pool building. With that, Roman stood up, said his goodbyes, and headed for the front door.

"Make sure you hide that money somewhere where *he* won't find it. You may need it soon," he said mysteriously.

Two days later, Roman had been sitting in front of the television, half watching it and half nodding off, when someone knocked at his front door. He got up to answer it. He had been waiting for his neighbour to come round and collect the moped and assumed that it was him. When he opened the door, four men forced their way past him, pushing Roman into the hallway and closing the door behind them. Morgan nodded to Mick, and Mick and Nick grabbed and held Roman's arms.

"I'll keep this short and sweet. I'm Morgan, this is Eddie, and this is Mick and Nick," said Morgan, as he pointed out to the people. "We're friends, Tony. Do you know Tony? The man that you think killed your dad. Your stepdad told me that you want justice. We're here to tell you to drop it. He's dead, end of. Not that I care what happens to Tony, but if he gets lifted, we might all be implicated. It was me who told Tony that his wife was having an affair. Unfortunately, for your dad, Tony killed the wrong man. The last thing we want is the coppers sniffing around our business."

He carried on talking. "I think that you are behind the fire at Tony's place, and I also think that you had his money. I don't care about that. But I am here to give you a warning. We know where you live, and if we have to come back, I will introduce you to Stanley." He took a retractable trimming knife out of his pocket and waved it under Roman's chin. "Now take your punishment like a man and hope that our paths never cross again."

With that, Mick and Nick gripped Roman's arms with a stronger grip, and Eddie, who had been silent throughout the conversation, punched Roman in the stomach. Roman gasped and sagged to his knees, but Mick and Nick pulled him up straight again. Eddie punched him a couple more times in the stomach and finished Roman off with a punch to his jaw. Roman lapsed into unconsciousness, and the two men holding him up let him slump to the floor. All four walked back out of the front door, closing it behind them.

A few minutes after the beating, Roman began to come round. He slowly crawled into the living room and pulled himself up onto the settee. He checked his face for blood. He hadn't been slashed, which was a bonus. He was in pain though. He got up to try and walk. He could walk if he walked slowly. He looked in the mirror at his face. It was already swollen up on one side. He could move his jaw though and so he didn't think that his jaw was broken. He walked into the kitchen to find the paracetamol. These men were bullies and gangsters, and the world would be a better place without them.

It was a week after his beating, and Roman put the first part of his plan into action. He had followed Morgan's henchmen around their drug dealing area for a few days, and he understood how they distributed their drugs. It was mainly cocaine in small plastic bags that they sold. He also got to recognise a lot of the buyers and users. Roman got to know a couple of Morgan's dealers who were lower down in the pecking order. These dealers only had small areas to deal with. Roman was unknown to them, so dressed in his black wig and glasses, he stopped one of them and told him that he had just been released from prison and was back operating out of the old workhouse. He then asked if the man would prefer to deal for him instead of Morgan. He told the dealer that he was going to be selling his cocaine at half the price of Morgans in Morgans area and that he was going to put Morgan out of business.

Roman had gambled that the dealer would be too loyal or scared of Morgan to take him up on his offer and would tell Morgan about this meeting as soon as he could. Roman gave the dealer his mobile phone number in case the man changed his mind about working with him. Within a couple of days, Roman received a call from Morgan stating that they would both be better off if they formed a partnership, with the profits split equally between the two of them.

Roman agreed and asked Morgan to come alone for a meeting between the two of them at the workhouse.

At the workhouse, Roman was working on the doorframe time portal. He knew that he could increase the number of coils surrounding the frame and increase the power to these copper coils by using mains electricity. According to his calculations, this should allow any potential time traveller to go further back in time and would mean that the potential time traveller would not have to crawl through a smaller wooden frame contained within the larger one. He had already calculated that if he wasn't using mains electricity to power the portal, he could attach a 12-volt power inverter to the cable between the battery and the timeframe, and this would boost the power hitting the copper coils to 230 volts. A massive increase, although this method would drain the battery faster.

Alternatively, he identified an incoming electricity feed that had been terminated at a metal fuse box on the basement wall. This cable went into the fuse box from the top. The box had a rusty metal handle type switch on the side to turn the power on and off. A struggling electric cable that exited the bottom of the fuse box and dangled about two feet from the basement floor was the live feed out. Upon opening the fuse box cover, Roman discovered that all of the fuses had actually been removed and the electricity, all 450 volts of it, had been wired directly to the feed out, making the cable permanently live when the side handle of the box was pulled down into the 'on' position. This was obviously the handiwork of the drug dealer that had been growing cannabis in the basement for a few years previously and would mean that anyone going through the portal door would have to mind that they didn't touch the copper wire coils on the way through if this option, the 450-volt option, was used.

In certain respects, the basement was well suited for growing cannabis. The concrete floor above, the basement acted as a barrier to heat and light identification from above, and the area was quite spacious. The electricity feed was not monitored, and so nobody would come around to read the electricity to see if there was actually a metre installed. The only drawback was that the wooden stairs that were needed to enter the basement had either been destroyed or rotted away over the preceding years. Entry into the basement was gained via a twelve-foot-long wooden ladder that was propped up from the concrete basement floor to the old doorway entrance on the ground floor, and the ladder was showing signs of rot.

So, in effect, if somebody was in the basement and the ladder was removed, they would probably be trapped in there unless they had some other means of scaling the eight-foot walls. During the Second World War, the basement had been divided into two areas, separated by a wooden wall with a wooden door built into it. Although the wooden wall remained, the door and doorframe were removed by the cannabis grower to make it easier to heat and light all of the cannabis plants and create extra growing room. Roman had decided to replace that doorframe with his own.

The portal was built. Roman had connected the copper coils to the 450-volt mains electricity without any mishaps, although he had been wearing rubber-soled Wellington boots and thick rubber gloves just in case. He hesitantly pulled the switch down and turned on the electricity. Other than a faint humming noise coming from the metal fuse box, there was no way of knowing if the electricity was flowing through the portal copper coils. He would have to try it by stepping through the portal, having a look around on the other side, and then stepping back onto this side. The room on the other side of the frame was dark. This side of the basement didn't have any windows, and Roman was reluctant to try and connect some light bulbs to the main electricity.

He braced himself to step through the doorway. He had removed all metal objects from his person in case the electricity flowing around the frame arced and gave him an electric shock. He mentally made a note to count backwards from five and jump through. He had just started to count when a voice came from the doorway opening above.

"I could pull the ladder up and leave you to rot down there." said Morgan. "But I really want the satisfaction of giving you a good kick-in first. Then you can rot down there."

Roman looked up at him. He had been caught completely unaware. Morgan was a day early.

"I had a gut feeling that it was you all along," said Morgan. "That's why I came alone. Well, just me and Stanley. I did warn you what would happen if our paths crossed again." He started to climb down the ladder.

Roman was trapped. A feeling of panic engulfed him. If the portal door didn't work, he would be trapped in the basement with Morgan, and that was never going to end well for him. Morgan reached the bottom rung of the ladder and stepped onto the concrete floor. He took out a knife from his pocket. Roman looked at the knife, then at Morgan, and then ran towards the portal frame.

Morgan ran after him, thinking that the boy may have a weapon in there that he could fight back with. Roman jumped through the doorframe and landed on grass, unscathed. A second later, Morgan jumped through. He gave an involuntary cry as the knife flew from his hand.

The metal knife had touched the copper coils on the way through. Morgan landed on grass on the same side of the doorway as Roman, but the knife had landed on the concrete floor on the other side of the doorway. Roman was on his feet immediately, but Morgan was stunned and semi-conscious for a few seconds after receiving the electric shock. Roman jumped back through the portal frame, into the basement, and into his own time. He ran over to the fuse box and pushed the lever switch up, cutting the power to the portal and trapping Morgan in the past. He would wait a few hours and then reactivate the portal to satisfy his curiosity about how far back in time the portal had taken them. He would take a wooden bat or something with him, though, just in case Morgan was waiting on the other side.

Chapter 7
A New Life Beckons

Morgan took a few seconds to come round. He wasn't sure what had just happened, but he was now lying on his back on the ground in a woods. He had no recollection of how he got there. Somehow, he had been knocked unconscious, which seemed unlikely given that he had no pain around his head or face, or he had been drugged and dumped into the woods at the back of the workhouse. That was it! The boy had obviously drugged him somehow. He had probably touched something going through the doorway, and he had absorbed whatever substance it was through his skin.

The boy must have known that he would follow him through that doorframe thing and smeared something on the sides of it to contaminate him. It would have been easy for the boy to move him and dump him outside if he had been rendered unconscious. He made a mental note to find the boy and leather him even harder when he got back home. He would cut him and break some of his bones.

Morgan could see that there was some sort of camp a couple of hundred metres away. There was a smoking bonfire in the middle of a few wooden huts. There were some signs of life—people moving—but they were too far away to make out their features. *Hippies,* thought Morgan.

"Long hair, flowery shirts, and flared trousers, no doubt." He took out his mobile phone from his jacket pocket, but it wouldn't switch on. Unbeknownst to him, the circuits inside the phone had fried when he went through the time portal.

Morgan got up and headed towards the hippy camp. It might actually be a camp of eco-warriors. Bloody eco-warriors—he hated them. A group of them had once superglued themselves to the road outside of his house. He had gone out to move them on, and a scuffle had broken out after he thought one of them had tried to glue himself to Morgan's jacket. A newspaper photographer had arrived at the same time as the scuffle, and Morgan's picture had made the headlines. From the photograph, it looked like Morgan was part of the protest group. Morgan was sticking two fingers up at the photographer at the time, and the newspaper headlines read "Crude Oil."

He looked around the camp. There were no plastic tarpaulins, no petrol, generators, and no vehicles. It dawned on him what it was. It was one of those social experiments where people lived for a few months as our ancient ancestors did. It was self-sufficient, living off the land, and survival research. He had seen a documentary about it once on TV. These people were actors.

Morgan had lost his bearings, though, because he couldn't see the workhouse from where he was standing. He walked over to a scruffy man who looked the most normal. The man was tall and thin. His hair was unkempt and merged with his unkempt beard. His small eyes and his mouth looked too small for his shaggy head. He was dressed in sandals, a baggy pair of trousers, and a sleeveless leather tunic that was fastened at the front by a leather cord. Judging by his unkempt appearance, *the man was obviously an actor or reenactor*, thought Morgan, but hopefully he would have a mobile phone stashed away in one of the huts. Though the man didn't look too helpful or friendly, Morgan was prepared to get physical if the man refused to help him.

"I need to borrow your phone for a minute to make a quick phone call," said Morgan.

The scruffy man stared at him but said nothing.

"I've been drugged and dumped here, and my cars at the workhouse. I need directions back to the workhouse," said Morgan.

The man stared back at him but still said nothing.

Morgan took a step closer, and the man took a step back.

"Look, just tell me where the workhouse is, and nobody will get hurt," said Morgan.

The man walked through the doorway of a wooden hut and emerged a few seconds later with a vicious-looking wooden club.

Morgan stepped back and pointed at the man with his outstretched finger.

"I know where you live, pal. Bad things will happen if I have to come back. I hope you're insured," he threatened.

The man still said nothing. Morgan wasn't sure if the man understood English; perhaps he was foreign and hadn't understood what Morgan had been asking for. He made another attempt at communicating with the man.

"Look pal. All I want is directions to the workhouse, and I will be on my way." The man still didn't speak but gestured with the wooden club in a wide-arc movement. Morgan assumed that the scruffy man didn't know where the workhouse was. According to his gesturing with the club, the direction could be anywhere from the left-hand side of the woods to the right-hand side of it. He decided that he would ask someone else.

A woman was crouching down and skinning a rabbit. Morgan walked over to her. She was obviously part of the setup as well. He noticed that she hadn't got a lot of clothes on. She stood up and offered him the rabbit skin. Morgan noticed her black and brown teeth. When she stepped closer, he could smell her. She smelt like a dead animal, and her hands were filthy too. She obviously hadn't washed in a while. The boils on her face looked quite realistic, though. Obviously, made from silicone or something. He asked her if she had any water, chocolate, or a mobile phone. She went into a hut and came out with a bowl of dirty water, with pieces of ash or something floating in it. If she thought that he was going to drink that, she was very much mistaken.

He thought about taking the bowl and throwing the dirty water into the woman's face. But he didn't want to get too close to her. She had the knife that she had been skinning the rabbit with tucked into her waistband, and if she lunged at him and scratched him with those long, dirty fingernails, there was no telling what infection he might get. She looked like the sort of woman who was riddled with disease. There was no telling what this lot got up to when the lights went out.

"Drink this!" she said. But Morgan refused. He stepped back to get away from her bad breath.

"Have you got any bottled water and a Mars bar or something?" He asked. He didn't fancy consuming anything that she might have handled. The woman was obviously taking her roleplaying seriously.

The woman looked confused. She cleared her throat and spat on the ground.

"I can pay," said Morgan, taking his wallet out. He also took out a pack of cigarettes. Both the man and the woman watched him light one up. He offered them one, but they refused. *I'm probably in a no-smoking area,* he thought. "Still, he hadn't seen any signs saying that, and he was outside, so who cared, and anyway, who was going to enforce the no-smoking policy? This lot?"

A couple of other men had appeared. One had a couple of dead crows and a battered squirrel or rat hanging upside down on a stick. Morgan couldn't make out exactly what it was, as its body had been battered and was quite bloody. He stared at the crows. There were flies buzzing around them. Surely, they weren't going to eat them. They were probably carrying them around to try to impress him. He wasn't impressed, though. One of the men offered Morgan something black in a wooden bowl. He made the motion of putting it in his mouth and chewing it.

This man was obviously the alpha male of the group, thought Morgan. He didn't know what was in the bowl, but it didn't look like food. The man was obviously taking the piss in front of the others.

Well, if he comes within arm's length of my arm, I'll put him on his arse. He thought.

"Workhouse," said Morgan to the man carrying the crows.

"Workhouse," repeated the man, looking puzzled.

Morgan stared at the man. The charade that they were playing was getting tiresome now. The tall, thin man walked over to the other two, and the three men started to talk amongst themselves. Morgan got the impression that they were plotting to steal his wallet or cigarettes. He decided it was time to leave, turned around, and walked back in the direction he had just come from. As he walked to the edge of the woods, he saw a cottage with smoke coming out of the chimney some way in front of him, and to his right, at approximately the same distance, he could see a large house with a perimeter wall around the gardens. It looked like a manor house, and there was a small gatehouse adjacent to the walled entrance, which you would have to pass to gain entrance to the manor house grounds. He decided to try the cottage first and, if there was no answer, to walk over to the Big House.

Twenty minutes later, he had reached the cottage and knocked on the front door. It was opened by an old man. Morgan explained that he needed directions to get back to his car. It was a Range Rover, and the man could direct him to the old workhouse. The old man was partially deaf. Morgan went on to say that he had been drugged and then dumped in a field near the woods. He pointed to the woods that he had just walked from. The old man hadn't heard what Morgan had said but had tried to lip read. He wasn't very good at it.

"I'm from Belgium, and I'm going to kill the king," Morgan said.

The old man was taken aback. He took a couple of steps backwards to put some space between himself and the murderer.

"You better come in for a while then; would you like something to eat?" said the old man, visibly shaking.

"I could murder a Ruby," said Morgan. "and Chug a toddy," he said looking up at a pot container that looked like it might have spirits in it. *It would probably be out of date though,* he thought, "or contain mead, dandelion wine, or something." Everything about the place seemed old-fashioned.

The old man had read Morgan's lips again. "I could murder a new-born and eat the body," Morgan said.

The man was starting to feel really frightened. The stranger was clearly dangerous. He went into another room and told his wife to go to the manor house and fetch help whilst he tried to keep the stranger here. Morgan looked around the room. There were no electric sockets or lights. These yokels really did live in the past. They really were averse to change. He looked at the old man as he came back into the room where Morgan was seated.

"Haven't you got a hearing aid?" he said. The man was obviously deaf and senile. "I just need directions to the workhouse."

The man said that he had sent it to someone, and they would be here shortly. They would take him wherever he wanted to go. They both sat at the table in silence. Thirty minutes later, the front door opened to reveal three men and the old man's wife standing there.

"Thank god, you've arrived," said the old man. "I was struggling to keep him here. He's from Belgium, and he's been sent to kill the king." The men entered the room, and Morgan looked them up and down. They must have come from a fancy dress or amateur dramatic party. They looked ridiculous.

The best-dressed man out of the three looked Morgan up and down.

"Yes, he's got the eyes of an assassin," he said. This was the third person this year who confided to the old man that they were going to kill the king. He had hanged two of them. Both had protested their innocence until the end. Ever since Cromwell killed the king twenty years ago, it seemed like everyone was jumping on the bandwagon.

The best-dressed man was Robert Layer. He was short and fat, with a round face and double chin. He was the lord of the manor for that parish and lived around half a mile away from the old man's cottage. He had an honorary army officer title and would therefore supply local parish men to the crown in times of war. He had, however, swapped sides during the civil war but was now once again a staunch monarchist. This ensured that he kept hold of his property and title. He was classed as rich by the standards of the day, and under certain circumstances, he was the local justice of the peace, judge, and jury.

He was a cruel man, and he had a lot of influential friends and influence in the surrounding community. He was a widower and had a daughter, aged twenty-one, who lived with him. His daughter doubled as his cook, cleaner, and gardener, and Robert was fiercely possessive of her. He made her accompany him to church every Sunday, and he had plans to marry her for money if the opportunity came along. For her part, the daughter looked forward to her church outing once a week, as this was her only release from the manor house grounds.

Robert's wife was hanged after being accused of witchcraft, a couple of years after tying the knot with Robert, and a couple of months after receiving her inheritance from her newly deceased father. The inheritance package consisted of the title, the manor house, the lodge, four cottages, and around one hundred acres of arable land. Conveniently, the manor house and its estate had been transferred over to Robert only a few days before his wife had been accused. A friend of Roberts', the area witch hunter and associate of the witch finder general, had claimed to have seen Robert's wife turn herself into a black cat when he had gone round visiting Robert's family.

He also claimed that he had heard her utter a spell to ensure that the local townsfolk's children would all die in a plague. A court trial was quickly arranged, and the woman was found guilty and publicly hanged in the village green.

The two men who entered the cottage with Robert were permanent workers on his estate. One, John Barrow, rented a cottage from Robert in the local village, whilst the other, James Hillyer, rented the lodge just outside of the manor house garden boundary. Seasonal workers came and went, but the two men with Robert were his permanent staff. Both were bullies, and they accompanied Robert when he went out every month to collect the cottage rent. They also carried out evictions for him. These evictions could have been spontaneous or acted out on a whim from Robert if someone living in the cottage or farming Robert's land had annoyed him or failed to pay their rent on time. Both men were big men, but both were overweight and looked to Morgan like they were rapidly going to seed.

Morgan got up from his chair, but one of the men pulled out a sword and pressed the point into Morgan's chest.

"Stay seated, you Belgian cur," said the man. "You'll be coming with us soon enough." Robert, the man who was obviously in charge, ordered the others to tie Morgan's hands behind his back.

Morgan looked at the man and then at the sword. The man's hand was shaking whilst he held it. Morgan knew the fear when he saw it, and he saw it in all three men. All four of these men in the room were scared. Homeowners, most of all. As the man with the sword edged closer, Morgan punched him in the jaw, knocking him unconscious. He picked up the chair he had been sitting on and beat the other two men about the head and bodies with it. When the other two men were also out for the count, Morgan made a dash for the door and ran outside towards the woods that he had come from.

He didn't know what was going on, or even if this was all a drug-induced dream, but if it was, it felt very realistic. The old man searched the three unconscious men for money, and when they came round, he told them that the fugitive had taken everything of value from them before he had scarpered.

Robert checked for his purse and found that the lanyard had been cut and that the purse was missing. This was now robbery and attempted murder. He made a mental note that when the fugitive was apprehended, he would make sure that he would be hanged slowly. He might even be able to hang the man until he was unconscious and then revive him so that he could hang him again.

Morgan got to the woods and entered it from a different side than the one that he had originally come from. There was a wide, muddy footpath to follow. It would obviously lead somewhere, probably to the workhouse. Or, at the very least, somewhere where he could get directions back to his car. Ten minutes into his walk, he came across a middle-aged man sitting on a tree stump. The man beckoned Morgan over. Seeing that Morgan looked hot and sweaty, he offered him some water out of a leather water bottle. Morgan took the water bottle and drank the lot. The man was eating some bread and some cooked meat. He offered Morgan some of it, but Morgan refused, saying he just wanted to get home. He asked the man about the workhouse, but the man didn't know where it was.

"Where is home?" inquired the man.

"Oxford," came the reply.

"You're in luck, my friend. Happens I'm going the same way. I can take you there. I'm just waiting on the transport," he said.

"Four-wheel drive?" said Morgan, looking at the rutted track.

"Aye, four wheels," replied the man. "Take this shilling to pay the driver and put your mark on this 'ere piece of paper. The paper was blank, but Morgan signed it."

"You've been schooled," said the man under his breath, looking at the neat handwriting. "You'll go far."

Morgan looked at the shilling. It was dated 1666 and had Charles II's head stamped on the front. The coin looked valuable. The man had obviously made a mistake, as this coin was no longer legal tender. Morgan kept his mouth shut, though.

Morgan sat down on the ground to wait for the transport. Has he stretched his legs out and started to relax, a man silently approached him from behind. With a flick on his arm, he hit Morgan on the back of the head with a short piece of lead pipe. He had hit many people in the same way with this piece of lead. He knew precisely where to hit them and how hard it was to render them unconscious with no permanent damage. Morgan sprawled out in front of him. He would wake up with a headache.

Morgan came around a few minutes later. He had a headache. He was in the back of a locked waggon being pulled by a horse. It looked like an old prison waggon that he had once seen in a film. It was wooden, with wooden wheels that were lined with steel. He looked at his clothes. His clothes had been stolen, and he was now dressed in a blue pair of flared trousers, a smelly white cotton shirt, and an old pair of worn leather boots with no laces in them. There were three other people in the waggon with him. All men. All younger than him.

"Welcome to the Royal Navy," said one. "Where did they get you?"

"On the back of my head, by the feel of this lump on it," said Morgan.

"No, whereabouts in this area."

"A wood just down the road. What about you?" Morgan began to wonder how he could feel pain if he was in a dream or hallucinating.

"Outside a tavern in Banbury," came the reply. "It will be three years at least until we get leave to go back, now that we've volunteered for the Navy."

"What do you mean, Navy? I've never been in the Navy."

The driver answered, "You're in the Navy now, friend, so get used to it."

"The Navy doesn't recruit like this," Morgan said sarcastically. "I've seen the adverts on the telly. I have to sign up and go through basic training. I have to have a medical and have my criminal record checked. You cannot be signed up with just a bang on the back of the head."

"You've taken the king's shilling and signed the contract," said the driver, holding up a piece of paper now with an enlistment contract written on it, with Morgan's signature below. "You're on your way home, mate. Your new home. The St Andrew. It's currently docked at Portsmouth."

One of the men who hadn't spoken began to silently sob. The other one sat silent and stared into space, deep into his own thoughts. Morgan got up and tried the waggon door. It was locked from the outside. Although the waggon was primarily built from wood, the majority of the wood had iron reinforcing in any potential weak spots, including the door. He sat back down and resigned himself to his fate. When they let him out, he would kick off. He would then contact a solicitor and sue the Ministry of Defence for the draconian way in which he had been recruited into the Navy. His head injury alone had to be worth a few thousand pounds in compensation. Then there were his missing clothes, all designer, and then there was his time and inconvenience. All in all, it should add up to a tidy sum.

The driver turned around and spoke to the group of men. "Are any of you educated men?" he asked. "Can any of you read and write?"

Morgan looked around. The three other men shook their heads but said nothing. *These men must be homeless men dragged off the streets,* he thought. "Everyone can read and write, surely."

"Can you read and write?" said the driver, looking at Morgan.

"Of course, I can," came the reply. "And I will be suing the Navy, big time."

"You're a big man, and you look tough," came the reply. "But there's bigger and tougher men that deal with men like you on a weekly basis. Can you count? Do you know your numbers?"

"Of course, I can count," said Morgan, clearly irritated.

"Well, I think you are officer material," the driver replied. "Take this advice. Keep your discipline in check, and you could be in command of your own ship within ten years. They will be hard on you at the start when you get down there, but you look like a man who can take it. They will be watching you. Keep your temper in check, and don't do anything that will get you flogging. I've seen good men with potential reduced to resentful deck hands after being flogged. They came to resent the Navy, and they rarely progressed in their careers." The driver didn't speak again for the next three hours.

The waggon rounded a bend, and Morgan could see the sea and, perhaps more importantly, the docks. A wooden ship with three masts took pride of place in the harbour. Men were scurrying around carrying boxes, sacks, and small wooden barrels. There was a human relay chain in operation, as everything was passed from man to man and deposited onto the ship. The ship was obviously getting ready to sail.

"Your training starts at sea on that ship," said the driver to the men in the waggon. "Keep your mouths shut unless you're spoken to by an officer. Keep your heads down and do what you're told, and you won't go too far wrong."

"Why do we train at sea and not on dry land?" said one of the men in the waggon.

"At sea, you can't run home at night," came the reply. "After three months at sea, you'll be allowed to stretch your legs on some foreign shore, but don't try to abscond. Desertion is a serious charge, and it carries a flogging charge. Whatever port you dock in, the locals will be on watch for deserters, and they will turn you in for a few pieces of silver. It's tempting to run, and if experience is anything to go by, at least one of you four will try it as soon as your feet hit dry land. Don't. Desertion flogging is particularly harsh. It has to be; it's a deterrent to the others on the ship."

Morgan shook his head as reality hit home. This was all a very realistic dream, or he had somehow gone back in time. He didn't know, but he had once read an article about a man who disappeared in full view of his family, only to return a few moments later sporting a ragged beard and ragged clothes. The man claimed to have stepped back in time to around one hundred years earlier and was trapped in that time period for a few weeks until he found the time doorway again and stepped back through, back into his own time. A few weeks in the past had equalled only a few minutes in his own time. Morgan began to accept his fate and realised that he would somehow have to get back to the workhouse and try to find the time doorway.

Chapter 8
The First Mistake

Tony was sitting alone at the breakfast table in his kitchen. An open letter was on the table in front of him. It was addressed to Tony, but Susan had opened it when she picked it up from their Victorian-style post-box at the end of their driveway after the morning postal delivery. Noticing that it had 'urgent' written across the front of the envelope in red ink and was handwritten in what looked like a woman's handwriting, she had accidentally opened it and read the contents. It claimed to be from Tony's girlfriend, stating that she was five months pregnant and wanted money from Tony to move out of the area.

It went on to say that if he didn't supply the cash, then she would have the baby, have a DNA test, and have a field day every day on the maintenance, Tony would be forced to pay her every month. Susan had confronted Tony whilst he was still lying in bed. After a massive argument, she stormed out of the house and drove round to a friend's house. Tony knew that the letter was fake, as he hadn't been in a sexual relationship with anyone other than his wife in the previous twelve months. He was annoyed, though. This was just another thing on top of several other things that were starting to go wrong in his life.

Tony's mobile phone bleeped to alert him that he had received a message. It was a message from an unknown sender asking Tony if he would like to buy the gold coins in the attached photo. There were a few of them, all old and all rare, and Tony was very much interested. The only trouble was that Tony didn't recognise the mobile number that had sent the message, and the message was anonymous. How did this person get hold of his mobile number, which he rarely gave out? He checked back through his mobile phone call log and discovered that he had spoken to this person before.

It was Declan, the television executive, who he met in the hotel lobby—the man who had somehow stolen his rare banknotes. Pretending that he hadn't made the connection between his previous meeting, Tony sent a phone message back saying that he was very interested in buying the coins and asked where the seller wanted the meeting to take place. The reply came back after a few minutes, saying that the exchange could take place in the basement of the abandoned workhouse, as this was where the coins had been found.

On the day of the meeting, Roman was ready to reactivate the time portal by connecting the wires to the high-voltage cable again. He had formulated a plan to send Tony back in time. Tony would probably meet Morgan on the other side if they were both sent to the same time period. Once Tony had stepped through the portal doorway, Roman would cut the power to the wooden frame and trap him in the past also. Roman had made a crude wooden table out of pieces of wood that he had found littered around the basement floor. He had nailed four wooden legs to a flat piece of wood and placed the gold coins on top, clearly visible from this side of the doorway but only retrievable by walking through the portal doorframe.

He would send Tony another message, telling him where the coins were and to examine them before thinking of a price to buy them. Once the trap had sprung, Roman would be rid of Tony, albeit a few gold coins poorer. But it would be worth it. He decided to climb up the rickety ladder out of the basement to create a hideout in a room on the ground floor where he could observe Tony's arrival and watch him enter the portal.

He had fastened a long piece of string to the live connection at the portal doorframe, which he would pull from the ground floor position, breaking the live connection, thus disconnecting the power to the frame when the time was right. He would connect the portal frame to the live electricity cable an hour or so before Tony arrived, as he wasn't sure if the portal would malfunction with the vast amount of electricity flowing through it for a long period of time.

The job would be slightly trickier now, as the metal on-off handle on the metal fuse box had broken and couldn't be turned, leaving the dangling cable permanently live.

Tony stopped the car and parked it up, before he reached the gated entrance to the workhouse. He was early. Mick and Nick stepped out of the car, and Tony followed. They walked to a part of the fence with a sign fixed to it saying, "Private keep out. Premises patrolled by reactive security." Metal panels had been worked loose at this part of the fence, and all three men crawled through the gap into the workhouse grounds. Tony told the two men to work their way around the back of the building by staying in the tree line and trying to gain entrance from the rear.

He would try to get into the building through a window on this side rather than through the door on the front. The door was clearly used by Declan, as it was still slightly open, and Declan might be planning some sort of surprise for whoever walked through it. Tony walked to the edge of the large pond that abutted the building. He would try to get through the window that didn't have a metal sheet fixed to it. This window was positioned partly above the pond, and that was why the security company hadn't bothered to board it up. To climb through this window meant standing in the pond, the deepest part of the pond at over two and a half metres deep. The pond was a good deterrent.

When Tony arrived at the window, he began to have doubts about the feasibility of climbing through it. He could definitely force it open enough to climb through, but he couldn't do it without standing on something solid above the water's surface. Why anyone would construct a pond tight against a building was beyond him. The brickwork that was visible through the water was green with slime. Surely some water must have leaked into the building. He tried a different window. A steel boarded window that was adjacent.

If he could get into this one, he could do it from dry land. Somewhat surprisingly, the steel boarding was screwed into the window frame using 'Philips' screws. Tony took out his multi-function pocketknife. It contained a Philips screwdriver. The screws were short but rusty, but Tony managed to remove enough of them to be able to force the steel sheet off by using brute force. The window catches also gave way. He climbed through the window and into a room inside the building. This was the old laundry room that Roman stood in over a hundred years ago.

Roman climbed up the ladder and stepped out of the basement. Tony's henchman immediately grabbed him. Tony walked over to Roman. "I want my notes, and I want my ten grand. I also want the gold coins you found here. Let's start with the coins. Where are they? I won't ask you twice."

"On the table in the basement," said Roman, nodding to the wooden ladder that connected the two floors.

Tony walked over to the ladder and looked down at the floor.

"Mick, you hold the boy. Nick, you hold the top of this ladder whilst I climb down it. It doesn't look overly safe."

Nick held the ladder, and Tony climbed down. Roman began to panic inside. Tony would collect the coins and then come back up the ladder. Roman had given half of Tony's ten thousand pounds to his mother and the other half to charity. He had also been discreetly selling off Tony's banknotes and making donations to various other charities. Tony and his henchmen would also blame him for Clem's death. They would most likely kill him and leave his body there. He tried to think. Tony had walked through the portal frame and picked up the coins from the makeshift table in the darkened room.

He walked back through the frame and into the basement area, where the ladder was. Because the wires hadn't yet been connected, the portal wasn't live. Tony walked over to the bottom of the ladder and shouted up to Roman.

"I want all of the coins, or you'll never leave this crypt," said Tony. "We can do it the easy way, or you can be laid to rest here."

"I'm not sure that there are any more!" shouted Roman in reply.

"Where's the rest of the coins?" repeated Tony, "This is only part of the trove that was hidden. I want them all. Last chance."

Mick walked Roman to the open doorway.

"Tell him where the money is, or I'll throw you down there," he said.

"It's hidden in the basement, but I don't know where. I've been here looking for the rest of it. It belonged to a man named Julian Wilson. He hid it there, I think, but died before he could retrieve it." Shouted Roman to Tony.

Tony looked around. The basement walls were damp, especially the external wall, which was covered with decades of green moss clinging to the brickwork. He spotted the large slate memorial stone that was built into the wall and was covered with moss. It had Julian Wilson's name carved into it. He smiled. "I know where the coins are, boys."

"Nick, give me hand," he said.

"I'll need Mick to hold the ladder," came the reply. "And he's holding the boy. The ladder looks as rickety as hell."

"Tie him up with some of this wire," replied Tony, folding and throwing a bundle of copper wire up to Nick. "Tie his feet and his hands, and then tie them together. We don't want him hopping off." He then took the Swiss army knife out of his pocket and threw it up to Nick.

Both men forced Roman into a lying position and tied his hands and feet together behind his back. They then ran a cable linking the foot to his wrists to hold him in that position. Nick then descended the ladder whilst Mick held the top of it, then Mick descended whilst Nick held the bottom. Once all three men were on the ground, Tony told them to find something to smash the gravestone with, as the money was behind the stone. The three of them looked around for something heavy. Tony found the hammer that Roman had used to build the table and nail the portal frame together.

"Stand back, men," said Tony, smiling.

He smashed the hammer hard onto the slate plaque. It bounced off, but a piece of slate flew off too. He took another swing and smashed the hammer into the slate again. A small crack appeared, and a trickle of water started seeping through. Tony didn't notice this, as he was looking at his henchmen after every blow with the hammer. The third blow shattered the slate completely, and instantly a deluge of water poured in. It was a giant waterfall, so powerful that it shot across the entire basement room, hitting the opposite wall and shooting back across the floor. Tony and his henchman were momentarily in shock. However, they quickly snapped out of it, and all three tried to move at the same time to get to the ladder first. Tony slipped on the floor.

Mick and Nick reached the ladder simultaneously, and both tried to climb it at the same time. Within seconds, the water was up to their ankles. Tony reached the ladder, and also tried to climb up. However, the weight of the three men was too much for the rickety ladder and it snapped in half, with the three men falling back into what was now turning into a swimming pool.

"Get the ladder up!" shouted Tony in a panic. "Give me a bunk up!" he shouted to the other two, but they were panicking as well. Tony had more reason to panic than the other two; he couldn't swim. He picked up one half of the ladder and tried to place it against the wall below the doorway, but the force of the deluge kept pushing it away.

"Hold onto the ladder, Tony; it's floating; you can float to the top," said Mick, as the water swirled around the bottom of his legs.

Tony grabbed the floating ladder and clung to it. He started to calm down. The water coming through the wall looked like it was slowing down slightly, and if so, it would be unlikely to level out above his chest. It had just about reached its knees. He shouted up to Roman.

"Make your peace with god, Son. We will be with you in no time."

"You've lost everything, Tony," said Roman. "Your pool house is half burnt down, and you have no insurance. You have no money in the bank cos your wife, ex-wife has just cleared you out. Clem's family knows that you killed Clem. They are waiting to have a chat with you."

Roman couldn't see what was happening in the room below him, but he could hear the noise of the outside pond water rushing in and flooding the basement. He remembered the live electric cable dangling from the electric fuse box on the wall and silently shouted down to the men to stay away from it as it was live. They obviously never heard of him. There was a loud bang and a bright flash as the water level reached the end of the dangling cable. The voices below him stopped. The only sound now was the sound of the water still rushing in, albeit slower than it had been.

Roman knew that there was nothing he could do for the three men. He was still tied up, and the now-submerged cable was probably still feeding an electric current into the water. With no fuses or electrical circuit breakers to cut the current, would the electricity flow indefinitely? Roman didn't know. He wriggled over to where Nick had left the pocketknife and opened out the blade behind his back. After twenty minutes of cutting, he managed to get through his wire restraints and make it through the exit door into the workhouse grounds. From there, he walked back home. He hadn't looked into the flooded basement.

A loud bang from the electric cable coming into contact with the pond water was heard by a dog walker. She had phoned the police when she got home, telling them that she had heard a gunshot coming from inside the workhouse. The police had arrived. Two bodies were discovered, and a police investigation was started as to why the two men had smashed through the memorial stone built into the outer brick wall. The most prominent explanation was that the men must have wanted to drain the adjacent pond for some reason but had been overwhelmed by the ferocity of the water deluge before they could turn off the basement electricity. The signs pointed to accidental deaths.

Roman heard the news and began to feel anxious. He knew that there were three people trapped in the basement that day, but the police had only recovered two bodies, Tony's and Nick's. What had happened to Mick? Did he escape? Would he blame Roman for the deaths and come looking for him to exact his revenge? Also, their friend Eddie would most likely start poking around for answers, and before long, he would probably come around for a 'chat' also. He stopped to gather his thoughts and look at the situation rationally. Three men were in the water when they made contact with the electricity cable.

If two men were next to the cable when contact occurred, they would have been electrocuted immediately or at least rendered unconscious and probably drowned. If the third man was further away, probably standing near the portal frame, the electricity would flow through the water, but it would be a much weakened electrical current that far away from the source. In theory, this current could have activated the time frame and dropped anyone that entered it into the past. This was the only thing that could have happened to Mick, reasoned Roman.

Chapter 9
Tying up Loose Ends

It was Sunday morning, and Eddie Monkton had decided to go for a run. He had donned his tracksuit and trainers and was about to run out of his garden gates when he noticed that someone had dumped a wooden doorframe in his driveway. It was standing upright and wedged between his garage and house. It had tightly coiled copper wire along the bottom, up the sides, and over the top. The wire looked like it was connected to a car battery via a small metal box, and there were some other electrical items connected to the frame that he couldn't identify. One wire stretched along the ground to the other side of his garage.

There was a metal security briefcase positioned a few feet behind the frame, but to get to it, you would have to walk through the doorframe. The briefcase was just too far away to reach it from outside of the wooden frame, so Eddie stepped through the doorframe completely to retrieve the case. At that precise moment, a watching Roman turned the power off on the portal, and Eddie disappeared. Eddie picked up the briefcase and turned around to step back through the frame, but the doorframe had gone. Disappeared. So did his house and garage.

He was standing at the top of a field. Looking down the slope, he could see people talking, walking, and generally going about their business. It was either market day or there was a fete. He walked down the slope, heading for a small group of people that were talking amongst themselves. As he got closer to the group, they stopped talking and stared at him. He was staring at them and then at their surroundings. Something strange was going on. The people were wearing silly clothes and talking in, weird English accents. They obviously lived in the old-fashioned houses that were dotted around the landscape. The whole place looked like it was stuck in the past. In a flash, the reality of the situation hit home.

He was drugged, kidnapped, and dumped on the Isle of Man. It was just how he imagined the place to be. It was obviously the work of his rival, Alan Bates, who must have wanted him out of the way for a bit.

He remembered talking to someone once who had made and then drank a brew derived from magic mushrooms and had imagined that he was being held prisoner by a giant lizard. Either this was all a drug-induced hallucination, or he really was in the birthplace of the tailless cats. He stopped short of reaching the group. He had the briefcase, and there was definitely something inside it—probably something that he wouldn't want this group to see. The case wasn't locked, and so he flipped the lid open. Inside was some sort of survival kit. There were packets of dried fruit, water purification tablets, a compass, a Swiss army pocketknife, a gold coin, a bottle of sun cream, and a packet of condoms.

His rival was obviously taking the piss. Condoms and suncream. Did they think they were packing him off for a weekend in Benidorm? What was with the gold coin? Did they think that they could buy him off with a single gold coin? They had crossed the line this time and will pay for it big time. When he got home, he would round up a few of his mates and finish off his rival for good. They had made the mistake of kidnapping him and leaving him alive. He took out his mobile phone, but it wouldn't switch on, and it smelt of burning. They had obviously disabled his phone to stop him, getting picked up and taken home. He walked down to the group of people in front of him and spoke to the man nearest to him. He told the man that he was from Oxford on the mainland and needed to get home. Could he fly from here?

"Fly!" came the reply, as the man flapped his arms and laughed. "There were boats if you wanted to go abroad. Most are sailing from Southampton."

Eddie looked confused. The man obviously did not understand his question. He repeated it, slowly this time.

"Can I get a flight to England from here? There must be an airport."

The man looked confused.

"Go down and ask at the inn," said the man, pointing to what looked like to Eddie, an old-fashioned tavern.

Eddie thanked the man and walked down to the tavern. He pushed the door open and walked inside. The place looked like it was done up to look like an olde-worlde pub from the past. There was nothing modern about the place at all. No pool tables, jukeboxes, pictures on the walls, optics, or even carpets. The pub was mostly empty, but there were a couple of people sitting at a wooden table adjacent to an empty fireplace. One man was smoking a clay pipe with a long stem. As Eddie walked to the bar, the two people in the tavern stopped talking and stared at him. The man behind the bar smiled and asked what Eddie would like to drink. He introduced himself as Gordon, the landlord, and went on to say that his alehouse was stocked with beer, ale, wine, brandy, and port.

He then said that he had hot mutton stew available if Eddie was hungry and that he had a small butcher's out the back if he wanted something else. He had bought ten rabbits only thirty minutes before from the two men sitting around the table opposite, and he could skin a couple and fry them if Eddie cared to wait. He looked Eddie up and down. He had never seen a tracksuit before, and he assumed that Eddie was foreign. Probably Spanish or French. He would encourage him to eat and drink as much as possible and then overcharge him for the drinks and food. He might also be able to persuade the man to stay overnight.

Eddie wanted a drink but was aware that he hadn't brought his wallet with him. He asked the landlord if there were any jewellers around that would buy the gold coin. He took the coin out of the briefcase and showed it to the landlord. The landlord looked at the coin in Eddie's hand, and so did the two men that were seated at the table. The barman slid a beer over to Eddie.

"It's on the house," he said, smiling. "What is that?" he said, pointing at the Swiss army penknife visible in Eddie's open briefcase.

"Just a pocketknife," said Eddie, taking it out of the case and opening up the attachments one at a time. He folded them back into the main body and passed it to the man behind the bar, who in turn opened the attachments one at a time. The man was visibly amazed.

"Would you sell it to me?" he asked Eddie. "I will give you five shillings."

He reached under the counter and took five silver shillings out of a wooden box and passed them to Eddie. The shillings dated from 1663 to 1681, with the ones dated 1681 shining as if they were newly minted. Eddie agreed to the sale. These antique coins would be worth a lot more than the knife. He would have swapped it for one coin if that was the first offer.

The man looked pleased. He gestured to the two men that were sitting around the table. The men walked over and were clearly in awe of the pocketknife. They each took turns unfolding, then folding the blades back again. Eddie watched all three men marvel at the knife. These knives were common everywhere. Everywhere but here, obviously. He began to think that the town was stuck in a time warp. He put the shillings into his pocket. He stared at the two men that had just walked over. Both were thinly built men whose arms seemed too long for their bodies. Facially, they both reminded him of a picture of two bears that he had once seen in a children's book.

To Eddie, they each looked like a cross between an orangutan and a bear. They were definitely related. Probably inbred. If Eddie had any doubts before that he was on the Isle of Man, these two men confirmed that he was. The two men ambled back to their seats around the wooden table.

"Why is everything so old-fashioned looking," Eddie said to the landlord. "Is it for the tourists? Surely the whole place isn't really this backward facing. I haven't seen a car, bike, or even an engine running. In fact, I haven't seen anything made from plastic—no streetlights or anything whatsoever that runs on electricity. How do you tell the time?"

The landlord looked confused but pointed out the rear window at the church sundial.

"That's how we know what time it is," he said. As for the other stuff, it has probably not made its way over here from your country yet. "What country are you from, if you don't mind me asking?"

'England' came the reply, "Oxfordshire in England," Eddie was studying the church out of the window. The church looked vaguely familiar to the church he had gotten married in. He began to realise that perhaps he wasn't on the Isle of Man.

"Whereabouts is this town?" He asked the landlord.

"Bampton," came the reply. "In the district of Oxford."

Eddie stared at the landlord. "I live in Bampton and have lived there for most of my life. This isn't Bampton."

The landlord called over to the man, now seated back around the table. "What is the name of this town," he asked.

"Bampton," came the unanimous reply.

Eddie stood silent as he tried to comprehend what was going on.

"What year is this?" he said to the landlord.

"1682," replied the landlord. "July."

Eddie took the coins out of his pocket and looked at the dates.

"Show me the other coins in your wooden box," he said.

The landlord lifted the box onto the bar, and Eddie went through them, examining the dates on every coin. Each coin was dated before 1682 and had the faces of various historical kings on them. He passed the box of coins back to the landlord, who placed it back behind the bar.

"I just need to check something," he said to the landlord. "I will be back in a few minutes."

He walked outside and into the street. He could see the church. If this was Bampton, then he should be able to walk around and see the manor house and the library. Both buildings were old, as he recalled. He turned a corner and realised that both buildings were there, albeit in their previous incarnations. The high street looked different, but the layout broadly followed the modern layout. He orientated himself to identify where his house should be, and he could see the field from which he first walked down. Either this was all a dream, or he had gone back in time. He thought back to the strange doorway that he had walked through to retrieve the briefcase. Was this a doorway into the past? If so, he needed to find it and step back into his own time. He walked back into the tavern to collect the metal briefcase. He had taken the gold coin out before he left, and that was in his pocket. The three people in the pub were gathered around the briefcase and discussing the contents.

Eddie explained to the group what each item was in the briefcase and gave the dried fruit and water purification tablets to the landlord. He gave the sun cream to one of the men that had been seated at the table when he first walked into the room and the condoms to the other one of the bear-faced orangutans. The man looked confused. Eddie laughed and opened one of the packets. He explained again what it was and what it was for, then put the open end into his mouth and proceeded to blow it up. When it was football-sized, he tied the end and tried to pass it to the man. The man recoiled in horror.

Eddie batted it at him with his open hand. The startled man took another step backward, knocking over a chair. Eddie burst out laughing, and the two brothers glared at him. Taking the compass out of the case and putting it into his pocket, he gave the metal briefcase to the landlord and bid the men au revoir. With that, he walked out of the inn and set off back to the field, where he had first materialised.

Twenty minutes later, he was at the top of the hill. He reasoned that this was the place where he came through the doorway, and so it must be the place where he could get back. *In two hundred years' time, there will be a house and a garage here,* he thought, as he walked about, crisscrossing every inch of the ground to try and find the portal doorway. After thirty minutes, he sat down on the ground.

Maybe the doorway only appeared at the same time every day, or maybe it appeared at midnight. He would have to sit and wait. The last thing that he wanted was to be stranded here in the past. He laid back on the ground and closed his eyes. Within five minutes, he had fallen asleep.

Eddie awoke with a gasp. Something was pressing on his chest and neck. He opened his eyes to find that one of the two orangutang brothers from earlier in the inn was sitting on his chest, pushing a thick wooden stick into his throat.

"Lie still, and you'll live," said the brother that was sitting on his chest. "We just want the gold coin."

Eddie was conscious that the other brother's hand was rifling through his tracksuit pocket. The man retrieved the gold coin and the five silver shillings. He put the coins into a purse that was hanging from some string tied around his waist. He removed a bone-handled steel knife from his waistband and knelt down against Eddie's head.

"I gut animals with this every day, and I will gut you if you start struggling," he said. "If you want to live, just lay there until we are out of sight."

The other brother stood up, keeping the end of the stick pressed against Eddie's throat. When he was standing, the kneeling brother also stood up.

"Remember, stay here until we are out of sight. You are all alone, don't forget, and it won't take us long to find you again if we have to. We know that you aren't armed, and we are. Take this as a lesson in travelling to places where you are not welcome."

With that, both men turned and started to jog down the slope towards the houses and shops. Eddie watched as they ran along the main street and got out of sight. He thought about following the men but thought against it. He was a stranger to the area and to this time. He wasn't armed, and the two brothers were. He could try and report the robbery, but to whom? Did they have police in the 1680s? He didn't know. He was alone. Friendless. Stranded in an alien environment, in a flimsy tracksuit, with no money.

He decided to go back to the inn to kill some time and then return to the top of the field at midnight, just in case the time portal opened up at that time. He walked down to the inn and through the door. He walked past a man seated at one of the tables, eating some stew, and then carried on up to the bar. The landlord greeted him again and started to pour him a pint of beer. Eddie stopped him by placing his hand over the top of the tankard.

"I've been robbed and haven't any money," he told the landlord. "It was the two men that were sitting there," he pointed to the table that the new man was seated at.

"Oh, well, at least you're okay. Have this on the house anyway, and there is a bed if you need one," came the reply. He lowered his voice and explained to Eddie that the man seated at the table hadn't any money either but came into the inn every day for his dinner and a couple of pints of ale. He never paid, and one time the landlord protested and asked for the money. The man punched him in the face and twisted his nose until it started bleeding. Ever since, he came into the inn every day and demanded free food and beer. Eddie turned around and looked at the seated man. He was a big man, aged around fifty years old, but looked massively overweight. Eddie walked over to him.

"Enjoying your food?" He asked the man. He then held out the palm of his hand. "Your free dinners are over, mate. Pay up and clear off. Don't ever come back."

The large man stood up. To Eddie, he looked scared. Eddie punched him in the face and the big man collapsed onto his back who Eddie thought he was. The big man collapsed onto his back. He was unconscious. Eddie grabbed both of the man's feet and dragged him through the inn doorway and into the street. He left the man lying there. He then walked back through to the landlord.

"I don't think he will be back. Not least whilst I'm here. You need a doorman pal, and I'm your man."

The landlord nodded cautiously. Was he substituting one hardman bully for another? Either way, he really did need some protection now, and so he agreed to employ Eddie for protection. He also agreed to clothe Eddie in some 'proper' clothes. Eddie stood and drank his pint. If the portal didn't activate at midnight or the following day, then this job would help him to survive in this time period until he found his feet. His mind was already formulating a plan for his future. The landlord was single, so he probably wouldn't be missed if he disappeared. Eddie would drop a few hints amongst the customers that he was interested in buying the pub to pave the way.

There were butchers out the back of the inn, and Eddie had experience cutting up meat. He had worked as a butcher for a couple of years when he first left school. Eddie reasoned that if he couldn't get back to his own time, he would take over the pub and butchers, look around the village for another profitable shop or business, and work out a way of taking over that as well. He also had the niggling thought that this venture into the past had something to do with that Roman lad. It was too sophisticated for his business rival, and the wooden doorframe that he was stepped through outside his house looked like one that he had seen in Roman's cottage, front garden.

If he got back to his own time, he would arrange an accident for the boy, and if he couldn't get back, then he would hunt down the boys' ancestors and kill them; this would stop Roman from being born, meaning that he couldn't build the time portal, meaning that he, Eddie, couldn't be sent backwards in time. He knew Roman's surname, and he would scour the area for people with the same name. It was a long shot. A massive long shot. But it was all that he had.

In mid-September, Eddie was the new landlord of the inn. He had a receipt for the sale of it and the butchery out back, and the old landlord had moved away from the area one night, unnoticed by anyone. This was Eddie's story anyway. Over the previous couple of months, Eddie had gained more influence over the running of the inn. He had pressured the landlord into buying two large pigs, which Eddie had been slowly starving over the past few weeks by reducing their food intake. On the day of the landlord's move, Eddie held a small new-owner welcome party for the regulars with free ale and meat pies, along with a meat and vegetable stew. The two pigs had at last been fed, and they would carry on being fattened up until the time of their slaughter.

Eddie became known throughout the surrounding villages as a man who would buy gold and silver, no questions asked, and would provide loans secured against jewellery or other items of value. He was a popular landlord and was often seen as charitable to the poor people of the village, especially the women and children, by giving small donations of money and food. This was all part of Eddie's plan. If he was ever sent to trial, these people would be the jury. If he was good to them, they would hopefully be good to him.

Unbeknownst to the people in the village, Eddie was also the leader of a small group of criminals. These men would commit robberies and house break-ins for him, and in return, Eddie would buy the stolen goods and provide the men with alibis for the times that the crimes had taken place. In his first week of working at the inn, Eddie also tracked down the two men who had robbed him of his gold coin. The following week, Eddie and two of his henchmen had beaten both brothers so severely that neither could use their hands anymore and only one could walk unaided. Eddie got his gold coin back. Over the next couple of months, Eddie employed a local couple to run the inn.

Both were uneducated, but Eddie had set them on without recommendations or references. The woman was a good cook and cleaner, and her husband could count. Eddie paid them identical wages at the end of every week, and for this, both the man and woman were grateful, trustworthy, and most important of all, loyal. In return, not serving in the inn every day, meant that Eddie could concentrate on acquiring a new business and tracking down the boys' ancestors. He had worked out roughly where the boy's cottage should stand in relation to the workhouse, but hadn't yet had time to investigate if either building had been constructed in this era. He would find out, though, even if it was the last thing that he ever did.

Chapter 10
A Meeting of Minds

The year was 1682, and Morgan was now fifty. He was still in good shape physically and looked younger than he was. Early on, after disembarking from the naval prison carriage, Morgan realised that this whole episode was not a dream or a drug-induced fantasy. He accepted that he had gone back in time, but he didn't know how or why. He knew that Roman was involved, though, and the time transfer had happened somewhere in the workhouse or on the workhouse grounds. He also realised that talking about his time travelling or previous life might not end well for him, so he decided to keep his mouth shut on that. Perhaps surprisingly, Morgan adapted to seventeenth-century naval life very well. Within a couple of days of being on the ship, he had fought and beat up the toughest non-rated man on there.

The fight was an organised bare knuckle fist fight in front of the ship's officers and crew. Morgan won easily and gained immediate respect from everyone who was watching. He found that he enjoyed the physical side of navel training and the additional responsibilities that the ship's captain began to give him. In just a few years, he had distinguished himself in battle, twice, and in just under ten years, he was promoted to captain and given his own ship. He was highly respected by his crew, not least because wounded men tended to survive better under Morgan's hygiene instructions and regulations. He was regarded as a hero in the local area. When on leave, though, Morgan would often travel back to a wooded area of Oxfordshire, from which he originally passed through time, to try and find a way back home.

On one of his trips back to Oxfordshire, Morgan had walked past the local church and met the daughter of the lord of the manor, Anne. Anne was now thirty-seven years old and still single. She was now allowed to attend church unaccompanied by her father, Robert Layer. This was partly due to Robert's ill health. His eyesight was failing, and he suffered from gout and so struggled to walk any distance. Morgan liked Anne at first sight, and he could see that the feeling was mutual. They started chatting, and when Anne realised who Morgan was and the navel reputation that he had, she invited him to the manor house for dinner and to meet her father.

Morgan had no idea that his path had crossed with Anne's father just over sixteen years previously. He decided to walk Anne home and would freshen up at her house whilst she prepared dinner and prepared the meeting between the two men. A couple of men had been invited to dinner before by Robert, in the hope that a spark of attraction would lead to marriage for his daughter. However, Anne had been repulsed by the old, ugly, chinless, rich men and had taken the dates no further. She felt different from Morgan, though. By the time they had reached the manor house, Anne felt ready for marriage. She hoped that Morgan would feel the same.

The dinner went well. Morgan recognised Robert from their brief encounter years earlier, but Robert didn't recognise Morgan. Faces for Robert were a blur, unless the face was just a few inches from his own. Morgan never let on that he had met Robert previously. Robert had heard about Morgan's reputation, and it was obvious to him that Anne had eyes for him. *Anne was not getting any younger,* he thought, and if the pair married, they could live at the house with Anne waiting on them both and providing heirs to keep Robert's bloodline going. All in all, Morgan wouldn't have been his first choice for a son-in-law, but in the circumstances, he would do. Morgan wasn't rich, but he had savings. He was a bit rough around the edges, but between Anne and himself, they could work on that. Morgan might also come in useful as an unpaid enforcer, especially since he had evicted James Hillyer out of the lodge house for demanding a pay raise a few months previously.

The wedding was a quiet affair and took place only three weeks after Morgan and Anne's first meeting. Morgan had resigned from his commission with the Navy, and was now unemployed, living at the manor house. The married couple mostly occupied the eastern wing of the house, but the kitchen and dining room were shared with Robert. The relationship between son-in-law and father-in-law had become strained after only the first day that they all lived together. Morgan had no intention of collecting debt for Robert or letting his wife slave to her father, and he secretly plotted a way to get rid of him. Permanently. Within two months of being married, Anne was pregnant, and Morgan's savings were steadily being reduced. Morgan had his eyes on Robert's considerable wealth and title.

It was a Sunday morning, and Anne had gone to church. She had gone by herself as usual, as Morgan only accompanied her to the Easter and Christmas sermons. Morgan had stayed at home and was entertaining a friend from his Navy days. The man was the ship's surgeon and had served alongside Morgan on his last ship. This man, Christopher, was a big, strong man. In his time as the ship's surgeon, he had gained a reputation for saving the lives of the injured. This was mostly due to Morgan's directive to keep the operating room as clean and sterile as possible. Christopher had also enjoyed rapid promotions within the navel service. Once again, this was largely down to Morgan's recommendations. He was a loyal man who readily acknowledged that he was in Morgan's debt.

Anne returned home to the sad news that her father had died. He had fallen out of his upstairs bedroom window whilst seemingly trying to adjust the curtains. Christopher had witnessed the accident from the ground and had pronounced the man dead almost immediately. Robert's neck was broken. The parish constable had been called and had accepted Morgan and Christopher's version of events. Robert was buried a few days later in a rather rushed burial service. Morgan had insisted that the service be a closed, immediate family affair, and he didn't bother to notify any of Robert's friends or extended family members about the death.

Morgan had insisted that Robert should be buried in a bound cotton shawl as opposed to a wooden casket and gave orders that the grave be positioned in an area of the cemetery that was permanently wet and prone to flooding after any heavy rain. This area was generally reserved for the poor people of the parish, as the permanently wet ground conditions rotted the bodies away quickly and allowed multiple burials in the same plots. Anne inherited her father's wealth, and thus, by default, it was Morgan who owned the manor house, grounds, properties, and money. Morgan was also lord of the manor.

As lord of the manor, it was Morgan who set the rent rates and collected the money. On his first trip, he was accompanied by Anne. Morgan reassured tenants and farm workers that he would only charge them a fair rate. He lowered the rents to a more manageable level for most people and quashed any arrears in order for them to start again with a clean slate. Morgan asked the tenants if they had any problems or grievances to speak to Anne first, and she would relay the messages to him. Morgan encouraged Anne to get out more and mingle with other women in the area outside of church hours. In response, Anne did get out more and mingled with local women.

With this newly found freedom, she went shopping at the local market and occasionally went for walks around the village perimeter. She had rarely been outside the village boundaries before, but she always timed her outings so she could be home to cook and then eat dinner with her husband. Within a year of being married, Anne gave birth to a son. Craig.

James Hillyer was now unemployed and homeless. He was a bitter man. He was evicted from the manor lodge by Robert for simply voicing his opinion that he should receive a higher share of the monies that he collected from the tenants on behalf of the lord of the manor. It was he who issued the threats and carried out the physical stuff—well him and John Barton, but Robert Layer, kept his hands clean. He was annoyed with John Barton as well. Both men had worked together for Robert for years and they made a good team. When James was sacked and evicted, John turned his back on James during his hour of need and refused him temporary food and lodging.

Yes, John had a full house with his wife and six children, but James was sure they could have squeezed him in somewhere. He decided to walk to the inn at Bampton. He heard that this was a good place to meet people and find manual labour jobs or other unskilled work.

James entered the inn through the front door. He strode up to the bar and asked to speak to the landlord. When Eddie appeared, James told him about his previous employment and how he was now homeless and unemployed. He explained that he could turn his hand to butchery, horse and cart collections, drop-offs, and debt collecting. Eddie was impressed and immediately offered him a room at the inn. He took James into the small butcher's room at the back of the inn and quizzed him about the type and whereabouts of the valuables that were in the manor house, the security employed there, and if there was any easy access to the premises. Eddie was also interested in the clothing that would be housed there.

He himself was dressed in stolen stockings, cotton breeches, a linen shirt, cotton waistcoat, and a frock coat. Even his buckled shoes were stolen. Good-quality clothing would be a nice earner for him if he could steal that as well. He would obviously have to be there in person for this robbery, something that he wasn't keen on. But he would have to evaluate each item before it was stolen and would have to be there in person to ensure the valuable metals and stones weren't pilfered by his crew before they reached him. He would also need a horse and cart to take away the stolen goods. He would keep the crew as small as possible, just himself, James, and a man called Lewis, who was his most trusted right-hand man.

Lewis is a large man and very strong. He had once been the village blacksmith and had been blinded in one eye by a shard of hot metal whilst hammering iron on his oak bench. With one eye, the trade he had built up around his intricate ironwork evaporated almost overnight. His problems with occasional double vision, depth perception, and distance judging made hammering, melting, and bending steel nigh on impossible. A new smithy was established just outside of the village, and the people from Bampton walked or rode the short distance to that one to have their horses shod and their weapons and tools manufactured.

Eddie led James to the spare bedroom and then walked back down to the butchery alone. In his mind, he was formulating a plan. On the night in question, he would have the cook give out free pig and sheep heads, trotters, and offal, as well as free hot broth. Most people in the parish never got to eat meat or meat-based cuisine because they were so poor, usually relying on bread, potatoes, foraged fruit, and vegetables with only the occasional rodent to supplement their meat intake. Free meat, fat, and especially broth would keep most people off the village's back streets that night.

He would let it be known that he was at the back of the inn, cutting and preparing the meat for his customers, and this would be his alibi. If the robbery went well, he would drop the stolen goods at a small, unoccupied building he had recently acquired adjacent to the inn. He would then arrange for Lewis to lure James into the butchery, where he or Lewis would kill him, and then he and Lewis would dispose of the body to his starving pigs. This would ensure that James couldn't blab his mouth off when he had drunk too much ale, and it would further increase his and Lewis's share of the profits.

Eddie smiled to himself and suppressed a laugh. Everything was too easy in this century. No DNA evidence, no forensics or fingerprints, no radio communications, and no proper police force, only an unpaid parish constable who appeared to be scared of the dark. Eddie moved up the ranks socially as well. In a few short months, he had gone from lower to middle class, and in a few short years, he reasoned that he would be part of the upper class. This was all part of the grand plan. He would transfer all his assets into gold bullion and then bury them. He would then return to his own time by killing Roman's ancestors and digging up the gold.

He would then be a millionaire in the twenty-first century. It was thrilling to him knowing that he could change history by killing someone now and erasing their ancestors lives in the future. He could kill Churchill's great grandparents and change the outcome of the Second World War if he wanted. He could invent the telephone, the steam engine or football or rugby. The future really was in his hands. He was a god.

Eddie had realised that the average life expectancy in this geographical area and probably throughout the country was around forty to fifty years old for the poorer communities. Only the wealthy people, seemed to live to be pensioners. The poor certainly didn't. It seemed to Eddie that the rich got richer whilst the poor got poorer. He intended to get richer with a vengeance. He did miss driving, eating convenience foods, watching television, and listening to music. He also longed for regular shaving and bathing with proper soap, hot water, and deodorant. He wished that people bathed more. Everyone that he spoke to seemed to stink of body odour.

James Hillyer was also making plans for his future. He had been living at Eddie's inn for six weeks now, rent-free, so long as he carried out Eddie's debt collections and ran his errands. The big one. The manor house robbery that he was going to be involved in would fill his purse substantially. Eddie said that he would appraise all of the stolen items on the same night as the robbery and pay off James and Lewis with cash. This meant that the other two couldn't be seen with any of the stolen goods and so shouldn't be linked to the robbery. When the robbery at the manor house was over and he had been paid, James decided that he would take a room in a different village for a few months, with the intention of buying a small plot of land. He would then build himself a small house on this land and look around for a bride. He knew that he could stay at Eddie's inn rent-free, and he had no intention of stopping working for Eddie, but he didn't trust Eddie completely.

A few times when he was in bed, he thought that he had heard Lewis or Eddie standing on the other side of his bedroom door. They seemed to be listening to see if he was asleep. Were they thinking of stealing his money? He was amassing a serious number of coins working for Eddie, and it might have crossed Eddie's mind to take it back. He also didn't trust Lewis. Quite often, when James casually turned to look at Lewis, he found that Lewis was already staring at him. Lewis would then grin at him, but the smile seemed false. It was almost like he was trying to reassure James that everything was okay, when really he was plotting something untoward for him. Perhaps Lewis was thinking of robbing him. He made up his mind to take a concealed dagger with him on the night of the robbery, just in case.

A few weeks later, Eddie decided to investigate the layout of the manor house and grounds. It was a Sunday morning, and so he assumed that the inhabitants of the house would be at church. Everybody seemed to attend church on Sunday, Eddie reasoned. He was with Lewis, whom he asked to wait for him at the bottom of the drive. He walked past the gatehouse and up the manor house, driving towards the manor house alone. As he walked past the stables, a familiar voice shouted out to him.

"Can I help you?" said Morgan.

Eddie stopped and turned around. He made a double take and then burst into a grin when he recognised Morgan's face.

"Morg!" he said, holding out his right hand.

"Eddie!" said Morgan in a confused tone. "What are you doing here?"

"I've got the pub in Bampton," replied Eddie. "Is this your place? Blimey. How long have you been here? Did that ginger kid send you here?"

Morgan proceeded to tell Eddie about how he was tricked into stepping through the time portal sixteen years ago and how he had served in the Navy and then married into money. He explained that for the first few years of this time period, he had wanted to get back to the twenty twenties and take his revenge on Roman, but over time he had come to accept his fate and was living a better life now. He was a respected war hero with money, property, land, and a wife and kid. On balance, he preferred his life here. Yes, it was a simpler life with none of the modern conveniences, but he was healthier for it. He kept himself in shape, he was respected throughout the community, and he was doing his part for charity. He was a major stakeholder in the building of the orphanage on the other side of his field, and he was building a stone cottage near it for his best friends' family to live in.

They would run the orphanage. The cottage would eventually be the cottage that Roman would live in. At this moment in time, he bore Roman no ill will.

Eddie was shocked. What had happened to the old Morgan a few months ago. This Morgan had gone soft. Civilised. He thought about asking Morgan if he wanted to be partners in his expanding crime empire, but he thought better of it. New Morgan seemed to have landed on his feet and wouldn't need the additional income or hassle. No, he wouldn't mention his criminal activities, and yes, he would still rob Morgan's house. What could Morgan do? He was one man against Eddie's half-dozen.

If Morgan suspected that Eddie had something to do with the robbery and came round to kick off, he would throw him out on his ear after giving him a hiding as a warning. Morgan was a big man in the twenty-first century. In this period, Eddie was the boss. In a parting comment, Eddie told Morgan that he wanted to get back to twenty-first century civilisation, and he had formulated a plan to make it happen. He was going to kill the people in the area that carried Roman's surname to ensure that Roman could never be born. He then ended the conversation with a handshake, turned, and walked back down the driveway.

Morgan watched him meet up with the big man at the bottom of his drive. This man was Eddie's bodyguard; that was obvious. Why would Eddie need a bodyguard to run a pub? He watched both men disappear. He was never overly keen on Eddie, and he never trusted him entirely. Eddie never did say why he was mooching around the manor house grounds, and he seemed cagey when Morgan asked him how he could afford the expensive clothing that he was wearing whilst living on an innkeeper's salary. Also, how did he take control of a thriving pub when he had only been here a matter of months? Knowing Eddie, it was something underhand that would have resulted in the previous owner being severely beaten or killed.

The worst part of the conversation, though, was the part where Eddie vowed to kill Roman's relations. Morgan couldn't care less if Roman died, but killing him before he was born would mean that Morgan, along with Eddie, would both be transported back to their own time, and Morgan didn't want to go back. He knew that he would somehow have to alert Roman about what was going on.

He walked into the house and sat down on a wooden chair. He reasoned that he had no way of interfering with the future, and so Roman would have to interfere with the past. But how could he alert him? The cottage that he was having built was the only link that could tie him and Roman together. Could he leave a parchment message built into the walls? Probably not. Someone else might find it over the following centuries, and there was no guarantee that Roman would find it anyway. Could he leave a message etched on the glass windows? No. When he went around to threaten Roman, he noticed that all the wooden windows and doors had long since been replaced with plastic. The stone lintel above the front door was original, though.

What if he had a message chiselled into the face of this? It would have to be a short message, and something that Roman would understand, but if the letters were cut in deep enough, they shouldn't weather away over time and thus still be legible. He got up from his seat and headed over to the stables. He would ride over to the stonemason's house and get him to replace the limestone lintel with a granite lintel with a message chiselled into it that Roman would understand. With a bit of luck, Roman may be able to reverse time for Eddie or at least drag him back into his own time.

A couple of weeks had passed since Morgan had met Eddie on the manor house grounds. Morgan still had a gut feeling that something about the meeting was suspicious. However, he put this to the back of his mind as he saddled his horse. He went to a parish meeting to discuss the progress of the orphanage. The meetings took place on the last Friday of every month and involved church representatives, some influential figures from the surrounding communities, and himself. The meetings usually only lasted for an hour, but Morgan would usually take the horse drawn buggy and drop his wife and son at a friend's house before the meeting and then pick them up on the way back. This meant that it was usually late before the three of them arrived home. Tonight, however, his child was ill in bed, so Anne was staying home to look after him.

Two hours later, Morgan rode back through the manor house gates. He stopped his horse just inside the gates, as he could see that further up the drive was a wooden buggy tethered to a horse, parked outside his front door. Something didn't seem right. Nobody visited unannounced, especially in the dark. He silently walked over to the buggy. A pile of men's and women's clothes had been placed in the back, along with some silver candlesticks. His first thought was that Anne was leaving him, but he dismissed this thought immediately. The front door was open, and he could hear voices, as well as the sound of his son crying upstairs. Instead of going through the front door, Morgan walked around to the living room window to see where the voices were coming from.

Anne was sitting on the floor, and a man who Morgan didn't recognise was pointing a finger at her and loudly asking her questions as to where the coins and jewels were kept. Morgan heard the man say that if they didn't leave with the jewels, then he would leave with her baby. Just as he was saying this, a big man entered the room with an armful of clothes.

"Clothes are done," he said. "Find out where the small stuff is, and let's get going."

Morgan recognised the man as Eddie's bodyguard, who had waited at the bottom of the drive when Eddie came around a couple of weeks ago. Eddie was obviously involved. Morgan could see that the big man was blind in one eye. Morgan silently slipped into the barn adjacent to the house. He picked up his wooden "Billy Club," from the shelf. The Billy Club was a two-foot-long carved baton with a heavy wooden sphere at both ends.

It was carved out of a single piece of oak and was capable of breaking a man's elbows or kneecaps if used properly. The club had accompanied Morgan for the duration of his navel career. Morgan swiftly but silently positioned himself in the shadows at the side of his front door. He held the club aloft. The big man looked strong and would be difficult to beat in a fight, especially if the other man came out to help his friend. Morgan reasoned that although he was a big man, he was blind in one eye, and as such, he wouldn't see the blow coming to the right-hand side of his head until it was too late to react.

Lewis stepped through the door, and Morgan swung the Billy Club. It caught Lewis cleanly on the side of his jaw, breaking his jawbone and knocking him clean out. Lewis slumped to the ground without uttering a sound. Morgan stepped into the living room. Anne's eyes looked up at him, and James, seeing her reaction, also turned around. Morgan brought the Billy Club down on James's head, knocking him out immediately. James slumped to the ground with a grunt. Morgan quickly grabbed the braided cord from the curtain tiebacks.

He rolled James onto his front and tied his hands behind his back. Once tied, he ran outside to Lewis and did the same. He then tied Lewis's feet together and dragged him by his feet over to the stables. Once inside the stables, he let go of Lewis's feet. His feet hit the ground hard, and Lewis started to wake up. He blinked and tried to talk, but just a gurgling sound came out of his mouth, along with blood-filled saliva.

"Don't you die," said Morgan. "Not yet anyway."

He ran back into his living room, and Anne passed him another braided cord. Morgan tied James's feet together and dragged him over to the stables. He dropped him next to Lewis.

"Sleep tight," he said. "You're going to need all your strength tomorrow. Oh, and don't try to wriggle out of your bonds. I'm a sailor, and I know my knots. You'll just end up with bloody wrists."

With that, he left the men and shut and bolted the stable door. He would send the militia tomorrow to take the men away, but not before he had gotten some information from them. Both men looked like they could stand a beating and so probably wouldn't be forthcoming with any information. Still, he had a large pair of horse teeth pulling pliers in his barn, and once these were introduced to the men's toes, they would tell him everything he wanted to know. Everything he wanted to know about Eddie. Morgan went back into the house to comfort Anne. She had picked up their son from his bedroom. Although the boy had stopped crying and had fallen asleep, Anne refused to put him back to bed.

Anne was crying, but it was more relief than fear. Morgan made an instant decision that he hoped would help to settle Anne. He told her that he would employ a friend, one of his old shipmates who he knew was out of work, to work as a security guard to patrol the house grounds at night. He would let him live in one of the cottages; the one that had just become empty after the death of the tenant, and that he would ride over the following day to see him. This did the trick, and Anne stopped crying.

Morgan went back into the stable with an ultimatum for the two prisoners. He explained their options to them. The first option was to be tortured with the horse pliers and then handed over to the militia to be hanged. He explained that he had considerable influence in the region, and if he wanted it, he could arrange for both men to be publicly hanged on the village green, without a proper trial, the following day. The second option was for them to tell him everything that he wanted to know. The men would still be handed over to the militia and confined to a house of correction, until their trial.

Morgan would see to it that the trial date came around quickly to limit the time that both men spent in the dirty, damp, overcrowded, and unhealthy conditions of their confinement. After the guilty verdict, he would arrange for both men to be transported to America for the remainder of their lives. In America, they would serve a five-year sentence at a new colony, where they would help to build new settlements. After five years, they would be free men. Admittedly free men in America, because under the law they could never return to England, but they would be alive at least. The men opted for the second option and told Morgan everything he wanted to know. Morgan handed both men over to the militia and sent word to his friend, the governor, that after the men's guilty pleas had been recorded, he should arrange with the judge to have both men hanged.

Eddie was waiting for Lewis and James to return, but when the time went past midnight, he knew that something had gone wrong with the robbery. Neither Lewis nor James had returned with the stolen loot, and Eddie was getting worried and suspicious. The two men might have come across some highly valuable stones or gold coins and ridden off with the proceeds themselves. Where would they go, though, where Eddie couldn't find them? Both men were born and bred in this area, and most folk didn't move too far away from their roots.

Anyway, it was unlikely that there would be enough valuables in the stolen stuff for both men to settle down into a new life, even if one did kill the other to increase his share. No, something had gone wrong, and it was more than probable that Morgan had something to do with it.

Knowing Morgan's temper as he did, it was highly likely that Morgan would come looking for revenge. Especially if James had hurt Morgan's wife. James seemed to be a bit that way. It was almost as if James liked to hurt women. Eddie decided to sleep at the tavern for a few days. He would keep his crew close at hand and always carry a knife. He would also keep a loaded pistol behind the bar. If Morgan walked into his place, he would be carried out.

Chapter 11
A Case of Mistaken Identity

Three weeks after his last visit, Roman had gone around to visit his mother again. This time he had made sure that George would be there by not leaving it too late in the evening. He knew that as soon as he sat down at the kitchen table to chat with his mum, George would get up and leave the kitchen to show his displeasure at Roman's being there, and then he would sit in the living room to watch the television, if he wasn't already in there.

Roman knew that George would leave the living room door ajar and turn the volume down on the TV, so that he could listen to Roman and Ruth's conversation. On cue, this sequence played out just how, Roman thought it would. In a slightly louder than normal voice, Roman explained to his mother that he had come into possession of some valuable gold coins. He never went into detail about where they had come from, but he said that he had hidden them for safekeeping. He went on to say that they were within walking distance of his mother's house and that he would leave shortly and bring a couple of them back.

George walked back into the kitchen and put on his coat and shoes. He explained that he was going to the pub for a meeting and that he wouldn't be back until later. Roman knew that George would be waiting in the shadows somewhere outside to silently follow him to the coin stash. This was all part of the Romans' plan. Roman walked along the roads and streets without looking back for twenty minutes until he arrived at George's old printing shop. The windows and door had been boarded up by the bankruptcy official. He walked to the edge of the building and pushed open the wooden side gate to the rear of the building. As he walked around the back, George arrived at the front and slowly followed Roman around.

A rear window had been forced open and was left wide open. By the time George had inched his way around, Roman was nowhere to be seen, but it was obvious that he had climbed into the building through the open window. It made sense to George now. This would be the last place that *he* would look for valuable coins. The building was secure, and it contained nothing of value when George handed it over to the official receiver. As silently as he could, George climbed through the open window and silently stepped through a standalone wooden doorframe that someone had left, blocking his entry into the workshop.

It was February 1944, and George Woodford, George's granddad, had just finished work for the day and was locking his workshop door. He was about to walk away when the internal light came on. He looked through the window and saw someone inside moving around. Immediately, he walked to the public telephone box a few feet down the road and called the police. As luck would have it, his detective handler and a uniformed policeman were just leaving the station on an unrelated matter, but they agreed to swing past George's printing workshop and arrest the burglar.

Ten minutes later, George Junior, who was crawling around on the floor looking for cracks and crevices in the bottom of the brick wall and floor, looked up to see two policemen standing there. One in uniform and one plain-clothed. George stood up and looked at both men. *The plain-clothed one looked like he had just stepped out of the nineteen fifties in that suit and overcoat,* thought George, and who wears a trilby these days, except for Clem?

"Who are you and what are you doing here?" said the plain clothes detective.

"George Woodford and I own the bloody place," said George. He looked around the workshop. He hadn't been back for a few months, but he began to realise that things looked different. He wondered if someone else had been secretly using the premises whilst he hadn't been there.

"And who are you, and what are you doing in my shop?" George Junior carried on.

"Inspector Rueben Johnson and police constable Henry Smith," said the detective. "And you are George Woodford, you say."

"Yeah," said George, nodding his head.

"Ahh okay," said the detective, smiling at the uniformed policeman and then at George's grandfather, who had by now followed the two policemen into the room. "I suppose you've got identification on you, George?"

"I might have something in my wallet," came the reply.

"Anyway, who is that?" asked George, pointing at his grandfather.

"His name is George Woodford," the uniformed policeman replied. "He owns the bloody place too."

"Where do you live, George?" said the plain-clothed policeman to George Junior.

"Spring Gardens, at the bottom of Spencer Street, it's a small council estate," came the reply.

The detective looked at the uniformed policeman. "You getting all this Smiffy?"

"Yes, sir," said Smiffy, brandishing his notebook and pencil. "But I can tell you now that there are no houses at the bottom of Spencer Street."

George looked incredulously at the policeman. "The houses have been there for around forty years. It's got a bad reputation for violent crime, especially at nights. I expect that's why you've never been down there," he said to the uniformed policeman sarcastically.

The detective looked at George again. "Who won the FA Cup last year, George?"

"Arsenal," came the reply. "How should I know?"

"It wasn't held," said the detective. "How many years has the king been on the throne?"

"One year," replied George. "Why are you asking me all these questions when he's the imposter?" he said, pointing to his grandfather. His grandfather stood silent with a bemused look on his face. He wasn't sure what was going on, but he had a niggling feeling that this may have had something to do with him being a police informer. Had his secret been discovered, and had this man been sent round to duff him up?

The detective was arriving at his own conclusion. He knew the real George Woodford was standing beside him. The real George Woodford was in his pocket. He met with him every few weeks. The two Georges standing beside him were about the same age, and they did look similar. It was obvious to the detective that the man in front of him was trying to steal the real George Woodford's identity. He had probably been chosen because they looked similar and he was obviously trying to pose as a legitimate British citizen with a legitimate British business.

"Have you been out of the country recently?" he asked George.

"No," came the reply.

"Oh wait, yes. I went to Calais on a booze cruise a couple of months back."

"You took a boat to France? What for?"

"Beer," said George. Looking at the policeman writing everything down, "I'm not the first, and I won't be the last."

The detective nodded to the policeman.

"Right then, Herr Woodford, or whatever your real name is. You've obviously been poorly briefed, and that suggests to me that you are just fodder. Before I arrest you, I'm going to give you some free advice. You will be taken to the Oxford police station, where you will be held until you are picked up and taken to London. The people from London are experts at getting to the truth. I suggest that you cooperate with them. It might mean the difference between prison time and having your neck stretched."

"I haven't got a Scooby, what you're on about, but this is turning into a nightmare," protested George as the handcuffs were locked onto his wrists. "He's the imposter. He doesn't even look like me. This is my workshop and my printing press. I want my solicitor."

George was escorted outside to a waiting police car. He looked at the car and started to panic inside. Something was wrong. The police car was old-fashioned. Police cars like this hadn't been used for at least seventy years. The two policemen looked old-fashioned. The uniform didn't look right, and they never had radios. Even the handcuffs on his wrists looked like handcuffs from a bygone age. Was this an elaborate ruse to spirit him away, beat him up, or kill him? He had been buying his drugs from a rival dealer recently. Had these men been paid by someone to do it, and had they concocted the story so that he would go with them without too much fuss? He had seen something like this in a film on television. But why the old car and uniforms? Then he relaxed, breathing an audible sigh. It was a wind-up. It was his birthday in a week's time.

He would be taken to what was supposed to be a police station, only to walk inside and be 'surprised' by some of his friends. It all made sense now. He remembered hearing some of the lads talking about something in the pub last week. They had all stopped talking when he strolled over. That was why. A surprise birthday party had been planned. No wonder they wanted rid of him that night. He decided to go along with the charade.

The uniformed policeman opened the car's rear door, and George got inside and sat down. The plain-clothed policeman opened the rear door on the other side, climbed in, and sat down next to him. The uniformed driver got into the driver's seat, started the car up, and then accelerated away. It was dark outside, and there were no streetlights on. In fact, there were no lights on anywhere. The roads were empty of traffic too. George began to get that niggling feeling again. He wasn't panicking, but something was not right again. He spoke to the plain clothes officer beside him.

"Been on the force long," he said, half joking.

"Ten years this year," came the reply.

"Why the old car?" said George.

"There is a war on, in case you haven't noticed," said the officer sarcastically.

George sat quiet for a few minutes and then tried to start a conversation again.

"You didn't caution me. That makes the arrest invalid, doesn't it? Anything I say can be used as evidence and all that. You never searched for me either; I might have a gun in my pocket."

"Have you got a gun in your pocket?" Came the reply from the police officer.

"My mobile phone doubles up as a machine gun," said George.

"I can tell if someone is carrying a weapon just by looking at the folds in their clothing. You aren't carrying a machine gun, or what did you say, a telephone?" said the driver.

"Well, you're half right," said George, putting his handcuffed hand into his pocket and pulling out his mobile phone. He looked at the screen. There was nothing to see. It wouldn't turn on, and it smelt faintly of burning.

"I don't believe it. It's only a year old, and it's stopped working. It smells like the battery has melted," he said.

"Let me look at that," said the detective, clearly intrigued, taking it out of George's hand. "It says *Siemens* on the front. What is it?"

"A phone—what do you think it is? It's made in Germany." Replied George.

"Foot down, Smiffy," said the detective to the driver. "I want to have a crack at him before the big boys get here."

George looked at the detective and then at the driver. The niggling feeling that he had been experiencing was now turning into considerable anxiety.

"Are we nearly there yet?" he said weakly, looking around the car to see if the other two smiled. They didn't.

"We're here now," said the driver as he pulled up outside the police station.

George was taken straight into the interview room. It was a small room with a wooden table in the middle of the room, two wooden chairs on one side of the table, and a single chair on the other side. A notebook and pencil had been placed on the table. As they entered the room, the detective asked George to put his hands in the air whilst Smiffy conducted a search. George agreed, and Smiffy removed George's wallet out of his trouser pocket and a packet of menthol chewing gum out of the other.

"No machine gun here," said Smiffy, winking at the detective. All three men sat down.

The detective opened George's wallet. He took out George's driving licence, a credit card, and then a five-pound note, a one-pound coin, and a fifty pence piece. He placed them on the table but didn't say anything. He studied the items, taking particular notice of the dates on them. He picked up the chewing gum, read the pack, and then noticed the "best before date." It reads May 2024.

"What year is it?" he said to George.

"What year do you want it to be?" came the reply.

"Just answer the question."

"Twenty twenty-three," sighed George. Things had been going on for long enough now, and he wanted to go back home.

Smiffy laughed, and Rueben shot him a look. Smiffy sat silent again. Reuben reminded Smiffy to write down everything that George said, word for word.

"What can you tell me about the war," said Reuben. "From the beginning until the present day."

"Look I'm no expert on the Second World War," George replied. "It started in 1939 and ended in 1945. Hitler shot himself in his bunker in 1945. The yanks dropped the atom bomb on Japan in '45. Russia and the west became enemies after the war. Alan Turin cracked the Enigma code at Bletchley Park. D. Day took place in Normandy in June 1944, and that was the beginning of the end for the Nazis. That's as far as I know. Oh, and Churchill dies in 1965."

Both policemen sat in silence for a few seconds before Reuben opened the interview room door and shouted at the desk sergeant standing a few feet away.

"Sergeant, I want you to take this man down to the cells. He must not talk to anyone, including you. He must be segregated from any other prisoners, if there are any in the adjoining cells. I want an armed policeman outside his cell at all times. He is to be stripped and searched. Some men are on their way up from London. When they get here, bring them to me."

He turned to Smiffy. "Sorry, pal, but you are here for the night too. You will be asked to sign the Official Secrets Act later, which unfortunately does mean that if you repeat anything that you have heard tonight, you will be imprisoned until the end of the war. We will both be interviewed by the men that are coming up from the smoke. They will probably accompany you home later to collect some clothes and stuff, and then you may be transferred to a different station for special duties for a few months. It's all a bit of a nightmare, but I will see that you get bumped up to an acting sergeant and obviously get paid accordingly."

With that, George was led from the room and put into an empty cell. Once he was locked in, a different policeman walked to the outside of the cell door, placed a chair on the floor, and promptly sat down with his back against the door. He sat in silence for a few minutes and then called out to the desk sergeant to bring him a cuppa and the newspaper that was folded up on the sergeant's desk. He sat back in his chair and lit up a cigarette whilst he waited. George started to voice his protest at being locked up. He now realised that this whole thing was real, and he wanted a solicitor. The seated policeman ignored him.

Two hours later, George was seated in the back of a different car. One man sat beside him but didn't say anything, the other man started up the car and proceeded to pull away.

"Where are we going?" said George, who was now resigned to his fate.

"Just try and get some sleep," said the driver. "It's a long drive to London in a blackout. You are an interesting and knowledgeable man, and some colleagues want to talk to you. All you have to do is be honest with them, and you will be sent home in no time. Just get some rest first; you've got a long day ahead of you."

George leant forward. "Can I ask you a question?" he said to the driver. "Are we in the middle of the Second World War?"

"Nearer the end of it, if your statement is anything to go by," came the reply. "It's February 14th 1944. Valentines' day."

George sat back in his seat. He felt confused, anxious, and scared. His legs and hands were visibly trembling, and he began to feel nauseous.

"Just sit still and relax," said the man seated next to him. "Try and get 40 winks. You have nothing to worry about. You might even come out of this as an important and wealthy man."

Two hours later, the car pulled up to the driveway of a large house. There were two big wrought iron gates at the entrance to the drive, and two big armed soldiers guarded the gates. The car stopped, and one of the soldiers looked inside the now-open driver's side window. He nodded to the driver and looked at the others in the car. The man beside George nodded to the soldier, and the soldier withdrew his head. He then gestured to the other soldier to open the gate. When the gate was opened, the car drove through and down to the end of the gravelled drive.

George could see that the whole of the ground's perimeter had a solid brick wall, at least eight feet high, circling it. The wall was too tall for anyone to peer over. Armed soldiers patrolled the grounds adjacent to the wall at intermittent spacing. George was led out of the car and into the hallway of the large house. *It was very luxurious by 1940s standards*, George thought, and definitely not a prison.

"Are we in London?" he asked the man standing next to him.

"Near London," the man replied. "We call this place the Big House. Follow me to your room. There is a comfy bed, some cotton pyjamas in your size, a plate of sandwiches, and a jug of water in there. There are no bars on the window, but there will be a man stationed outside of your room. You will need to ask him to accompany you if you need to get up and use the lavatory during the night. I must stress that you are not a prisoner, and as such, you will not be treated as a criminal, but you are being detained for your own protection."

The pair stopped at the bedroom door. "One more thing. Don't attempt to talk to anyone; they all have orders not to speak to you," said the man to George. "Get some sleep. You will be woken up around 08.30 tomorrow for your breakfast, and then it is a day of interviews for you with different people. Stay relaxed, tell the truth, and we will see about getting you out of here." With that, he opened the bedroom door, watched George step into the bedroom, and then closed the bedroom door behind him.

George walked over to the bed and sat down on the edge of it. It all felt like a dream, but it was obviously really happening. He picked up a sandwich and put it in his mouth. Bread, butter, and cheese. No sauce or pickles. But he was hungry, and so he ate it all. He laid back on the bed and stretched out. He would change into the pyjamas in a few minutes. He realised just how tired he was. He closed his eyes for a few moments and instantly fell asleep. He was awoken by a knock on his bedroom door and a soldier walking in.

"Eight thirty, mate," said the soldier. "I'm here to accompany you to the lavatory and then to the breakfast hall. There will be other people having breakfast there, but you've got a table on your own. Please don't attempt to talk to anyone in there." With that, he led George out of the room.

An hour later, George was seated in a room that looked to him like a small library. It was all very informal. The chairs were leather-backed and comfortable. Four people were already seated with their chairs facing George. Two men were in uniform, both smoking cigars. Obviously, the officers thought George. Two other men were dressed in civilian suits. He recognised one of the men from his trip down from Oxford last night. The suited man whom George had met yesterday offered George a cigarette. George's mobile phone, wallet, bank cards, and coins were all on display on a table in front of him.

A uniformed woman carrying a notebook and pen walked into the room and sat down on the only available spare chair. She didn't speak to anyone in the room, and nobody spoke to her. When she was seated and ready to take notes, the meeting began.

It started with George being asked about his personal details and then being asked to describe the items on the table. From there, the questioning progressed to details about life in the 2020s and then on to what George knew about the Second World War. The questions remained informal and were asked by all four of the men in the room. During this session, George told them about how England beat Germany in the 1966 World Cup. How America put a man on the moon in 1969. How the berlin wall came down around 1990, but he couldn't remember the exact date. He went on to state that King George died in 1952 or 1953, and Queen Elizabeth was crowned in 1953 and became the longest serving monarch. This meeting went on until 1pm, whereupon the meeting was stopped for an hour for lunch. At 2pm, the meeting resumed. George explained how he had followed Roman into the printing shop. Yes, the boy could have invented a time machine. He was always repairing or upgrading computers and mobile phones.

The mobile phone on the table was passed to George, but he couldn't get his phone to work. However, after a bit of fiddling with the on/off button, the backlight came on and 'Siemens' briefly flashed across the screen, and so in theory, at least the phone wasn't totally beyond repair. The men in the room admitted that their boffins were stumped by the technology contained within the phone. The story about George's grandfather and the forged ration books was checked out, but George was not made aware that his grandfather was a police informer. The printing shop was duly closed, and an armed soldier was placed inside the premises in case the time portal door was opened again. The meeting went on until 5pm and was then stopped for the day, to be resumed at 09.30 the following day by three American intelligence officers. The men in the room had no choice but to accept that George was indeed from the future.

Later that night, George was given an army uniform. It was the uniform of a captain, complete with three shoulder pips. He was shown how to salute and stand to attention, but warned that he must not engage in conversation with anyone outside of the people that he talked to in the library. He was told that wearing the uniform would make him look less suspicious around the place and deter people from trying to engage in conversations with him. He was told that he was free to come and go around the grounds of the house but must be accompanied when moving around the house interior. Once again, this was for his own protection, he was told. George was happy.

He had always seen himself as an officer. He had almost joined the army when he left school but had turned up late for his interview with the recruiting sergeant and had received a telling-off. George promptly turned around and walked out of the office, then walked back home. Walking around the house grounds, George would sometimes beckon one of the perimeter guards. He would then inspect their uniforms and chastise them if they had mud on their boots or creases in their uniforms. For once in his life, George felt like an important man. Someone with authority. He quite fancied a young female typist who would come outside on her lunchbreak to smoke a cigarette and eat her sandwiches. George would try to impress her by arriving ten minutes before she arrived and being in the act of either inspecting a perimeter guard's uniform or bawling someone out for slacking on the job. In George's mind, he was the quintessential army officer.

George's behaviour had not gone unnoticed by his handlers. He had been with them for a little over two weeks, and he was getting ideas above his station. He wasn't a real captain, although George thought that he was. In George's mind, the months of training that were needed to receive a commission had been bypassed and condensed to around an hour for him. He was obviously an important and special man. He just hoped that he wouldn't be put in charge of a platoon of men and sent abroad to fight. He quite liked being a captain on home soil, though. His handlers were in a predicament. They had interviewed him almost every day and had exhausted everything of importance that George knew.

George had to be continuously monitored as he was always trying to strike up a conversation with someone outside on the grounds, despite frequent warnings about this on a daily basis. The handlers were in a dilemma, though.

For all intents and purposes, George became a liability. He was harmless to a certain extent, but in his mind, he carried some dangerous information about the war. If they imprisoned him, he would have to be kept in solitary confinement to prevent him from talking to anybody, but what could he be charged with? He hadn't done anything wrong. He was, after all, just a victim of circumstance.

There was another alternative. A woman had recently been charged under the Witchcraft Act and would most likely face jail time if convicted. She had revealed details of a sunken warship to a group of people during a séance. Prison would keep her from revealing any more secrets that she claimed to know. Could they somehow hold George on a charge of witchcraft and convict him after a secret trial to keep him out of the way until the war ended? It was a possibility. But there was another option. They could arrange for George to be freed for one afternoon to meet the young typist that he so obviously had a crush on. They could drop him, in a park a few miles away and tell him to wait around for his date. He would be warned to speak to nobody else and given an emergency telephone number to contact his handlers in case of trouble.

George would be dressed in his captain's uniform with no identification on him. They could arrange for him to be arrested by the local police for impersonating an officer, and then when he made his emergency telephone call at the police station, they could deny all knowledge of him. They might even say that George fit the description of a dangerous lunatic that they had received information about and to take him straight to the local asylum to be dealt with. As with all the hospitals, prisons, and asylums in the area, the government had placed people in positions of power within them, and these would screen the new entrants and deal with them accordingly.

George would probably be drugged for the remainder of the war and possibly return to the community afterwards if he was up to it. This would probably be unlikely, though. People who were turned into zombies for more than a year rarely made a full recovery.

George was given the good news about his meeting with the typist the following day. It had been cleared by the top brass, and it had been agreed that he would be allowed to stay out until eight pm, and then both George and the typist would be collected by car and brought back to the Big House. This would give him ample time for lunch, dinner, and a trip to the cinema. George felt excited. The girl had obviously agreed to the date, and freedom with female company for just a few hours was a hundred times better than the continual confinement to the house.

George stood and waited for the car to arrive at the house entrance steps. The typist had left earlier, apparently, and she would be waiting at the park for him. He took out his cigarettes and fell in his pocket for his lighter. It wasn't there. He remembered that he had left it on his bedside cabinet. Although he had been given orders to wait here for the car, he decided to run back up the stairs to his room to retrieve the lighter. It would only take him a couple of minutes. He ran up the steps into the hallway and then up the stairs to his room. He reached for his bedroom door and was shocked to see a cardboard sign saying 'vacant' taped to the door. He tried the handle. The door was unlocked, and so he walked inside. The room was empty.

He looked around in amazement. The bed had been stripped, the mattress had been removed from the bed frame, and it was now leaning upright against the wall. All of George's clothes, pyjamas, underwear, and toiletries had also disappeared. The room was a shell. He didn't understand. He was supposed to be coming back to this room this evening after his date. Obviously, he wasn't, he thought.

He walked back down the stairs and out onto the driveway. The car still hadn't arrived. He was now, growing suspicious of his handlers. They rarely interviewed him now and they wouldn't give him an identification card, even though he had been fingerprinted, photographed, and asked for one daily. Surely he would need one if he was wandering about the streets this afternoon. He had also been told quite firmly that he wouldn't be wearing civilian clothes for the date. This now seemed odd. Surely, a civilian walking the streets would attract less attention than an army officer.

Also, George almost had to beg for the cash to spend on this date. His handler had reluctantly given him some money, but this reluctance seemed odd when it was well known to his handler that George hadn't gotten a single penny to his name. How did they expect him to pay for anything? George started to feel anxious again. It was obvious to him now that he wouldn't be coming back. But where were they going to take him, and what would they do with him when they got him there? As important as he thought he was to national security, it was obvious to some people that he had outlived his usefulness. The car pulled up beside George and stopped. The driver stepped out and opened the passenger-side door.

"Welcome aboard, captain," said the uniformed corporal. George noticed that the soldier hadn't saluted him. This was a normal disciplinary offence. Why had the soldier called him captain but failed to salute? To all junior ranks, he was being paraded around the grounds as an officer, yet this junior non-commissioned officer had obviously been let into the secret.

The soldier started making small talk. It seemed to George that this was designed to put him at ease. It wasn't working, though. The soldier asked why George looked nervous. George replied that he hadn't been on a date for a long time and was feeling queasy as the date got closer.

"You'll be fine," said the driver. "She'll do all the talking for both of you. She's a proper little gas bag."

George noticed how the soldier never once called him "sir." He thought about reprimanding the corporal but decided against it. He wanted to keep things friendly. He wanted to escape the situation that he was heading into, and he wanted the driver to drop his guard. Ten minutes later, they entered the park gates. They drove close to a concrete bandstand, and the car stopped.

"She's going to meet you here," said the driver. "Women are always late, so just bide your time. I'll be going now, but I will pick you up at eight." He shook George's hand. "I'm Mark, by the way, Mark Reid; I'll see you later." And with that, he drove away.

Pick us from where? thought George. "I never told him where I'll be."

George looked around. Two hundred yards to his left were the park's public toilets. He decided to wander over to them. Upon reaching them, he casually looked around before entering. It came as no shock to George to see the car he travelled down in, with Mark sitting inside, parked at the edge of the car park. From this vantage point, the driver could observe anything that went on at the bandstand and at the public toilets. George pretended not to notice the car and walked inside the gents. Once inside, he tried to figure out his next move. He was able to make a run for it, but the park was surrounded by six-foot-high railings. By the time George had struggled to get over them, if he could get over them, Mark would be upon him, and he was probably armed.

He looked around the toilets. There was a long, narrow window that was built into the rear wall. It was frosted glass, and it was open slightly from the hinges at the top. George pushed the window open to its limit. It was not overly wide, but he thought he could probably squeeze through if he climbed up onto the toilet pan first. He had started to climb through the window almost before thinking about doing it. He had to be quick. The corporal would no doubt walk over to investigate if he didn't exit the toilets soon.

Once through the window, George dropped to the ground. He was out of sight from the car but still surrounded by the six-foot fence, which he knew he couldn't climb. He laid down on the grass and slowly peered around the corner of the toilets. He immediately spotted that the corporal had exited his car and was heading towards him. He had to think fast. Mark would no doubt walk into the gents and spot that the rear window was open. He would then run around to the rear of the building to see if George was round there. If he couldn't see George, he would have to summon help to look for him.

George immediately removed his cap and dropped it in plain sight on the other side of the railings. There were trees on the other side, so if someone was hiding amongst them, they would be difficult to spot. He then waited near the entrance door to the lady's toilet.

The corporal arrived at the gents and shouted to George that there had been a change of plan. When he didn't get an answer, he walked into the toilets and pushed open the cubicle door. He noticed the open window immediately and ran around, as expected, to the rear of the building. In the meantime, George had slipped into the ladies' toilets just as Mark had entered the gents. Two cubicles were occupied, but the third had the door open. George rushed in and locked the door from the inside. He knew that he could never outrun the corporal. Mark immediately spotted George's hat on the other side of the fence. He started to run towards his car and passed two ladies exiting the toilets.

"There's not a man in there, is there?" he asked the woman closest to him.

"Chance would be a fine thing, you cheeky bugger," the lady replied, feigning irritation.

"There might be a man up my skirt," laughed the other lady. "If you'd care to take a look."

Both ladies started laughing, and Mark carried on running to his car.

George continued to wait inside the cubicle.

Chapter 12
Roman Makes a Decision

Roman watched George step through the portal frame and then disconnected the cable that was clipped onto the live car battery terminal. He thought about dismantling the frame and leaving the building, but a feeling of curiosity overcame him. He sat down on the floor for a few minutes and pondered whether to reconnect the wire to the battery terminal and then step through the doorframe for a few minutes himself, just to see where George had ended up. Disconnecting and then reconnecting the live wire should send him back to roughly the same time, as the battery voltage was consistent and the charge wouldn't have fluctuated much in the few minutes between the time hops. Roman knew that he had to be careful, though.

If he travelled through the time portal in the past, the portal must be kept active for him to step back through in order to return to his own time. If the power supply was interrupted, the time doorway would disappear, stranding him in the past. If by any chance he could build another portal whilst being in the past, say by taking an unassembled one with him, this would only take him even further back into time. It wouldn't take him forwards. He also didn't know if stepping through the electromagnetic doorway would damage any mechanical or electrical items that he would have to take with him to construct another timeframe.

Roman connected the wire and cautiously stepped through the frame. He was in the same building, but now the workshop was dimly lit with a single light bulb hanging from a ceiling pendant. Clunky looking printing machinery filled a good portion of the workshop floor, but it was silent, and the room looked empty.

Roman realised that he hadn't gone too far back in time in relative terms, but looking at the printed posters on the walls, he realised that he must be in the 1940s or 1950s. Just as he realised that he could smell cigarette smoke, two hands grabbed him from the side. In a panic and thinking that George had grabbed him, he struggled and threw himself backwards through the doorframe. The person who was grappling with him also fell backwards and landed on top of Roman, swearing as he did so. The two bodies grappled for a few seconds longer, and during the struggle, a soldier's boot kicked out and caught the car's battery. The live lead fell off the terminal.

"Come on, lad," said the soldier to Roman. "The game is up. You're coming with me to answer a few questions."

Roman stood up and looked at the soldier, then at the battery, and disconnected the cable. He didn't say anything but allowed the soldier to gently push him through the doorframe. The soldier followed closely behind him. Both walked through, and both realised that they were still in the same room; they were both still in the same time and in the same time era. Roman turned and looked at the soldier.

"You're trapped in 2023, and I'm the only person that can get you back to your own time," said Roman. "That's if you want to go back."

The soldier looked around the room. This was definitely not the same room that he had been stationed in for the previous few days. He knew every square inch of that room. He took a step backwards and steadied himself against the wall.

"I've got a new-born and a wife," he said to Roman. "I can't leave them behind."

"As we stand here, your child is an old-age pensioner," replied Roman. "I can send you back within a few days from when you left, but I won't be coming with you."

The soldier nodded. "Okay. Within a few days," he said. "I will have to take something back with me, or they'll think I've been awol. My name's Roger, by the way."

"Roman," said Roman, patting his pockets. He took out his mobile phone and wallet.

"Take this phone," he said, pushing it towards Roger. "You won't have a signal when you get back, but you might be able to listen to my playlist."

He took the phone back, scrolled through to 'We are the Champions' by Queen, and pressed play. The song started, and Roger was visibly astounded. He gratefully took the phone.

"I've got a five-pound note and a two-pound coin, but that's all the money I've got on me," he passed the money over to Roger. "This should convince everyone that you've been to the future."

"Before you go, can you tell me what happened to the other man that stepped through the portal?" said Roman.

"Brass has got him somewhere. It's all very hush-hush and on a need-to-know basis. I've only been told very limited information. Basically, I was told to wait to see if anyone else appeared and then hold them for questioning if they did. The printing workshop has been closed until further notice by order of the police," replied Roger.

"Okay," said Roman. "Step through the doorframe when I say. Good luck and all that."

Roger smiled and stuck up a thumb. "I'll most likely be dead before you're born. If you remember, have a look for my headstone in the cemetery. Roger Neeve, born November the sixteenth, 1919."

With that, he put the phone and coins into his pocket. Roman connected the wire to the battery and asked Roger to step through the doorframe. As soon as Roger stepped through, Roman pulled the wire off the battery terminal and laid on his back on the floor. He let out a long sigh of relief. That had been a close one. He had nearly been stranded in time himself. He made a mental note not to follow anyone else through time, no matter how curious he was. He laid there for a few minutes longer, and then he got up and headed home.

Roger Neeve arrived back at his own time only a few hours into the future. He immediately reported to his superiors his time-travel experience and was driven down to London. Here he was fully debriefed, and he handed over the mobile phone. The circuits were fried, but he explained how he had listened to music on it. He had decided to keep the money, though, and so never mentioned that he had been given that. He explained how he had grabbed the boy and how the two of them had struggled and fell through the portal doorway. He confirmed that he hadn't seen anything outside of the building. He was then asked to describe the doorway as best that he could from memory and then asked to draw the frame, copper coils, and battery.

After completing this, he was informed that he had now been removed from guard duty and seconded to the Big House because of the knowledge he now held. He was told that he would be here for the duration of the war. He was then asked to sign the Official Secrets Act and, given a low-level security clearance.

Two weeks into his new job role, Roger was called into a meeting with George's handler. He was told that George had escaped and that Roger was now part of a small task force that would be sent out to hunt George down and then silence him for good. He was given all of the useful information they held about George, including his grandmother's connection to Haverford West in Wales and her relatives across the sea in Ireland. He was also told about the family connections in Oxford. As an added incentive, Roger was made acting sergeant, with a permanent promotion if he completed the job satisfactorily.

Roger accepted the job but had a few misgivings. First, he was going to be away from his wife and child for as long as the top brass at Big House deemed appropriate, and he was already missing them. Secondly, he was now a plain-clothed detective, not a soldier, and he had a warrant card to prove it. Thirdly, he had been given a small, concealable pistol to always carry with him. He had been told not to engage in conversation or try to arrest George if he found him, but simply to shoot him in the head or through the heart immediately. They couldn't risk him running away again or talking to the enemy. No charges would be brought against Roger for murder, and the whole thing would quietly go away.

Killing someone in cold blood didn't sit right with Roger, even if the man was a spy. Even spies had the right to a trial before they were executed. He never said anything to his superiors, but he mentally decided that he would bring George in if he found him and let someone else take over from there. He collected his pistol and ammunition and jumped into a car with three other members of his team. They looked like a hard bunch of characters. Probably SAS or commandos. He began to wonder why he had been chosen for the mission when they all looked like they were perfectly capable and would be perfectly comfortable killing someone in cold blood. He also had a niggling thought that he was a loose end and that these men had probably been ordered to sort him out at the end of the job.

Roger sat in the front seat and introduced himself to the three men in the car.

"Mick," said the driver. "John," said one man in the back seat. "Steve," said the other man in the back. John started the conversation.

"We're a bit in the dark on this one, and we were told that you would brief us on the mission. We know it's a job hunt and may take some time, but that's about it. Can you fill us in?"

"Okay," replied Roger. "The man we are after is a spy. Brass wants him dead, and he could be anywhere by now."

Steve carried on the conversation. "You're civvy police, aren't you?"

"I'm ex RAF police. I was transferred into the army in late thirty-nine. I'm now a soldier who's just been seconded to the civilian police. I think it's to give rank over, any police we encounter or need help from," replied Roger.

"Good," said Steve. "We prefer to work on our own. Have you seen any action? By action, I mean, have you killed anyone before?"

"I let off a few shots at Dunkirk before I was evacuated," said Roger. "I don't know if I actually hit anyone, though. I've been in an office job since I got back from France. What about yourselves?"

"We're all part of a small team that's been operating in France," said Steve. "We've been running around hunting Nazi top brass and killing them. We were recalled to England yesterday, and we will fly back when the job is done over here. Don't you worry about killing the spy; all you have to do is identify the man and then leave the rest to us. All we need is a positive ID from you, then it's tea and medals for you, and we go back to France."

Roger felt relieved. He just wanted the mission to be over as quickly as possible. These men were the experts. He would do his part to the best of his ability and then go home to his wife. He had been promised two weeks' leave when the mission was over. He sat back in his seat and relaxed.

"Personally, I don't think he's gone to Wales or Ireland. Not yet, anyway. I think he'll hide in London and then try to get back to Oxford."

"What's your reasoning behind that?" said John.

"Well, I think he's intelligent enough to know that the train stations and ports are being watched. His officer's uniform must be getting dirty and dishevelled by now, and he's lost his cap. He's probably unshaven, and he has very little money, and that will go on food and drink anyway. To anyone in authority, George will look like an army deserter. The other three agreed."

"So how far do you cast the net?" said Steve?

"We can start with ten miles around London and twenty miles around Oxford," said Roger. "London can be very unaccommodating to strangers, and I think he will head back to what he's familiar with. We'll let the local police do the legwork. I've got two hundred printed wanted posters in my case to leave at various police stations. I don't think we need to go to the papers yet, but it is an option if it drags on for too long."

"Can we walk into a police station and tell them to put up a poster and keep a lookout for him? After all, we are the military, not the police," said Mick.

"Yes, you can!" replied Roger. "But ask them; don't tell them. Some of the inspectors have a massive chip on their shoulders. If they ask on whose authority, give them this telephone number and tell them to speak to Colonel Brannagan at the Big House. He will put them straight."

The car drove on, and the atmosphere became more relaxed. Roger discovered that Mick had been a professional football player before the war and that John had played semi-professional rugby. Steve had been an English master at Eton, and that's why he talked so poshly, he joked. Mick stopped the car at the entrance to a tube station, and everyone got out. Roger divided the wanted posters and gave everyone fifty sheets each.

"Mick, you go north. Do you know which way north is?" he asked, winking at Mick. Mick grinned back and took the posters. "Steve, you go south, and John, you go west. I will park the car and then go east. We will meet up at that hotel tomorrow afternoon," he pointed at a small hotel on the main street.

"The rooms will be booked for you, and so will an evening meal. We can all freshen up and discuss the next moves from there." With that, they all went their separate ways.

Roger took a small map of London out of his pocket. He then took out a pen. He decided to do some leg work himself before handing out the posters at the police stations. He thought about his East End search area logically. George would be avoiding the posh areas of London and, by now, would be with the poorer people or the down and outs. He coloured out parts of the map. George would be avoiding the main and high streets, and he had no money for hotels. He would barely have enough for a shared room. He coloured out more of the map. George had no identification, no money, and no change of clothes. He also had no ration book. Roger reasoned that the small amount of money that George had would have been spent on cigarettes and cheap cooked food.

He would also need clean drinking water. George had no employment skills and so couldn't get a job as a chef, builder, etc. He might get a job as a builder's labourer, but from what Roger had been told, George was not the physical type. The weather was wet, and the nights were cold, so George would need some type of shelter. Wooded areas were out of the question, as George would have only limited shelter building or other survival skills during the wild. Roger coloured out more of the map. George would feel safer at night than during the day, but breaking into someone's garden shed carried its own risks these days, especially during the blackout.

The main underground stations were frequented by the police, the military, and air raid wardens, so sleeping in them carried a small but significant risk. Under the train bridge arches, with the other homeless, anonymous people, would probably be George's best bet. Roger marked the bridges on the map and set out to find George. It was a long shot, but it was all that he had.

For the best part of six hours, Roger walked the streets of the East End without luck. He had one more bridge to try, and then he would start on the underground. It was nine o'clock at night, and it was getting cold. He thought about his bed and evening meal at the hotel. He had missed his dinner. He rounded a corner and walked to the archway. There were around six bodies on either side. Most of the people were sitting, talking, and smoking, but two people were lying down with discarded carpets, newspapers, and rags over their bodies. Roger walked to the first person. It was an old woman. He walked on to the second person. It was George.

Roger gently tapped George with the toe of his shoe. "George, come with me," he said. "We need to talk." George sat upright. He looked scared and dirty.

"Who are you?" said George, the fear in his voice making his speech waver.

"Police!" said Roger. "And I'm armed. I have been told that you are a spy, and I'm here to take you in."

"I'm not a spy," said George. "You won't believe me, but I travelled through time, and I know too much about the future. I think they want to get rid of me in case I blab to the wrong person. I told them everything I knew."

"Does the name Roman mean anything to you?" asked Roger.

"He's the boy that tricked me into going through the doorframe," said George.

"Yeah, I went through it too. At the printing shop, near Oxford. I'm from this time, though, and not from the future."

"Small world," said George dejectedly. "What happens next?"

"The police and the army are looking for you," said Roger. "You have a target on your back. I can take you to Oxford, but you'll be on your own from there. I can get you a change of clothes, some money, and some food and drink, but there's not much more that I can do for you. It's orders from the top and all that."

"Sounds like the best offer I've had in weeks." Replied George. "What do you want me to do?"

"Wait here and cover up," said Roger. "I'm your only hope, so don't run away; you won't last a day. I'll fetch the car and stuff and be back here in a couple of hours. We can travel through the night. It will be safer." Without waiting for an answer, Roger turned and walked away. George lay back down and covered his face with a newspaper.

Two hours later, Roger pulled up in his car and parped his horn. George sprang up and quickly walked over to the car. He opened the door and climbed inside.

"There's a pile of clothes on the back seat," said Roger. "Here's a couple of quid. There's a spam sandwich in that paper bag, and the water bottle is full of cold water. We'll drive straight to the printers' shop where you originally appeared, as this will be the safest place for you to hide in, when I get rid of the soldier on watch in there."

The pair set off. George fell asleep almost immediately. As he did so, Roger unwound his window. George certainly does stink, he thought. They had a good time and arrived within a couple of hours. George walked up to the printing shop, front door and opened it. He stepped inside. He couldn't see anyone in the dimly lit light, but the strong smell of pipe tobacco alerted him to someone's presence.

"At ease, soldier," said Roger, "I'm here to relieve you."

"Amen to that," came the reply, as a soldier walked over.

"I'm police," said Roger, "and we'll be taking over for the next couple of weeks." He showed the soldier his warrant card. "I bet you're bored stiff," said Roger.

"This is only my second night," replied the guard. "To be fair, I'm struggling to stay awake."

"Well, go back to your unit, and we'll make contact again in a couple of weeks' time to tell the army to relieve us."

The soldier picked up his personal belongings and headed for the door.

"If you want, I can leave you this book," he said. "I finished it earlier."

"If you don't mind," said Roger, thinking of George. "You can have it back in a couple of weeks." With that, they said their goodbyes.

Roger waited a few minutes and then gestured for George to come into the building.

"Is there a cellar or an attic in this place?" said Roger, looking around. "Somewhere that you can make comfy and that is quickly accessible."

"There's no space in the roof, but the floor is a suspended wooden floor for the most part," said George. "It's solid where the heavy machinery is, but there's an eighteen-inch gap under the rest. There's a hatch somewhere under those boxes. If I wall it off with those crates, nobody will find it. I could make a bed out of all these magazines. It should be relatively comfortable in the circumstances."

"Good," said Roger. "Get cracking on that whilst I get your stuff out of the car. There's a toilet out the back and a sink over there. I can see there is soap over there too. Have a wash as soon as you get the chance. You smell awful, and a trained nose will smell that someone is hiding in here if you get a surprise visit."

Roger returned with the clothes out of the car. He looked across at the telephone in the corner of the room and decided that he would call his wife. He had been on the phone for a couple of minutes when she remembered a message that she had taken for him. She recited it to Roger. It was from Roman.

"He's being forced to go back to 1944. He will come back on the sixth of August, to the same place as last time, but he doesn't know what time during the day or night. He thinks the man forcing him to come back will kill him when they come through the time frame. The man has already beaten him up. Can you help him?"

Roger ended the call. The sixth was the day after tomorrow. If the lad came back, then he could take George back with him. That would mean that after a few weeks, the search would be scaled down. If he could lose the SAS men for a day, he could get George away and arrest Roman's tormentor. He walked over to George and explained his plan. George would have to remain hidden on that day until Roman and the other man came through. Roger would arrest the other man, put him in handcuffs, and then lock him in the other room whilst George and Roman went back to the future. The other man would not have seen any of this, and so, wouldn't be able to tell anyone at his subsequent interviews. He advised George not to leave the building under any circumstances. George agreed.

The two men said their goodbyes, and Roger headed back down to London. It was early morning when he got to the hotel, but he decided to have a couple of hours of sleep anyway. He got up at seven o'clock and went down for breakfast. He hung around the hotel lobby afterwards for a couple of hours, reading the newspaper, and then went out for a walk to kill some time. At midday, he went back to the hotel to make his daily phone call to Colonel Brannagan and to wait for the team to arrive.

During the phone call, Colonel Brannagan informed him that a man matching George's description had been seen buying cigarettes from a shop in Oxfordshire. It may have been a false sighting, but it was worth checking out, as the colonel had insisted. He gave Roger the general location and told Roger to split the team up. He was to leave one man in London in case he was needed quickly and to take the other two men with him. Roger put down the telephone receiver and cursed under his breath. George had one job to do. Stay out of sight for a day or two, and he wandered off to get some fags. Well, he only had himself to blame if he took some lead through his heart.

Roger met up with the other men and told them that there had been a potential development. John was to stay in London, whilst Steve and Mick were to accompany him to Oxfordshire. They would set up an observation point overlooking a printing workshop and wait for George to turn up. The men agreed, and the three men climbed into the car. Two hours later, the three of them were working out a plan. Roger took the lead and went into the printing shop alone to make sure it was unoccupied. He emerged five minutes later after berating George for being so stupid about going out for cigarettes.

He warned George to stay out of sight because there were now two armed men outside with orders to shoot him. He told Mick and Steve that he had conducted a thorough search of the place and that the workshop was empty. He then told both men that the three of them would split into two teams and keep an eye on the place full-time. He would be one team, and both men would be the other. They would set up in the bedroom of the unoccupied cottage next door by forcing entry via the back door. He went on to explain that they would do six-hour alternative shifts. The cottage offered a good all-round vision of the workshop, and so when one team was on, the other team could sleep in a back room or go out for something to eat and drink. The men agreed, and Roger took first watch.

The observations went on throughout the night and the following day. The sixth of August arrived, and Roger decided to break observation protocol. He told the other two men that because the workshop had one window at the side, which couldn't be seen from their observation point, he would enter the workshop alone and hide in there for the day.

The other two were to move from the cottage to the small shed in the workshop grounds, which was connected to the workshop by an open doorway. The two men would have been immediately at hand if Roger had called out George's full name. The men looked slightly aghast at the move, but Roger reassured them that George was unarmed and that he had a gut feeling that George would arrive through the side window sometime that day. He explained that his gut feelings were rarely wrong. He walked to the window and discreetly unfastened the catch.

Chapter 13
Roman Alerted

Upon waving Roger Neeve off back to his own time and leaving George's printing works, Roman had walked through his garden gate and headed to his front door. He took his door key out of his pocket and stopped briefly to check that there were none of Tony's or Eddie's friends waiting for him to arrive. He glanced at the stone lintel above the door, which looked out of place with its deep grey colour compared to the light grey stone that the rest of his cottage was built from. It was strange that he had never noticed this before. As he got closer to the lintel, he noticed that there were some words carved into it. The words had been cut deep into the granite, and the crevices were filled with yellow and brown lichen, but he could still read the engraved words.

Roman. Eddie is killing your ancestors. Morgan. 1682

Roman read it again and again. He sat down. Eddie must have landed in the same time period as Morgan. He was obviously holding a grudge. If he was killing Roman's ancestors, it was only a matter of time before Roman would have never existed. Did his ancestors come from Oxfordshire? He didn't know. If not, Eddie was killing the wrong family tree. Still, it was now imperative for him to go back and stop Eddie from killing anyone with the same surname. He rushed into the house. First things first. If he went back in time and couldn't get back, what would happen to his house? He decided to make a quick will and testament, leaving all his belongings to his mother. The will probably wouldn't stand up in a court of law, but he didn't have the time to go and see a solicitor, and anyway, his mum was his next of kin.

After writing the will, he tried to formulate a plan. He couldn't use the workhouse basement as it was no doubt still flooded, and the security fencing had also been improved. He might be able to set up the portal on the other side of the building, as this would land him in roughly the same place as Morgan if he could gain access to the space through someone's back garden. The brief glimpse of the landscape that he got when Morgan and he jumped through the portal looked like a wooded landscape area with no sign of the workhouse or orphanage, and so this was probably before the workhouse had been built. The trouble was how far into the past he would need to go and how much electricity would need flowing through the copper coils to take him there.

When Morgan went through, the coils were operating under a massive electrical load from the workhouse power supply. Could he get there via a car battery? Unlikely. A lorry battery? Probably. He would probably need a portable generator. But how big though? He had no idea. He tried to calculate the voltage-to-time ratio from his own trip into the past and from Morgans. Roman went back to the 1800s under a 12-volt car battery. His grandfather had gone slightly farther back on a fully charged 12-volt car battery. Eddie went back on a fully charged 24-volt lorry battery and met Morgan, who went through on around 400 volts. Perhaps 24 volts was the optimum, and any voltage over that didn't take you back any further? Perhaps the time frame only had the capacity to take you back into the seventeenth century at most.

Roman had left the doorframe and lorry battery at the side of Eddie's garage, and he didn't want to go back and pick them up. He decided to try the portable generator that was still stored in the garden shed to see if it worked. He wheeled it out of the shed and onto the lawn. The petrol tank was nearly empty but probably had enough in there to start it up. He flicked on the choke button and pulled the pull cord. After the fourth time, the generator came to life. It coughed and spluttered a bit, then ran for a few minutes before cutting out.

Roman assumed that it was out of fuel. He went into the house and opened his laptop to do an internet search on the generator model in the garden. Apparently, the generator would give out 230 volts for a maximum of six hours on a full tank of petrol. Roman's generator was quite old, so six hours would probably be the *absolute* limit. It would probably only run for five hours, and that was with a service beforehand.

Roman topped up the generator's petrol tank to the brim. He had given the generator a service to the best of his ability, and it now started first time and ran until he switched it off. He had decided to use his back garden again as the launch place and would head into the village once on the other side. He decided to take a survival rucksack with him, which included a one-man pop-up tent, some food, a knife, and a first aid kit. He also carried a Second World War bayonet that had belonged to his grandfather, tucked into his trouser waistband. He tried to dress as inconspicuously as possible by wearing dark jeans and a dark pullover, and he had his pockets filled with the remaining gold coins retrieved after his previous excursion into the past.

Roman had made a doorframe by stripping lengths of wood from the garden shed. He kept the resonators and electromagnets after using them at Eddie's house and spent a few minutes calibrating them. He sourced more copper wire from the back of the shed, and once the copper wiring had been tightly coiled around the frame and wired to a plug, he was ready to go. He thought about calling his mum and telling her that he loved her, but thought against it. He had never told her that he loved her before, and she had never said the same to him, so saying that would only make her suspicious and lead to her worrying.

She seemed happier now since George had walked out on her, and Roman didn't want to do anything that would change her frame of mind. Roman turned on the generator and took a deep breath. No matter what, he had only six hours maximum to do what he had to do, although he didn't really know what he had to do, and to get back through the time frame before the generator ran out of fuel.

If he didn't make it, he would be stuck in the past forever. He shuddered. He set up his digital watch—the only watch he owned—to stopwatch and stepped through the frame. He was now in the field behind his house, and to his right was the nearly completed orphanage. It was a lot smaller than the one he knew, and it had obviously been substantially extended over the following years. He glanced at his watch, but it had stopped working and smelt faintly of burning.

Roman headed towards the village. He orientated himself with various landmarks that he could see in the distance and that were still there in the twenty-first century. The church in the distance was his main focal point. As he got closer to the village, his footsteps slowed. He felt the bayonet in his waistband, and this gave him some sense of comfort. He decided to head to the church or the pub if the village had a pub, as these two meeting places would be the best places to glean any information about Eddie's whereabouts. He would avoid as many people as possible on the route, though.

Roman came to the village's outskirts on the top of a small hill. *This is roughly where Eddie's house will be built a few hundred years into the future,* he thought. He could see a row of terraced houses in the distance, at the bottom of the slope, and one building in particular caught his eye. It looked like a pub. He slowly walked down the slope towards it. On arriving at the pub entrance door, he took a deep breath and then stepped inside. As he walked into the room, he noticed a couple of hard-looking men seated at tables, either side of the front door. Both were smoking clay pipes, but neither were drinking. He walked towards the bar. He could see the barman standing in the doorway of the bar and the entrance to a back room. The landlord had his back to Roman.

"Excuse me!" said Roman, trying to talk in a voice that disguised his nervousness.

The landlord turned around. There was a brief split second before Eddie and Roman recognised each other, then Eddie shouted at the two men seated in the doorway to grab Roman and take him into the back room. The men lunged at Roman just as Roman, tried to pull the bayonet out of his waistband. The man who got to Roman first knocked the blade out of Roman's hand, and it clattered to the floor. The man immediately grabbed Roman's arm and twisted it behind Roman's back. The other man grabbed Roman's other arm, and the two men led Roman into the back room.

"Roman," said Eddie. "As I live and breathe. I've waited months for this meeting, and to be fair, I never thought that it would happen. And here you are, bold as brass, strolling through my front door." Eddie rolled his eyes upwards. "Thank you, Lord," he whispered loudly.

"Tie his hands behind his back, but don't gag him," said Eddie to the two henchmen. He looked at Roman. "We are going to have some fun when this place closes, but I want to chat first. Sit down."

Roman sat down. "Now, I want to know how to get back," said Eddie. "You're going to take me back, or at least tell me where the doorway is. I have a large chest that I need to take with me, on a barrow, but I can't retrieve it until it gets dark."

"It can't be done," said Roman, shaking his head. "If you're going, it's got to be within the next three hours. I can show you where the doorway is, but I can't explain where it is, as it's in the middle of nowhere. If we don't go through before the diesel in the generator runs out, we will both be trapped here. Forever."

Eddie stared at Roman. "If you're lying, boy, I will kill you. Slowly," he said.

"I'm not; I can take you there now," said Roman. "But we've got to be quick."

"I'm not leaving without my gold," said Eddie. "And I can't collect it until it gets dark."

"You can't take it then," said Roman. "Not unless you let me go back and top up the generator and then come back for you."

Eddie stood silent for a moment. "Okay, here's what's going to happen. You're going to go back and top up the generator. Then you're coming back for me and my gold. If you decide not to come back, I will carry on killing your ancestors until you were never born. That way, I will get back eventually because all of this will have never happened, but you won't have happened either. I burned down a cottage in the next village where a couple lived with the same surname as you. Obviously, these were not your direct descendants, or you wouldn't be here, but I'm prepared to kill every single person in this area with your surname if I have to. You can look at me as a King Herod type figure, like the one in the Bible. Believe me, I am capable, and I will do it."

"Okay. Untie me and take me back. I will show you where the doorway is, and you can meet me there later." said Roman, raising his arms.

"Untie him," said Eddie to his henchmen. "You can have the pub when I'm gone." Eddie looked at Roman. "I did have some unfinished business with Morgan up at the manor house, but that will have to wait now. Still, you never know; I might pop back in a few months and finish him off anyway. I might even come back and put my name on the deeds to his house. Imagine what that's worth in our time."

Roman stayed silent. Obviously, Eddie was thinking of seizing the time portal for himself. What had he really got in store for himself, wondered Roman.

Eddie and Roman walked up to the portal doorway. Just as Roman braced himself to step through, Eddie reminded him of the consequences of not coming back. Roman shuddered and walked through, back into the future.

Chapter 14
Roman Reunited

Once back inside his own garden, Roman dismantled the wooden time frame. He didn't trust Eddie not to follow him back with some ulterior motive in mind. The last thing he wanted was for Eddie to pop through the doorway into his garden, unannounced. He decided to move the portal entrance further away. Eddie was the type of person who would be waiting on the other side of Roman's garden, with the intention of harming Roman when he went through, and then coming home to the twenty-first century alone. This was more than a possibility if the time frame was left in the same geographical place. He decided that he would move the doorway to the hedge that surrounded the workhouse. This part was sheltered from the public, so nobody should question why Roman was hacking a hole through the branches and brambles. This spot would also give him a good vantage point to look out for when in danger and give him a chance to quickly get back if need be.

It was late afternoon by the time Roman had wheeled the generator, the frame, and the electrical components to a suitable part of the hedge. This part of the hedge was the thinnest point in its length, but it still took an hour for Roman to hack a doorway sized hole through it with his machete. After setting up the frame, he started the generator and prepared himself to step through. He was sweating from the hacking and decided to take a few minutes to cool down and recuperate his energy before he went through.

He sat down and looked up to see two men standing about three metres away. Both men looked as if they were in their thirties. One had a baseball bat in his hand, whilst the other had a piece of wood in his hand that looked like a chair or table leg. It was obvious to Roman that the one holding the bat was a close relation of Eddie's; they looked so similar.

"I'm not sure what you're up to," said Eddie's brother, "but no doubt you're up to no good. We think that you're involved with Tony's death and the disappearance of my brother. We're here to get some answers, and we can do it the hard or easy way."

Roman stood up. "Your brother is through there," he said, pointing at the doorframe. "Follow me, and I will take you to him."

With that, Roman hurled himself through the frame. Thinking that Roman was trying to escape into the derelict building, both men ran through the door frame after him. They arrived on the other side a few seconds after Roman, but these few seconds gave enough time for Roman to position himself to the side of the portal and then step back through into his own time, immediately after his two pursuers charged through. Both men stopped and turned around to chase Roman back, but the doorway was gone. The hedge had also gone. Upon arriving back at his own time, Roman had pulled the live wire that was connected to the generator.

Darren, Eddie's brother, and Andrew, his gangster friend, looked around. The workhouse was gone. They were at a building site where a smaller version of the workhouse was under construction. There were no diggers, dumpers, or in fact, anything that a modern building site required. Was it some sort of self-build project where the owner ran out of money? Had the scheme been abandoned? Was the owner trying to build the place on some sort of ecological basis? No diesel machinery, no cement. But this didn't answer the question as to how a large brick and slate building had disappeared within less than a minute, to be replaced by a much smaller building. Both men looked at each other. Speechless. It was a lot to take in.

"Are we dead?" said Andrew. "Are we on the other side?"

"I don't know," replied Darren. "There's nobody about. I'm sure my mum and some other relatives would be here to greet me."

"I don't think we're dead," said Andrew. "I twisted my ankle when I turned round to run back through that doorframe. It's killing me. I don't think you'd feel pain when you die."

"Yeah, I agree," said Darren. "There's a big house up there," he said pointing to the manor house in the distance. "Let's get some answers up there. If we don't get any joy, we can walk over to that cottage on the other side of the field." With that, both men set off to the house in the distance.

Morgan walked out of his house and headed to the stable block for his horse's saddle. He was going to ride out for a few hours to get the lay of the land around Eddie's inn. He had made up his mind to enter Eddie's place through a back door or window and attack Eddie inside the premises before the inn's front door was opened to the public and before the room filled up with Eddie's friends. As he lifted the saddle onto the horse's back, he noticed two people at the bottom of his drive, walking towards him. As the men got closer, he recognised Eddie's brother, Darren, and another man who he didn't recognise.

Morgan walked back into the stable and picked up a small iron bar. He put this inside his tunic, out of sight, and waited a few seconds for the two men to arrive. As the men drew closer, Darren looked at Morgan, and his face opened into a smile.

"Morgan, what are you doing here? Where are we? What's happened to us all?"

Morgan relaxed slightly. Both men were dressed in twenty-first-century clothing, and both were clearly confused. Darren held out his hand for a handshake. Morgan shook his hand. The other man introduced himself as Andy.

"What are you doing here?" repeated Darren. "How long have you been here?" he said, looking at Morgan's grey hair. "What's going on?"

"Did that Roman kid trick you into stepping through a door frame?" said Morgan.

"Yeah, we chased him through one, but he doubled back on us. We couldn't get back through the hedge in time to catch him, and then the doorframe disappeared, trapping us here. Everything had disappeared. All the houses have gone. It's just fields and the odd building. We saw this place and headed over to it. I couldn't believe it when I saw you. What's going on?"

Morgan proceeded to tell both men about how he was tricked into going through a doorframe and how the doorframe was in fact a doorway into the past. He explained how he had lived here for years, even though Darren had seen him in Oxford a few weeks ago. Morgan went on to tell both men how they were now trapped here forever. He never mentioned Eddie at all, though. The men looked aghast. What about their families? What about their properties? their jobs? Andy said that he felt sick.

Morgan realised that he had to get rid of both men. The last thing he wanted was for them to team up with Eddie and come look for him. He had to think on his feet. He told both men to wait in the stables, out of sight, whilst he fetched them some clothing. He warned them both that walking around in the clothes that they were in would make them stand out and would probably make them a target for robbery or worse. They might even be accused of witchcraft and be hanged.

Both men sat down on a pile of logs whilst Morgan went into the house and collected some clothes. The clothes had belonged to Anne's father and would be too big on both men, but they could tie the trousers and tunics with string to make outfits that they could both wear comfortably. He returned with the clothes and gave them to the men, along with half a loaf of bread each and a jug of water to share.

"You really need to get to London," said Morgan. "You'll fit in and blend in there. I can drop you off at a pub where you can take a carriage. It's Thursday today, and if I drop you off at the pub in Marston, you can ride down from there. Tell the barman that you are new to the area and don't have any money. He will probably give you a couple of pints of beer on the house whilst you're waiting."

"Don't tell him or anybody else that you are here from the future," continued Morgan. "You will either be locked up as madmen or hanged as witches."

The two men stood silent and chewed the bread.

"Time to go," said Morgan. "You need to be at the pub in good time. The carriage leaves at three, and it won't wait."

Morgan fastened two horses to his wooden carriage. He told both men to lay down in the back with a blanket over them until they were out into the countryside. He warned them that they didn't want to draw attention to themselves during the forty-minute journey. The men did as they were asked, and Morgan rode off with the men.

Approximately forty minutes later, they arrived at the tavern. Morgan helped both men out of the back.

"That's the pub. Speak to the landlord and wait for the coach. The coach is a bit rough and ready, but it's free. Luxury hasn't been invented yet." said Morgan, "I'm going this way, so good luck."

With that, he climbed aboard his carriage and rode off down the road. Andrew and Darren walked through the tavern door and up to the bar. They beckoned the landlord over.

"What can I get you, gentlemen?" said the landlord, looking at both men's baggy clothes.

"We're new to the area and haven't got any money," said Darren. "But we were told that a coach leaves here at three, and we can get a lift on that."

"No problem," said the landlord. "No problem at all. Would you like a beer whilst you're waiting? It's on the house."

Both men grinned. Morgan was right. "Yes, we'll have a beer," they said in unison.

The landlord walked to the end of the bar and filled up two tankards with ale. He brought them both over. Darren and Andy downed the pints without drawing a breath.

"Same again?" said the landlord.

"Yes mate. Same again," said Darren. "You do realise that we haven't got any money to pay for them, don't you?"

"It's all on the house until the coach gets here. It's tradition," said the landlord.

"Keep them coming then," said Andy. "I don't turn anything down that's free."

Both men were on their fourth pint when the inn door opened, and a man walked in. He walked up to the bar.

"Ale, please, landlord," he said to the barman, taking off his hat and rubbing his bald head.

"Two here for the waggon," the barman replied.

The coach driver looked at both men. They were obviously in stolen clothes. Nobody would buy such expensive clothing if it didn't fit.

"Where do you want to go?" he asked.

"London!" came the unanimous reply.

"You're in luck, then. That's just where I'm headed. Have another pint on me and put your marks on these pieces of paper. This will act as your travel warrant. How much money do you have?"

"Nothing," said Darren. "We were told that the ride is free."

"Ah!" said the man thoughtfully, rubbing his chin. "It should be a shilling apiece, but I'll tell you what. I will give you both a shilling, and then if we are stopped on the way down, and you are asked to pay, you can pay with the shillings. If we don't get stopped, you can give them back to me when we reach London."

"Sounds fair to me," said Andy, nodding to Darren. "Five pence sounds cheap for a trip to the smoke anyway."

"Twelve pennies, you mean?" said the driver, making a mental note that at least one of the two men didn't know his sums. "It's not cheap when you see the standard of your transport. It's very basic, to say the least. Very short on comfort, but it's the only one travelling to London this week."

"I'm sure we'll survive," said Darren, grinning. "When do we go?"

"Just as soon as I've finished my drink," came the reply. "Swill yours down. We won't be stopping for drinks until we get there."

With that, all three men finished their drinks, and the coach driver gave the landlord a two-shilling piece out of his pocket. They all made their way to the front door. When they got outside, the effects of the alcohol began to hit them.

"Blimey, that beer was strong," said Andy as he climbed through the door into the back of the waggon.

"You can sleep it off on the way," replied the coachman, as he held the door open.

Darren climbed into the waggon, and the coachman locked the door behind him.

"If you need to pee, pee through the slats, 'cos we are only making one more stop on the way."

Both men sat down on a long bench fixed to the side of the waggon. On a bench on the opposite side sat two teenagers, each about fifteen years old. One of the boys was sobbing. Darren looked around the waggon interior. The waggon was very sturdy. It was almost like a prison waggon he had seen in a western a few years ago. He began to feel uneasy.

"What if I need a crap before we stop for the other passengers? Do I ask you to stop the waggon?"

"There's a bucket under your seat," replied the coachman as he positioned himself in his seat and got the two horses moving. "Just get yourselves comfortable. It's a long trip. Try and get some sleep."

The boy who was sobbing started rocking back and forth.

"I can't join the Navy. I can't go to Portsmouth," he sobbed. "Please let me out. You can have your shilling back," he pleaded with the coach driver.

The coach driver ignored him and kept the waggon moving. The other boy sat there quietly, his eyes drifting into space. He had already resigned himself to his fate.

"Nobody can force you to join the Navy," said Darren to the crying boy.

"I took the king's shilling," came the reply.

The boy opened his hand to show Darren the shiny new shilling.

"Did you sign a contract?" said Darren to the boy.

"He put his mark on the oath," said the coach driver, turning to look at Darren. "Same as you two."

"We never signed any such thing," said Darren indignantly.

The coach driver reached inside his tunic and pulled out the two pieces of paper with Andy and Darren's signatures on them. He held them up so the pair could see.

"I will fill in the gaps when we stop."

"I never signed up for anything, except for a ride to London," said Andy.

The coachman laughed but didn't reply.

"Did you take the shilling as well?" the crying boy opposite asked Darren.

"Yes, he did. They both did," the coachman replied. "You have all joined the Navy, and you are all on your way to the docks. Don't try to get out of the waggon. You won't. Bigger men than you have tried, and if you damage any part of it, you will be punished when we stop. Just sit back and sleep the beer off. This is the easy part."

Darren stood up and started kicking the door. It wouldn't budge. He walked around the waggon and tried kicking the sides. Still no joy. He began to make threats to the driver, but the driver ignored him and carried on driving. After a while, Darren sat back down. The driver started talking again.

"Ten years is nothing these days. When I joined, it was *fifteen* years hard. Now sailors eat well and sleep well. You might all retire with a rank. You might all take a wife on some foreign shore. The Navy will make men of you all."

With that, the driver took a clay pipe out of his pocket. He had no tobacco, but he sucked the empty pipe anyway.

"Driving without smoking makes me grumpy," said the driver, turning his head around to Darren. "Don't try to smash your way out or make any more threats against me. Sit back and be quiet, and I'll forget what's just gone on. I still hold a rank, and I can have you flogged if I have a mind to when we stop. We will be stopping by soon to pick up some more volunteers. When you do, stay seated. A couple of muskets will be trained on you, and the Jack's holding them have itchy trigger fingers. They would rather see a dead sailor than a deserter, so keep that in mind."

With that, he turned his head forward and carried on sucking on his empty pipe. The waggon fell silent, and horses drove on.

Morgan arrived home at dusk. As his carriage approached his gates, he saw someone waiting there to meet him. As he got closer, he recognised that person as Roman. The boy hadn't changed at all. He stopped the horses.

"You look familiar," he said to Roman, smiling. "You got my message, then?"

Roman smiled back. "I've come to take you back," he said.

"Nah, I don't want to go back. Said Morgan. I'm used to it here now. It's a healthier lifestyle if you know what to eat and how to keep yourself clean. I'm married and settled down now. I've got a wife and a kid, and another kid on the way. I'm the lord of the manor into the bargain. I was made for this life."

"What about Eddie?" said Roman. "I'm supposed to be taking him back later today, but I don't trust him. He said that if he gets hold of my time portal, he may come back and kill you and put your manor house deeds into his name."

"Did he indeed?" said Morgan thoughtfully. "Where is your doorframe set up, and what time are you leaving?"

"In about two hours," replied Roman. "The generator petrol will run out in three hours, and once that happens, whoever's here stays here. The doorframe is set up at the back of the workhouse, directly opposite the front door, about twenty metres further back. You can't see it from this side. Eddie thinks it's further along the field, in my cottage's back garden."

"Leave it with me," said Morgan. "Happy travels."

With that, he drove his carriage through the gates. Roman set off at a slow pace towards the workhouse.

It was dark when he got there, and he decided to inch his way around the field to try and spot Eddie and see what Eddie may have in store for him. He reached a secluded spot and almost immediately spotted Eddie pushing a small wooden barrow up to where he thought the portal door was going to open. Roman still hadn't formulated a plan. He would have to play it by ear.

Roman watched Eddie lift a small chest out of the barrow and place it on the ground in front of the hedge. It was obviously heavy, and Eddie strained to pick it up. He then moved the barrow to the side of the hedge. This would be difficult to see by the person emerging through the hedge from the cottage garden side. Roman wondered if Eddie had anything else concealed in the barrow. Roman waited a few minutes longer and then decided to reveal himself to Eddie. He stood up and started to walk over to where Eddie was standing.

"Have you got everything you want to take through with you," he said loudly.

Eddie was startled momentarily; he was expecting Roman to appear through the hedge beside him.

"Where is the doorway?" he asked.

"Along that way," said Roman in a generally sweeping motion. "Pick up the chest and follow me. Leave the barrow. It's not far."

"This is not what we agreed," said Eddie, clearly irritated.

"I couldn't get it to work just there. Come on, or the petrol will have run out," said Roman.

"I will need the barrow for the chest," replied Eddie. "It's too heavy for a man of my age."

Roman watched as Eddie put the chest back into the barrow.

"Lead on, Macduff," said Eddie, misquoting Shakespeare's Macbeth.

He picked up the wooden handles and started to push the barrow towards Roman. Roman turned and walked towards the portal gateway, with Eddie a few steps behind. Roman was nervous. He couldn't leave Eddie in this time period, but he didn't really want to lead him home. Eddie was too calm and pleasant about everything, and it seemed to Roman like an act. A few metres before the portal gateway, Roman stopped and turned to Eddie.

"We are nearly there. Take your chest and leave the barrow. The barrow won't fit through the frame."

Eddie hesitated, but stopped and lifted the chest out of the barrow. He was now in a predicament. It took both of his hands to carry the chest. He also needed to carry the eighteen-inch, loaded, wheel-lock pistol that he had concealed in the barrow. This was to be Roman's fate when the portal doorway was revealed. As he momentarily pondered the situation, Morgan appeared, seemingly out of nowhere.

"Are we going to sort it, Eddie?" he said, looking directly at Eddie. "Man to man. I know you carry a concealed dagger in your tunic. I've got one too." Eddie looked at the knife in Morgan's hand, and then he looked at Roman.

"You two in this together?" he asked Roman. "Well, no worries," he looked back at Morgan. "I do carry a dagger, but I'm not crazy enough to take you on with it. However, I do have this," he said, lifting the wooden pistol out of the barrow. "I will just say my goodbyes the old-fashioned way."

He levelled the pistol at Morgan, and simultaneously, Morgan threw the knife at Eddie. The pistol went off with a bang and a flash of fire and smoke. Eddie cried out in pain as the knife penetrated the top of his arm. He dropped the pistol and attempted to pull out the knife. Morgan was also struggling. The lead ball had passed through his side. It was a clean shot, though, in through the front and out through the back, and it appeared to have missed his vital organs. Morgan pressed his hand over the wound at the front to try to stop the blood from flowing out.

"Roman, get through the doorframe," he said. Nodding in the direction of the frame.

"I'm not leaving you here to die," replied Roman. "Come with me and let me get you to a hospital; they will save you."

"I'm fine," said Morgan. The ball went straight through. Brains there has had the lead ball out in the cold for too long, and it's solid. It never broke up. I can sort it out. I've been shot before. In battle, and I know what to do. Eddie, on the other hand, is going to die from an infection. I rubbed the knife blade in sheep shit on the way up here.

Eddie pulled out the knife with a grunt. His wound was deep, but he could still carry the chest for a short distance. Roman started to run towards the portal gateway.

"Send me another message to let me know you made it," he said, as he started to run. Eddie also started to run after him with the chest. Morgan was too far away and in no condition to stop Eddie, and so he was reduced to being an unwilling spectator. Roman hit the doorway first and threw himself through it. He landed hard on the ground but scrambled to his feet. He ran to the generator to pull off the live cable that was connected to the frame. Eddie had reached the doorframe a second before this moment, and as he tripped and half-stumbled through the frame, he dropped the chest into the Roman's side of the doorway. At this exact moment, there was a flash, a scream, and Eddie disappeared. Roman sat down on the ground to catch his breath.

One electrical resonator was disconnected. *That scream was disturbing, though, and where had Eddie gone?* Thought Roman. Passing through the timeframe with both resonators slightly misaligned was dangerous enough, but to attempt to pass through with only one working, which had nothing to synchronise with, was beyond dangerous. If Eddie was still alive, and it was a big if, Eddie would be nowhere. Everywhere. Somewhere, where nothing exists. In a different dimension or plane. Roman shuddered. Poor Eddie. Yes, he was going to kill Roman, but would Eddie have been better off dead?

Roman stood up and turned the generator off. He picked up the electrical items and carried them over to his garden. He then went back to collect the generator and returned a little while later to dismantle the door frame. Once everything was put away in his shed, he walked around to the front of his house and dropped the chest full of gold inside. He walked back outside and looked up at his stone lintel. It now reads: *Roman. Made it. Morgan.*

Chapter 15
A Race Against Time

Darren and Andy were still seated in the waggon when it arrived at the next tavern. When the waggon stopped, Darren could see that there were two people sitting on a bench outside of the tavern, and a soldier was seated opposite with a musket laid across his lap. *These were obviously the volunteers*, thought Darren. He looked around and quickly noticed that there was only one soldier, not two, as the coach driver had warned. He also noticed that the soldier was barely more than a teenager himself. Darren nodded to Andy and rolled his eyes. Andy nodded back. This was probably the best chance that they would get to escape from the waggon. The waggon driver got out of his seat and walked around to the back of the waggon. As he did so, Darren spoke in a whisper to the still-sobbing boy opposite.

"When the door opens, stand up and tell the driver that you need to be sick and you don't want to throw up on the waggon floor. He will let you out."

"Will he?" said the boy, visibly perking up.

"Yes," said Darren. "Just make sure you are standing in the doorway as soon as the door opens."

The boy got up and positioned himself at the rear of the waggon. The door was unlocked and swung open. The soldier stood in front of the door with his muzzle trained on the open doorway.

"Sit down!" shouted the soldier to the standing boy.

"I feel," he never got a chance to finish his sentence. Darren stood up behind him and gave him a violent shove out of the doorway. The boy fell onto the business end of the musket, which went off at the same time. The boy died instantly as the lead ball tore through his chest, but the momentum of the shove, combined with the boy's dead weight, sent the soldier sprawling, his musket falling from his hand. Darren, then Andy jumped out of the doorway. Andy grabbed the musket, whilst Darren kicked the prone soldier in the face a couple of times, rendering him unconscious. Andy pointed the rifle at the coach driver and told him to lie down on the ground.

"You've no powder or ball," said the coach driver. "It won't shoot. If you run, I'll see you both hang. As it stands, get back into the waggon, and I'll report this as an accident."

Andy walked over to the driver. "Report this," he said calmly, then smashed the rifle butt into the coach driver's face. The driver fell to the ground, his smashed mouth and nose pouring with blood.

"Which way to London?" said Darren to the two volunteers that were still seated on the bench.

"Back the way you came ten miles away, then turn right. Stay on that road; it will take you most of the way," came the reply.

Darren walked over to the waggon door and ordered the other boy out.

"It's your lucky day, Son. Get away and stay away from your home area for a few months; they'll probably come looking for you."

The boy jumped out of the doorway and started running down the road. When he was approximately one hundred metres away from the tavern, he turned into some woodland at the side of the road, out of sight of everyone. Darren shut the waggon door.

"Can you drive this?" he said to Andy.

Andy shrugged. "How hard can it be?" he replied.

Both men got up onto the driver's bench, and after a couple of attempts, Andy managed to turn the horses around so that they were facing the opposite direction.

"Home, James," grinned Darren. "Let's get there before they come looking for us."

Five hours later, the pair had reached London. They had unhooked the two horses and were leading them by the reins on foot. They had abandoned the waggon down, a muddy track, but with nothing available to light a fire with, they couldn't set fire to it. They walked through the town's outskirts and headed towards the centre. They had already formulated a plan to sell the horses to the first person that showed an interest in them, whether this be a blacksmith, coach or courier service, or butcher. They would then use the money to find lodgings. From here, they would do what they had to do to survive. To survive long enough to take their revenge on Morgan, whom they blamed for this whole episode. Darren was also formulating a plan in his head to take his revenge on Roman.

He and Andy may be stuck in the past for the rest of their lives, but Roman could never be born if his ancestors were murdered. After keeping a low profile for a few months, they would return to Oxfordshire and systematically rub Roman's ancestors out of history.

It was Sunday, and Roman was sitting at home at his kitchen table. His mother had just left after eating a meal cooked by Roman. Roman was now scrolling through some historical web pages for the local area. He felt content. It had been a few months since his last excursion into the past, and now the timeframe and the related equipment were gathering dust in his garden shed. He still had Eddie's small chest of gold, and he reckoned that he had more gold than he needed to get by. He had been meaning to search out Morgan's family history online for a while, to see if any of Morgan's relatives were around during this time period. If they were, he would give them some of the gold. He felt that he owed Morgan that for saving his life.

A few days prior, he had searched the local cemetery and located a couple of graves with Morgan's surname on the old stone headstones. This led Roman to believe that Morgan's descendants had survived well into the eighteenth century, at least.

As Roman flicked through the web pages, he decided to check his own family tree, stored on a separate file on the computer, and cross reference both his and Morgan's to see if the two families overlapped at any time in the past. It was unlikely, but people did tend to marry people from their local area in those days, so he and Morgan might share some common ancestry. The research would also kill at least an hour before he went upstairs for a shower. He opened the file labelled 'My Family Tree' and scrolled through the names.

Something was wrong. On previous occasions, Roman traced his father's ancestors to the fifteenth century, and the family tree was wide with the number of relatives he had listed there. Now the tree was narrower. Some of his grandfather's and great-grandfathers' families were missing from the tree. Roman sat up straight. His mind started to race. He jumped out of his chair and raced over to the cupboard. He took out a cardboard tube and pulled out the rolled-up paper that was in there. He placed this printed version on top of the table and compared this paper version with the file that he had on the computer screen. They were different. The paper one had a lot more family members on it.

He sat back down in his chair to think clearly about what this meant. Was there a glitch in the computer file? It could be. He decided to double-check. On the second viewing, he was shocked again. The paper file was now identical to the computer file. Now with fewer family members. He sat down again. Now he was in trouble. Some were changing history—their history—in real time.

Roman forced himself to stay calm. He was here, alive, and if one of his distant relatives had died recently, there would surely be a gap between that death and another one. Nobody could go around killing people willy-nilly, even in those days. He needed to reason out who it was. He spread out his printed family tree on the table again. The branches that were disappearing were definitely from the seventeenth century. Eddie couldn't be there and was unlikely to be Morgan, so thinking logically, it had to be Darren or Andrew. Based on the fact that most of his ancestors lived in Oxfordshire, these two must be systematically searching his relatives out in this area to kill them. There was no electoral roll in those days, reasoned Roman, and so it must all be done by word of mouth.

That should hopefully be a slow process, and it would hopefully give Roman time to formulate a plan if he travelled back. He could definitely get back to the right place, but the tricky part would be getting back at the right time. Another concern was that when Eddie had disappeared because of the disconnected resonator, Roman had noticed that the resonator's digital face kept flickering when he checked it to see if it still worked. It did hold up to a later calibration test, but the flickering numbers were a concern. If it jumped out of synchronisation, he would be stranded, or worse still, he could join Eddie wherever he was.

Four hours later, Roman was standing at the hole in the hedge that he had made the last time that he had jumped through time. It was partly overgrown now, but the frame still fitted into the hole with a bit of wriggling. The generator was topped up to the brim with petrol and it had started with the first pull of the chord. Five hours wasn't long to carry out much investigative work, but if he kept popping back to top up the generator and then stepping forward through the frame afterwards, he reasoned that he should be okay. Whilst checking his family's history online, he discovered that the bulk of his relatives had lived within a ten-mile radius of the orphanage, and so he had a very basic map in his pocket of the places to visit.

He had also decided to visit Morgan at the manor house to see if he had heard anything about Darren and Andy. Roman strapped his rucksack to his back. Inside was his survival kit, which this time also consisted of his black, floppy-haired wig, an analogue watch, and a small handful of gold coins that he had taken from Eddie's small treasure chest. The coins were in a leather purse, tied at the top with a leather drawstring. Roman was dressed as a person living in the seventeenth century.

He visually checked the resonators one final time and stepped through the doorframe. He was on the orphanage grounds, but a few years into the future after his last visit. The orphanage was finished and occupied. He took a couple of steps forward and realised that he was being watched by a tall, teenage male. He was about to step backwards when the boy called out to him.

"Excuse me. Is your name Roman by any chance?"

Roman froze. He didn't answer. His initial thought was to hop back through the portal and return again at a different time, but curiosity got the better of him. How did this boy know his name?

The boy started walking over. As he got closer to Roman, Roman could see the resemblance between him and Morgan. This boy was obviously Morgan's son.

"Did you just step through the time frame?" he asked. "Are you from the future? My father told me all about it. I'm Glenn."

"Yes, I'm from the future," replied Roman. "And my name *is* Roman. You are obviously Morgan's son. Is Morgan at the house? Can I go and see him? What year is this?"

"1701," replied Glenn, "and yes, you can go and see him, but don't stay too long. He's getting weaker by the day, but my mother is with him constantly, so he's not wanting for anything. I will walk with you, if you have no objections. I've finished here for the night anyway."

The pair headed towards the manor house. During the conversation, it transpired that Glenn was the under-governor of the orphanage, still in training for the top job. He enjoyed the work and was outside walking the building perimeter at the time that Roman appeared. The sudden appearance of Roman had frightened Glenn at first, but almost immediately he remembered the story that his father had told him and his brother a few years ago. Morgan had sworn both boys to secrecy. Morgan was the main benefactor of the orphanage but was not involved in its day-to-day running.

Morgan was ill, though. He had been down to London to see the hanging of Captain Kidd. Morgan didn't know Kidd personally, but he had served with some of the crew on Kidd's ships. Morgan knew these would be at the hanging, and it would be a good time and place for a catch-up. On the way back from

London, Morgan had stopped at some woodland to relieve himself and had been bitten by a tick. The bite had become infected, and Morgan was now going through the fever phase of sweating, shaking, pain, occasional delirium, and a massive lack of energy. He was confined to his bed, and it was unclear if he was expected to survive.

"The irony is that my father was stabbed when he was my age," said Glenn, "and once in battle, and he has been shot twice as well. Each time, he has been fine. Now, one small tick bite, and this might finish him off. He is a strong person, though; even the doctor said as much. The doctor thinks that he would be dead already if he was going to die. Everyone at the church and in the orphanage is praying for him."

"Well, I will pray for him too," said Roman, who deep down felt responsible for everything that happened to Morgan.

"Can men really fly in your time?" said Glenn. "My father said they can, and he said that they have put people on the moon."

"Yes, it's all true," replied Roman. "Although I'm not sure that it's such a good thing. Man is destroying this planet like you would not believe. Men are killing men on a scale never seen before in history. There is a lot to be said for this century."

They had arrived at the manor house. Roman was asked to wait inside the hallway whilst Glenn went up to see if his father was receiving visitors. Glenn came back after a few minutes and told Roman to go to the bedroom directly in front of him at the top of the stairs.

"He's weak, but he can hear and talk," said Glenn.

Roman nodded to Glenn and then climbed the stairs. Morgan's bedroom door was open, and so Roman walked over to it. He looked at Morgan lying there. He had aged considerably since they had last met. Morgan smiled at Roman and attempted to raise his hand for a handshake.

"I'm as weak as a kitten," said Morgan. "But I can feel myself getting stronger every day. I do feel very vulnerable lying here, though. What brings you back to my century?"

"Eddies, Brother," replied Roman. "He's killing my ancestors."

"Ahh!" said Morgan thoughtfully. "He's got the pub in the village. The one Eddie had. Darren and Andrew have it between them; I think they killed the landlord and then told people that they had bought the pub off him. Darren and Andrew don't get on now, apparently. Each one wants the other to buy him out, so I've been told. Andrew doesn't do too much regarding the running of the pub. He's an alcoholic, or very nearly one. He also smokes a lot of weed. I don't know where he gets it from, but he's totally paranoid. I caught them snooping around here a few years ago, and I warned them that if they came near me or my place again, I would fit them up and have them hung on the same day. It's just live and let live now, but I'm still not one hundred percent about Darren though. I don't trust him an inch."

"Have you any advice on how I can dispose of them?" said Roman. "Especially Darren."

"I can't help you from here," replied Morgan. "But you know where they are, and you're welcome to take my sword or pistol if you think it will help. My advice would be to do Darren at least, and then clear off back to your own time and never come back."

Roman shook Morgan's hand and passed him a glass of water. He then wished him luck with his recovery. He knew Morgan was right, but he didn't think he could carry out such a cold-blooded murder. He did have the basis of a plan in his mind, though, but he would have to hurry. He only had about three and a half hours before the petrol in the generator ran out.

Roman jogged to the village's outskirts. It was dark, and nobody was around. As he got nearer to the tavern, he stepped into the shadows and put on the wig. He also pulled a scarf over his mouth and nose, leaving only his eyes and a black fringe on show. He knew where the tavern was, and he knew where the wall was that surrounded the attached piggery. He reached a part of the wall around the back, where it was darkest. The wall was around six feet tall, but Roman easily pulled himself up to look over. There was only one pig in the yard. There was lots of straw and a large sack, presumably containing pig food, dangling off a thin rope, so that the food was kept off the ground, near the tavern's rear entrance.

Roman needed to get to the sack. It was risky, though. Would the pig make a lot of noise when he dropped into the yard? *Are pigs good guard dogs?* he thought. Well, he would soon find out. There was candlelight shining through the cracks in the rear entrance door, and although the yard was dark, someone was obviously in the back room, and if they opened the door, Roman could be compromised and unable to escape. He shuddered at the thought.

Climbing to the top of the wall, Roman positioned himself so that he could hang and drop his body into the yard. Once inside the yard, he noticed a small, five-bar wooden gate leaning against the perimeter wall. In case of emergency, he could scramble up this and launch himself over the wall to freedom. The pig watched Roman's every move but remained silent throughout. Roman quietly moved over to the hanging bag and unhooked it from a rusty iron hook. He untied the string, grabbed a handful of the foul-smelling food, and threw it to the pig standing on the opposite side of the yard. The pig started to eat it. Roman rolled up his sleeve and took out the leather pouch containing the gold coins. There were five in there. He took out one and put it in his pocket, then tied the pouch and pressed it into the pig food. He pushed it just below the surface but left the leather drawcord laying on top.

He was about to walk over to the propped-up gate and make his escape when he heard voices coming from the other side of the door.

"Jesus, Andy. Can't you smoke that shit outside?" said Darren. "I can hardly see it in here because of the smoke. I'm getting high, and I don't even touch the bloody stuff."

The door handle turned.

"Not out there," said Darren. "The pig's already struggling. The last thing I want is for that to keel over. Go and smoke it in the street."

Andy never replied, so Roman surmised that he had walked through the bar room and through the front door into the street. Roman shimmied up the gate and dropped over to the other side of the wall. He checked that his wig was showing and pulled the scarf up tightly around his nose and mouth. It was now or never. He casually walked around the wall and along the road to where he could see Andy standing. Andy was alone. Roman took the gold coin out of his pocket.

"You're Darren, aren't you?" said Roman to Andy. Before Andy could answer, Roman carried on with the conversation.

"You've overpaid," Roman said, handing the gold coin to a speechless Andy. "Jack told me to tell you that it's two gold coins for a murder, not three. He also said that he will need a full description of your partner so that he doesn't kill the wrong man. Oh, and one more thing, I wouldn't keep your gold in that bag of pig food out back. It's not safe. Certain people know that's where your coin is kept, and there's talk of robbing you."

With that, Roman hurried back in the direction that he had come from. He reasoned that he had only one hour's worth of petrol left in the generator and so he would have to get back to the time frame quickly. He would have liked to have stayed and watched the outcome from a safe distance, but he could always come back tomorrow.

Andy stood speechless as he snapped into reality and mentally digested what he had just been told. He looked at the gold coin in his hand and then walked back into the tavern. Darren was sitting at a table talking to two men. Were these three plotting his demise? *Quite possibly*, thought Andy, had he hurried along to the piggery out the back? Once there, he unhooked the feed bag and opened it up. He spotted the leather lanyard sitting on top of the food and pulled it. The leather purse popped out. Andy opened it and saw the four gold coins.

He took them out and put them into his pocket before pushing the empty purse back inside the pig's food. He stifled a laugh. He had Darren's gold. This was more than enough to buy a different pub somewhere else if he wanted. He could either sell this one to make even more money or he could keep it and run the two. Either way, he was quid's in. Darren wouldn't need the money, not where he was going. Also, the assassin, Jack, didn't know what Andy looked like; the young lad had told him that, so he wouldn't be coming after him. He wondered if he could get the other two coins back from him.

The next day, Andy was up early and waiting at the tavern door for Darren to arrive. When Darren did, he was mildly shocked. Andy rarely got out of bed this early.

"You off on a reccy trip?" said Andy to Darren.

"Yeah, I'm going this way and asking around the villages up by the woods," said Darren, pointing to some distant woodland. "I just wish that there was some way of knowing if the boy is dead or not. I'm going to have to draw the line somewhere."

Andy nodded. "I'll come with you. Two mouths are better than one."

The two men hitched up their horses and rode at a leisurely pace towards the woods. Andy rode slightly behind Darren, all the time formulating a plan in which to dispose of Darren for good. He didn't hate Darren. They had gone through a lot together. But the gold coins were proof that Darren was holding out on him, and they were supposed to be partners. But for Darren to pay someone to have him killed? It went above and beyond. It's a dog-eat-dog world, reasoned Andy. Do it to him before he does it to you.

He patted the dagger that he had hidden inside his tunic. Andy's mind went back to the day that Darren discovered that Eddie had once run the tavern that they were in now. Once he had found out that a ginger boy, most probably Roman, had visited Eddie on the day that he had disappeared, Darren had vowed revenge on the boy. For months now, Darren had been plotting, then carrying out, the murders of Roman's supposed ancestors.

The two men rode slowly up the track towards the woods. Andy had been to the small village up here before. He knew that there was a tavern there, and he was thirsty for some beer. His mouth went dry every time he thought about killing Darren. Darren was stronger than him, and he would beat him in a fair fight. Andy would have to catch Darren unawares to have any chance of riding home alone. This thought made him nervous, though. He would have to stand really close to stab Darren in the back, and if he didn't catch him right, Darren would turn around and fight until his last breath. The top of the track opened onto a long, narrow street. There were houses on both sides, and the tavern was down the left-hand fork.

"You take the right, and I'll take the left," said Andy. "We'll meet back up in the tavern."

Darren nodded. He had a speech rehearsed that he had used many times previously, whereby he would knock on a random door and then tell the owner who he was looking for. He would then show the person a purse filled with money and say that this was part of an inheritance payout, and did he know anyone in the area with that particular surname? It had worked before, but it was a laborious process. He set off on a slow trot, and Andy trotted away in the other direction. He had no intention of knocking on any doors. He was going straight into the pub. He tethered his horse around the back and walked through the front door. The pub was empty, apart from a middle-aged man standing at the bar, sipping a beer.

"Pint of ale landlord," said Andy, to a man he could see at the end of the bar.

"Certainly," came the reply.

"Let me pay for this," said the man who Andy had first seen when he walked in.

Andy looked at the man and laughed. "You wouldn't have a shilling on you that you could lend me," he said, realising that the man was trying out a similar tactic to ensnare volunteers into the Navy that someone else had tried on him all those months ago.

"I'm too old for the Navy anyway," said Andy, walking over to the man. "You keep your money in your pocket and let me buy you a beer."

The man smiled and accepted the offer, realising that the game was up.

"I'm Lawrence," said Lawrence, holding out his hand for a handshake. Andy shook his hand. "I'm Elvis. Elvis Presley," said Andy. "I'm an innkeeper too," he said to the landlord, who had now walked over to the two men.

Andy looked at Lawrence. Lawrence was in his mid-thirties, handsome, and looked very fit. Andy began to formulate a plan.

"Just out of interest, do you keep a list of deserters at all," he said to Lawrence.

"We do. We check the name of every volunteer in case we manage to get the same man a second time round," said Lawrence. "Why do you ask?"

"Oh, I rode up here with a man who says he deserted from the Navy some months ago. He said he killed a recruit to escape and beat up two soldiers in the process. His name is Darren Monkton. Apparently, he's armed and very dangerous. He will be calling in here soon."

Lawrence walked out of the tavern and over to his horse. He opened the leather saddlebag. He took out a paper scroll and studied the list of names on it. The second from the bottom was the name "Darren Monkton." He walked back into the bar room and took out a flintlock pistol from his trouser waistband.

"He's armed, did you say?" asked Lawrence as he methodically loaded the pistol.

"He said he is always armed. But I never saw a weapon as we were riding up here."

"Does he trust you?" said Lawrence. "Can you get him to confirm his name in front of us?"

"No, I'm not a man of violence, and I will have left before he arrives. Stand behind the bar and pretend that you're the innkeeper of this place. Say that you recognise him from the village tavern. Engage in some chitchat and get him to drop his guard. It shouldn't be too hard for a clever man like you."

Lawrence nodded, and Andy finished his drink. I'll be saying goodbye to you then. Good luck.

"Thank you, Elvis," came the reply. "I'm much obliged to you."

Andy walked out of the door and climbed onto his horse. He rode down the road and then turned his horse into some woodland. After stopping the horse, he climbed off and tied the horse to a tree. He then walked swiftly through the trees towards the tavern. When he had a decent vantage point, he sat down and waited, staying totally concealed from anyone outside of the tavern. He didn't have to wait long. Darren rode up, tethered his horse, and walked through the inn door.

He strode up to the bar and ordered a drink, then sat down at a table to wait for Andy. He was on his second pint when a waggon rode into the yard. Andy recognised it as a naval transport waggon. A man was locked in the back. He decided to finish his drink fast, but without attracting any attention, and left. He would wait for Andy down the road and warn him to avoid the tavern. The driver of the coach walked into the inn. He glanced at Darren but ignored him. He walked up to the bar and was mildly surprised to see that his colleague in arms was serving.

Lawrence shook his head and directed a nod towards Darren, who had almost finished his drink and was getting ready to leave. "Wait outside," he said in a low voice. The driver immediately turned around and walked out of the door. Darren watched the man leave. He began to feel as if something wasn't right.

"Can I get you another drink Darren," said Lawrence.

"No, I'm fine, thanks," replied Darren, immediately realising that he hadn't told the barman his name.

He turned to look at the barman and immediately realised that he was pointing a flintlock pistol at him.

"What's this all about?" said Darren, trying to sound calm. "You've obviously got me mixed up with someone else."

"No, you are Darren Monkton, wanted for murder and two assaults on officers of the crown. Your friend Elvis Presley, who you travelled up here with, confirmed this to us. You will come with us, and you will be tried and then hanged for your crimes."

Darren looked around; the barman had lowered his weapon but was still pointing it in Darren's general direction. It was now or never. Darren picked up the tankard he had been drinking from and raised it to throw at Lawrence. Lawrence calmly discharged the pistol before the tankard left Darren's hand. There was a loud bang, a flash, and a puff of smoke, and Darren was writhing in agony on the floor. The soft lead ball had entered the top of Darren's boot, and had blown off all of Darren's toes. Blood was seeping from the hole in the boot and Darren was screaming. The coach driver walked through the door.

"Take the man from the waggon and get him to help you lift this one into the back," said Lawrence. "I will keep my pistol trained on both men in case any of them try to run off," he looked down at Darren's bloody boot. "I don't think this man will ever run again though," he said, smiling.

Andy was watching from the bushes as Darren was carried out. Darren was screaming. "I'll get you, Andy. They'll find you. I'll tell them where you are. I'll get you if it's the last thing I ever do."

Andy sat in the bushes until the waggon had ridden out of sight. He then walked back to his horse. He realised that he could never go back to the pub or the village. To be on the safe side, he would leave the area completely. He would head back down to London. He had money, and he had gold. He smiled to himself. There were always cheap pubs for sale down there. He would change his name and become a landlord again.

Early the following morning from Roman's previous excursion into the past. He travelled back again. He found out that this time it was 1702. He walked up to the manor house, only to be told by Morgan's wife that Morgan never recovered from the tick bite and had died two days after Roman had left his bedside. He wandered down to the village and cautiously opened the tavern door. A different landlord was behind the bar.

"Are you the innkeeper?" asked Roman.

"Yes, I am!" came the reply.

"What happened to Darren and Andy," said Roman.

"Oh, Darren was hanged at Tilbury," said the landlord.

"He was wanted for murder, apparently. Soldiers came here looking for Andy, but he had disappeared. He's probably dead by now; drank himself to death, no doubt. He did like his rum."

As it happened, Andy did make it to London but survived only long enough to die in suspicious circumstances. Andy purchased a cheap backstreet tavern in a seedy part of London and quickly settled down with a woman called Catherine Bosse. Catherine had fled Paris some years earlier, and it was rumoured that she was wanted for murder. She would often tell people when she was drunk that she was a cousin of Marie Bosse, the notorious poisoner who was burned in 1679 for supplying poison to women who wanted to kill their husbands.

Before moving in with Andy, Catherine had been in three separate relationships since moving to London, and all three relationships had ended with the accidental deaths of her partners. Two of her partners died after drowning when they fell into the River Thames whilst drunk. A third had fallen into an open fire and burned to death whilst drunk. Andy didn't know about her past; only a few people did, and Catherine went to great lengths to keep it that way.

Andy and Catherine were both serious drunkards and would drink throughout the day and night. They would argue with each other regularly, especially when Andy voiced his suspicions that Catherine was having an affair with a burly ex-soldier that frequented the tavern most nights. In November 1703, a hurricane that lasted several days hit Britain and destroyed houses, forests, and other buildings, as well as around one fifth of the Navy's ships. During the storm, Andy's dead body was uncovered under a pile of bricks when a tall garden wall collapsed on top of him, smashing the back of his skull. There were only two witnesses to the accident, Catherine and the ex-soldier, and three months after Andy had been buried, the two of them married each other and jointly took on the responsibility of running the tavern.

Having said his farewell to the new innkeeper of Darren's old inn, Roman turned around and walked out of the door. He walked back to the portal frame and then through it. He then dismantled it and packed it away in his shed. He felt happy knowing that Darren wouldn't be going after his ancestors anymore. He vowed to redouble his efforts to find Morgan's living relatives, and to give them the remaining gold that was still in Eddie's treasure box. He owed Morgan that. Morgan saved his life. He made a mental note to never go through the portal into the past again. At least, not for revenge purposes. He might go slightly too far back in time to meet Eddie or Darren again, and this time the outcome might be different.

Chapter 16
Mick Takes Control

It seemed like any other normal day to Mick when Tony and Nick picked him up in Tony's car. He had been asked to provide some muscle at the forthcoming meeting when Tony would confront Roman about his missing money and banknotes. Unbeknownst to Mick, this was to be his last day in the present year. It was to be the day that he would disappear from the workhouse basement and reappear thirty-five years into the past. Mick wasn't that keen on Tony, but he kept his feelings to himself. *Tony was a bully, a smartie*, thought Mick. Soft inside but surrounded by a hard shell. Tony paid Mick decent money though, and so Mick went along with most of Tony's schemes. They had arrived early at the workhouse basement and had caught Roman unaware.

When Tony had smashed the stone feature on the wall and the pond water had flowed in, Mick was already thinking of ways to get out of the water and make his escape. As the water rose, and with nobody knowing how high the water would rise, he was already formulating a plan to assist Tony's drowning and then using Tony's dead body as a float to help him rise higher up the basement wall so that he could climb through the doorway onto the ground floor level. Once he was out of the basement, he would throw the tied-up Roman into the water and let him drown. At the time of the rising water touching the live electric cable, Mick had waded into the basement's other room to retrieve a hammer he had seen in there, to hit Tony over the head with in all the panic and confusion.

Mick had been vaguely aware of a bright flash and a loud bang and had then found himself lying on the basement floor. His trousers were wet, but the floor was dry. He picked himself up and walked back through the doorway into the other basement room. This room was also dry. There were no signs of any water, and no signs of Tony or Nick. The stone wall plaque, smashed by Tony only minutes before, was intact in its rightful place. A set of wooden steps were in place to walk up and exit the basement level and enter the ground floor area of the workhouse. Mick walked up the steps.

The boy was gone, almost as if he had never been there. The room that he had been in was also considerably tidier than it had been when they first arrived. Mick exited the ground floor to the sound of music coming from an adjacent building. He walked over and was surprised to be standing outside of a mechanics workshop. The door was open, and a Ford Escort was on a set of ramps. The radio was playing eighties pop music, but the mechanic was nowhere to be seen. Mick walked into the workshop to take a look around. The first thing he noticed was a steaming mug of tea on the workbench, indicating that somebody was not too far away, and above this was a calendar pinned to the wall, showing the year 1988. The noise of a toilet chain being flushed caught his attention, and so he waited to see who came out through the toilet door.

A fifty-year-old, grey-haired man in oily overalls opened the toilet door and walked into the workshop. He smiled at Mick.

"What can I do for you?" he said.

"Err I was just looking for a price on some new tyres, for a Ford Escort," said Mick. "Something like these," he pointed at the wheels on the car beside him.

The man looked at Mick's wet trousers and shoes. "You fell in the pond?" he asked.

"Yeah, something like that," Mick replied. "I was just admiring your wall calendar. June is a good month," he said, pointing to a topless model that adorned June's page. "What's the date today?" he asked the mechanic.

"Fourth," came the reply. I don't usually work on Saturdays, but this is a rush job as the woman's driving to Brighton tomorrow. He looked at the car tyres. "I can do you a set of four, fitted, for a hundred pounds cash."

Mick said he would have a think about it and walked out of the workshop and into the workhouse grounds. Something was obviously wrong. Had he died in the basement? Was he in a coma and dreaming about this? Had he always been in 1988 and imagined the following thirty-five years? He felt into his pocket and retrieved his mobile phone. The phone had stopped working, but it was his own modern phone. This type of phone was definitely not around in the eighties. He started to think about it rationally.

He had turned his back on Tony when he waded into the other basement room. Had Tony thought about his own survival along the same lines as Mick had? Had Tony hit *him* over the head to procure a floating body buoyancy aid? It was just the sort of thing Tony would do in order to protect his own life. It all made sense now. He was in a coma, on a life support machine, having a weird dream. No doubt Tony would visit him in hospital, and play the innocent, but Mick had reasoned the truth, and he would take his revenge on Tony at a later date.

Where had Nick been in all this, though? Had he assisted Tony? They would have a serious talk when he woke up. If he woke up. What if he died, though? What if he was already dead and this was his life flashing before his eyes? It wasn't exactly flashing, though, but who was the mechanic? He was sure that he had never had dealings with him in the past. He would have to keep an open mind.

He walked out of the workhouse grounds and headed towards the village. He had no money on him, so he didn't bother waiting at the bus stops that he passed. Plenty of cars passed him. All with number plates on or before 1988. As he approached the village, he remembered an acquaintance who lived on the village outskirts. The lad was a few years older than him, but they were sort of friends. He decided that he would call around his house and cadge a lift home. He arrived at the house and was about to enter the front garden gate when a woman opened the front door. A child was with her. A boy around four years old.

"Come on, Kieran," said the lady to the boy. "We will miss the bus, and that will be another visiting order wasted. Your dad will think that we don't want to see him. Hurry up! Just leave Teddy there 'til we get back."

The boy grabbed his mother's hand, and they walked down the path to the gate. Mick carried on walking past the house. It was definitely Kieran and Kieran's mother, and Kieran's dad had been in prison for most of Kieran's early life. Mick walked along the road to a small pocket park and sat down on a bench. This was all too real. There were no pink elephants floating around in this dream. He wasn't walking around naked, and he couldn't fly. He punched the arm of the wooden bench. It hurt. Bearing in mind that you couldn't feel pain in a dream, or so he had read once, this couldn't be a dream. It must be reality. He was in the same geographical area, but at a different time. 1988. That year, Holland beat Russia 2.0 in the Euros. A plan began to formulate in his mind.

He would thumb it to Oxford and pawn his watch. Even in 1988, it had to be worth a couple of hundred quid. He would put the money in the bookies for Holland to win Euro 88 2.0, with Gullit and Van Basten bagging the goals. He could then put the payout from this on Tyson to beat Spinks in the first round and Mechelen to win the UEFA Super Cup. Nobody would give Mechelen a chance to win the cup; most people had never even heard of them. The odds would be fantastic. He would clean up big time if he spread the money around wisely.

Mick knew the workings behind high-street bookmakers and how much to lay down in each one in order to not raise suspicions. With his knowledge of most things sports-related, he knew that he had a shot at becoming very rich in a very short period of time. He would need to invest his money, though. Not in stocks and shares, which he didn't understand, and not in banks. He would invest it in ecstasy production, large-scale cannabis farms, and then put the subsequent money into property. He would need a buffer between the production and marketing of the drugs in order to appear respectful around the community. He did not want any visible trails that could lead to him being arrested.

He would need to open a legitimate business to launder the money, and his first thought was a car breakers yard or a recycling facility. A lot of cash was bandied around in these places, so it would be an easy place to hide money. He would also need a small warehouse or shipping container in somebody else's name to store his stock of drugs.

Nine months passed, and Mick was a relatively rich man. He was also a powerful man in the local area, living a double life. He had friends in the police force and friends on the district council. Over the previous months, he had been buying up derelict or run-down properties in the area and obtaining various planning consents and permissions to demolish, rebuild, extend, or change the buildings' use. Local councillors backhandedly ensured that the operations went smoothly. He was a silent partner in a local scrapyard, on land that he had purchased only a few months previously, and he had future plans to buy, then demolish, the workhouse in its entirety and build houses on the site. Life was good. He was engaged to a woman, and he had a child on the way. He also controlled a lot of the drugs in the area, with his biggest rival being Arthur Babbage, Tony Babbage's father.

Mick and Arthur agreed to work alongside each other and pool their various resources. This made more sense than trying to fight it out. Arthur thought that Mick was a newcomer to the area but knowledgeable, and because he dealt different drugs to Arthur's cocaine and heroin, there were no conflicts of interest.

On paper, Mick was a newcomer to the area, as he had had to assume somebody else's identity due to the fact that he hadn't been born yet.

With the birth certificate of a dead child, he had legally changed the child's name to his own and applied for a passport, provisional driving licence, and national insurance number, claiming that he had been living abroad since he was a child. He passed his driving test for the first time, with the help of a wad of cash. Although Arthur didn't see Mick as a rival, Mick saw Arthur's empire as an extension of his own. He wasn't quite ready to take it over yet; he wasn't that powerful, but he stored the thought on the backburner of his mind, knowing that in a few years' time he would make Arthur disappear.

Mick also had designs for opening a bookmakers' business on the local high street. There was one there already, and Mick was already seeing this as his rival, even though Mick hadn't opened his yet. With Mick's knowledge of future sporting event outcomes, he had been sending various friends to the bookmakers and placing large bets. The owner was slowly going under whilst Mick's wealth was increasing. Mick was already acquiring a nickname as Mister Big, and he had made a conscious decision to destroy anyone that could be seen as a threat to his authority.

A few months later, Mick was the biggest drug dealer in Oxfordshire. He could also lay claim to being one of the top four biggest dealers in the country. His rivals included families in London, Manchester, and Cardiff, although Cardiff was technically in Wales. There was a family from Scotland that were big, but Mick had no dealings with them as they mostly confined their activities to the north of the border, and so he never counted them as rivals. There was an uneasy peace between the families, but all agreed that it was better for everyone to keep the peace in order to keep making money. Mick wasn't satisfied, though. He wanted to run a drug empire without geographical restrictions, and he was forever toying with ideas on how to bring the other families under his control.

Mick was paranoid, and this paranoia was growing at the same rate that his drug empire and drug addiction were. Every day, he smoked cannabis and snorted cocaine in ever increasing amounts. Every day he was watchful in case his organisation had been infiltrated by rival gang members or the police. He was suspicious of everyone and permanently anxious and mistrustful. He had taken to carrying a concealed knife strapped to the bottom of his leg and a smaller knife taped to the top of his arm, concealed under his long-sleeved jumper. He reasoned that what he needed was a way to dispose of the top men in the other gangs without leaving a trace, and more importantly, no retribution trail back to himself.

He had long since determined that his own trip back into the past was something to do with that Roman lad, and it must have involved a time machine of some kind. This time machine must have been constructed in the workhouse basement and must have been activated when he waded through the door. What he needed was his own time machine. Something that he could use to dispose of the other gang leaders and any police, judges, or informers that could possibly pose a threat to him. What better way was there? No bodies, no witnesses, and no more worries.

Mick pondered on this thought regularly. He had mentioned it to his trusted sidekick, Ricky, a few times, but Ricky couldn't grasp the concept of time travel or time machines made in basements and secretly reported to his real boss, Gino, in Manchester that Mick was slowly going insane. Mick, however, couldn't let the idea go. He was living proof that time machines were real. He recognised that Roman hadn't been born yet, but if that dopey, ginger-haired layabout could build one, so could someone else. He hatched a plan to kidnap a physics student from Oxford University and make him construct a time machine in his basement. Better still, in one of his derelict property house basements. This wouldn't leave a trial for the police to follow if anything went wrong.

Two weeks had passed, and Mick had imprisoned a student in his rental house basement. He had advertised student accommodation for one of his properties but insisted that it was for physics undergraduates or higher only. He had forced the youth, Sean, into the basement at knifepoint and ordered him to build a time machine. Fearing for his life, Sean had agreed to build one, and not wishing to antagonise Mick, who was obviously insane, he got started immediately. Mick told Sean to write out a list of everything that was required, and he would buy it. He also promised to release Sean once the machine was completed. He even agreed to pay the boy ten thousand pounds on completion. Sean was locked in the basement for twenty-four hours a day. He had a bucket latrine and was brought sandwiches, cakes, and bottled water every day from a nearby service station. He was given a comprehensive toolbox of tools to get things underway.

Four days later, the time machine was complete. The basement was large, and the student had divided it into two halves with floor to ceiling wooden studwork, which he overlaid with plasterboard. A single door frame separated the two areas, and above this doorframe was a sign that read "Time machine." Up both sides of the doorframe and over the top were a continuous strip of small, flashing LED lights and a small box, not dissimilar to a smoke detector, that pinged every thirty seconds.

This sound resembled the sound of a battery-operated smoke detector when the battery was running low. On the left-hand side of the wall was a large clock. The glass clock face had been removed, along with the clock's hour hand, and various wires were attached to the remaining minute hand. Written against each number was a time in history. Against the number three digit, it read "1600s," against the number four digit, it read 1700s and against the number nine digit, it read 400 BC. The dates were not in chronological order, but Sean explained this as being too difficult to do.

The student had also moved a single lightbulb that dangled from the middle of the ceiling to just inside the basement entrance door. He explained that a lightbulb inside the time machine could interfere with time itself, putting everyone in the basement at risk. He also added a second light switch that could turn this lightbulb on and off at the very bottom of the doorframe. This could be operated on by someone's foot. Various magnets and switches were placed around the walls, and a 'High Voltage' warning sign was visible to everyone that walked down the stairs into the basement. Sean told Mick that the time machine was up and ready for use.

He said that only last night he had slipped into the 1500s for a few minutes. He invited Mick to walk through the portal, but Mick was wary. What if the student controlling the switch refused to let him back into this century? He asked to be shown how to operate the time switch and told Sean to go back in time once more. Sean refused. "You can only go back once," the student said. "A second time would be fatal."

Later that day, Mick invited the heads of the three crime families down to Oxford for a demonstration of his time machine. If all went well, he might be able to trick the men into stepping through the doorway and dispose of them forever. If he was unsuccessful at this, he would offer to dispose of the men's enemies without trace for a large fee. He would also need to be made the head of all three families as part of the bargain. After Mick had phoned the three men, the three men phoned each other. Was this a trap? None of the three men trusted Mick. Had he really got a time machine? Ricky had told Gino that Mick had an Oxford physics graduate trapped in his basement, and so, as unlikely as it sounded, there was a small chance that it might be true. All three were sceptical, though, and each decided to arm themselves before travelling to Oxford to look.

The men arrived the following morning, and Mick greeted them at the door. The basement door was still locked, with the student inside. Mick grinned.

"I've got a demonstration for you all, and a surprise for the boy," said Mick. "He doesn't realise that he's going through it again."

Mick unlocked the door, and the men filed downstairs. They stood opposite the plasterboard wall that led into the time machine and looked around the walls, then to the nervous student standing next to the time machine doorway. Gino had to stifle a laugh by pretending to cough and clear his throat.

"Pick a century," said Mick to the three men.

"Fifteen hundreds," said Gino.

"Set the clock for the fifteen hundred and switch the machine on," ordered Mick to the student. Sean did as he was told.

"Right Son, step inside," said Mick. Sean hesitated and then stepped through the doorway. Immediately as he did so, the basement light went out. The three men grabbed for their concealed weapons, but Mick turned on the light switch on the wall. The basement ceiling light came on. All three men looked through the doorway into an empty room. Mick grinned. "And then there were four," he said.

"Has he really gone?" said Gino, obviously sceptical.

"He's probably dining with Henry the Eighth as we speak," said Mick.

The three men walked over to the door frame. One put his arm through the open space. Nothing happened. There was a brief silence, and then a cough came from inside the time machine. Gino stepped inside, only to find the student pressed against the stud wall to the side of the doorway. He grabbed the boy and bundled him out into the basement with the other men.

"Right, what's going on," he said to Mick. Releasing the student. The three men crowded round Mick menacingly. Sean, seeing his opportunity, silently nipped up the stairs and exited the basement doorway. He stopped and turned around when he realised that he wasn't being followed. He could hear raised voices below him, and it sounded like things were getting ugly. He pushed the basement door closed and slid the two bolts across. He then ran outside into the fresh air. Immediately, he ran to a house across the road and asked the owner to call the police. The owner obliged, and within ten minutes, two police cars had arrived at the house. Sean explained the situation of being kidnapped, held in a basement for a week, and ordered to build a time machine for a bunch of psychopaths. The policemen looked incredulous but walked through to the basement door anyway.

"I think they're armed," said Sean in a low voice, as the men were battering the door from the inside.

The policeman shouted to the men at the other side of the door. "It's the police. We are armed. Come up from the basement one at a time with your hands in the air." He then opened the basement door.

The four men filed through the basement doorway with their hands in the air. Each one was stopped, searched, and handcuffed as they stepped through. Mick came through last. His face was swollen and bruised, and his nose and lips were bleeding. The men were all placed in police cars, and two policemen walked down the basement steps. The time machine lights were still flashing, and the smoke alarm was still beeping when they got down there. They took turns to photograph the outside and inside of the room with their mobile phones.

"I don't even know where to start with this one," said the officer in charge, shaking his head. "They must all be mad. Insane. I wonder what their defence will be? A time machine, though? And did you see the weapons that they were carrying? The one with the black eyes had knives taped to his arm *and* leg. Do you think it was some kind of weird cult thing? They probably thought that they would kill the boy and then disappear into the future. The small one did look a bit like 'Captain Kirk'. He probably thought that he was in Star Trek. Oh well. It'll all come out in the wash."

Chapter 17
Mick Comes Clean

Mick was sitting in his cell, mulling over the previous day's escapade. Something didn't sit right with him. Three other men were charged with carrying offensive weapons and then released on bail. He, on the other hand, had been charged with a range of offences, ranging from kidnapping and false imprisonment to carrying offensive weapons, and was still in custody. An idea was forming in his mind that the charging officers at this station were in the pockets of the other three crime bosses, and this was all an elaborate conspiracy to take over Mick's drug empire. He thought about his interview with his solicitor a few minutes earlier. His solicitor had told him to keep quiet and to do a 'no comment' interview with the police. This was standard. It was the norm for most criminals, but Mick thought that he smelt a rat. Was his solicitor part of the conspiracy? He decided to come clean at the interview.

Ten minutes later, Mick and his solicitor were sitting in the police interview room. The tape was switched on, and the interview was started. Mick started the interview by saying that he was actually from the future. He went on to say that he wished to go back to his own time, and that was the only reason why he had imprisoned the student—to force him to build a time machine. A half-wit called Roman had built one, so it couldn't be that hard to build.

No, they couldn't interview Roman; he hadn't been born yet. Yes, he took drugs. Yes, every day, but what has that got to do with anything? So, what if the police had tested the time machine in the basement and it didn't work? The boy had obviously cocked something up. Mick went on to state that he knew the police were in on a conspiracy to frame him, alongside three other men, but that was all he was going to say on the subject. The interview was terminated at that point, and Mick was led back to his cell. His solicitor followed him in.

"Brilliant," he hissed as the custody officer closed the door. "An insanity plea. Brilliant."

Roman was at home and had logged onto the internet again. He had been scrolling through old local newspapers to see if there was any information about Morgan's relatives. There wasn't, and he was getting bored, so he started to read the more recent headlines. He was shocked to read one headline.

"Local man imprisons a student to force him to build a time machine." Mick's mug shot was also on the front page. Roman read the full story. Mick, who was obviously using a different name, hadn't been convicted yet, but he had been charged. Roman flicked through the following newspapers to catch up with the story. Three newspapers further along, the story read that the charges were dropped after the student witness failed to turn up to court. Mick was convicted of carrying an offensive weapon, though this only culminated in a suspended prison sentence.

When Roman did a search backwards through the newspapers, a separate, smaller article came to light about Mick being fined after being convicted of threatening words and behaviour. This incident happened almost six months before the incident with the imprisoned student. The six-month time span between the incidents in Mick's past equated to mere weeks in Roman's present. Roman largely understood the theory of time dilation—time slowing as speed increases—but this concept was new to him. Perhaps this was nature's way of stopping people from abusing time.

Roman sat back in his chair. Time *was* obviously moving at two separate speeds between the two worlds. His granddad had alluded to this in his notes. He had realised early that time wasn't a constant. Roman picked up a pen and paper and tried to work out a formula using his own trips backwards and forwards through time. In theory, time moved faster in the past than in the present, but this was unnoticeable to the time traveller. As the time traveller got closer to the time in which he had originally left, time should slow down for him, but even allowing for time to slow down for the time traveller as the past caught up with the present, Mick would probably be greeting Roman in fifteen to twenty years' time.

It was three months after the basement incident, and Mick's drug-fuelled mental health was getting worse. As well as daily cannabis and cocaine, on Gino's suggestion, Ricky had offered Mick small amounts of LSD, and this was tipping him over the edge. After the first encounter with the drug, Mick thought that he was Maverick, out of *Top Gun*. The second time, he thought that he was

Jason Orange. Both outings as both men didn't end well and Mick got into two separate street fights. Mick was also not rehabilitated from carrying a knife. Quite the opposite, in fact. After watching 'Taxi Driver' on television, he made his own version of a slide-up-your-arm weapon.

In the film, Robert De Niro attached a knife to the sliding part of a drawer and fitted it to his arm. When he flicked his wrist, the knife shot forward for him to hold. Mick's version was an improvement on this. He used the sliding part of the drawing idea but mechanised it with a skeletonised battery-operated car tyre inflator that pushed air up a thin tube. This, in turn, pushed up the slide with the knife attached. The tyre inflator derived its power from a battery pack that Mick wore around his waist and could be turned on by pushing a button strategically placed under his armpit. The slide worked quickly enough to get the knife into Mick's hand, but the only drawback was that the pump was a bit noisy. Nonetheless, Mick arranged a meeting with Gino, where he intended to slash Gino's jugular vein. He had ground the knife blade razor-sharp in anticipation of the meeting.

The meeting time arrived, and Mick was making small talk. A few minutes into the conversation, Mick pretended to yawn and stretched out his arms. He pretended to scratch his armpit and pushed the button of the tyre-inflator. The motor sprang to life, and Mick's sleeve started to inflate. The sharp edge of the blade had cut the air tube that controlled the knife's ascent out of his sleeve and into his hand. However, there was at least some air being forced through the tube, and the blade did eventually reach the edge of Mick's sleeve, but the mechanism ran out of air just as the tip of the knife exited his shirt sleeve, and Mick couldn't bend his wrist enough to grip the blade and put the knife into the palm of his hand. Mick carried on making small talk as if nothing unusual was happening.

Gino just watched. He had heard the motor start up and saw Mick's sleeve inflate. He thought that this was a way of Mick trying to intimidate him by pretending that he had massive arms. If Mick thought that he could intimidate him with one giant arm, he was sadly mistaken. He thought to himself that he wouldn't need to destroy Mick, Mick was doing that himself. Mick had really gone mad!

The meeting ended, and Mick went home. It hadn't gone as well as he planned, but at least he had gotten his idea across that it was time to run all the families along the lines of the Italian Mafia, with himself as the main man. The godfather. Gino had agreed to put the idea forward to the other families. Mick was sitting at the table when his wife walked in. She didn't say anything to Mick. She just picked up a teaspoon and walked back into the room that she had just come from. Mick was pleased that she didn't speak to him.

He had been observing her behaviour lately, and he was concerned that she was turning into a giant crow. He knew that this was impossible, but something had been niggling away at him for a few weeks. His wife's hands sometimes looked like talons, and her nose was starting to resemble a beak. Even her speech was changing. He was convinced that his wife occasionally dropped a 'Caw' into her conversations. No wonder she looked at him with disgust when he drank his raw egg protein shakes. Mick began to wonder if he would be better off without her.

Ricky came around, and Mick's wife told him to go through to the kitchen to Mick. He sat down and mentioned how he had seen a massive rat near the bins outside of the kebab shop.

"I want you to clean up the streets in this area. I want the rats gone," said Mick, looking at Ricky. "I want every rat gone that's living in this area. I don't want my kid to catch any diseases off them."

Ricky looked at Mick. "You want them all gone?" he said, sounding confused. "How?"

"Just sort it said Mick," clearly irritated. "And keep your wits about you. I think Gino might be planning a move against me and the other heads of the five families."

Ricky got up to leave. "I'll see you tomorrow, boss." he said.

"Don't call me boss," came the reply. "It's Capo."

Ricky left the house and phoned Gino from his mobile phone to give Gino his daily rundown on Mick.

"He's well and truly gone, mate. I think that the acid I'm slipping into him may be too strong. Still, I've managed to shave off more areas on Mick's patch, and they've all said that they will buy from us."

Mick sat at the table alone, and his mind kept wandering towards Roman. The boy was evil, and he would surely be born in a few years' time. Roman's name even sounded a bit like Satan's. He tried to look at this rationally. Roman's name contained five letters. So did Satan's. If you took some of these letters away and then added some different ones, Roman's name was SATAN. But what was Roman's purpose on earth? Mick wondered. Was he here to destroy mankind? Satan needed to be stopped, and he was the man to do it.

The following day, Ricky arrived at Mick's early. "I got rid of the rats," grinned Ricky.

Mick just stared at him with a blank expression. Ricky carried on.

"We were round Barry's 'til six this morning, playing poker. I'm two hundred quid up," said Ricky, tapping his pocket. "I may need some matchsticks for my eyes later. I can hardly keep them open. I've only had an hour's sleep. I'll make us a cup of tea," he said, fingering the small dropper bottle concealed in his pocket.

Mick still said nothing but continued to stare at Ricky's face. It looked different from what it usually did. Something was wrong with it. It seemed very puffy, almost like a mask. Then it suddenly dawned on him. It was a mask! Someone was wearing Ricky's face as a mask.

"Roman," gasped Mick.

"Sorry," said Ricky, looking confused.

Mick looked again. This *was* Roman. He was going to have to play it cool. He couldn't let Roman know that he knew. He thought about fitting the tyre-inflator knife combination to his arm. He had repaired the air tube with some tape but thought better of it. It took a long time to fit it properly, and Mick hadn't gotten a long time. There was no telling what Roman was plotting. He stood up from his seat.

"Come on, we're going to London," said Mick. "By train."

Forty minutes later, the pair of them were standing on the station platform. As the train pulled in, Mick positioned himself at the back of Ricky.

"It ends here, Roman," said Mick, and pushed Ricky into the path of the train.

Ricky, caught unawares, didn't stand a chance. He died instantly under the train.

There were too many witnesses to the murder for Mick to walk away without blame. In his defence, his barrister had said that Mick had in fact been trying to stop a suicidal Ricky from jumping, by grabbing hold of Ricky's coat. However, Ricky's momentum had prevented Mick from doing that, and Mick was powerless to prevent Ricky's death. Mick's barrister had also gotten various medical reports pertaining to Mick's state of mind at the time of the incident. Mick was diagnosed with drug-induced paranoid schizophrenia, and this was blamed for his psychotic behaviour during the police interviews.

When the two witnesses to the murder changed their testimonies, the Crown Prosecution Service deemed that there was not enough evidence to secure a conviction, and the murder charges were dropped. Mick was charged with drug possession, though, and he agreed to attend a drug rehabilitation centre for six weeks. Here he was weaned off the illegal drugs and put on ever decreasing doses of antipsychotic medication to help him function as a 'normal' person. His wife stood by him throughout, and although she had sold his drug stock to Gino and let Mick's drug empire crumble, she ensured that Mick still held various title deeds at a range of domestic and commercial properties throughout Oxfordshire.

The rent that they received from the properties alone gave the family a comfortable living. Mick was now drug-free and, to the outside world, a respectable businessman. He freely admitted to having lost a few memory cells whilst he was using drugs, and his memory of his past life was just a memory. He still remembered Roman, though, and blamed him for all the negativity in his life over the previous months. Yes, he was richer now than he would have ever been in the twenty twenties, but he was content before without being rich, and Roman spoiled this. He knew that sometime soon he would be able to contact Roman, albeit Roman as a child.

But when he did make contact, he would do something to him that Roman would remember every time that he looked in a mirror. It took time for Mick to adjust to life without drugs, but he had a strong character, and with the support of his family, he persevered. He was no longer Mr Big, but he was Mick. Mick is the memory man who was still quite good at recalling facts, just not as good as he used to be.

On more than one occasion, Mick had contemplated visiting his younger self to give out some advice about the future. Each time that he got nearer to his old house, though, he started to get a headache. The headache got steadily worse the closer Mick got to the house that his younger self lived in. Once curiosity got the better of him and he climbed into the rear garden of his old house to at least look through the patio doors at his younger self. The pain in his head became excruciating, and he thought that he was about to burst a blood vessel, so he retreated and stayed away. He put this experience down to the fact that two people, the same two people—couldn't occupy the same space.

Perhaps this was a universal law. It made sense. Mick didn't know the actual answer or the perceived reasoning behind the theory, and neither did anyone else, according to Mick's research via the *Encyclopaedia Britannica*.

Roman killed time by flicking through historic local newspaper stories online. He did this partly to check for any changes in the past that he should be concerned about, especially with Mick still running around only a few decades behind himself. He came across a headline about a mother who had acid thrown at her by a man wearing a balaclava. Roman recognised the woman as his old next-door neighbour from when he was a child and was still living with both of his parents.

The newspaper told the story of how the lady had exited her garden gate and was confronted by a man holding a water bottle. The man had tried to throw the contents of the bottle into the lady's face, but the woman had turned her back to the man in time to protect herself. Fortunately, most of the acid had hit the back of her coat, and only a few drops had landed on the back of her neck, causing only minor burns. The man had run away to a waiting car, and once inside, the driver had sped off.

This was too much of a coincidence to not be linked to Mick. The gate that the woman had walked through was a shared gate for Roman's family and the next-door neighbour. The intended target did resemble Roman's mother to a certain extent. This criminal operation had been planned in advance, even if it had gone awry. Obviously, Mick had paid someone to carry out the assault, and the man had cocked it up. This meant that Mick was still harbouring a grudge, despite being a wealthy man with a family. Roman made the decision to go back in time to bring an end to the situation. First, though, Roman had to do his homework on Mick.

Two weeks later, Roman was set for another adventure into the past. He had set up the doorframe at the bottom of his own garden and wired it via an extension lead connected to the mains electric, with a current limiter fitted between the socket and the frame. This would allow him a lot more time in the past, as he wouldn't need to keep coming back to top up a generator with petrol, every couple of hours. The only thing he feared was a power cut, as this would strand him in the past. He had put the time frame amongst a patch of weeds in an area of his garden that was rarely frequented in the past. just in case someone or something unexpectedly stepped through it and arrived in 2023 from a previous time.

Roman arrived in Mick's time and made his way to Oxford by bus. This time he would have to confront Mick on Mick's own patch, and Roman was feeling slightly apprehensive about this. Mick was unpredictable at the best of times, but coupled with this, he was also very intelligent. Getting him to walk into a trap wouldn't be easy. However, Roman had spent a considerable amount of time trawling through old newspapers online, as well as carrying out checks with the Land Registry and researching Mick's friends and rivals, and he felt as prepared as he could be in the circumstances.

After getting off the bus, Roman first walked around to the street that Mick lived on. He identified Mick's house and then walked away to an office block that Mick jointly owned with a business partner. Renovation work was being carried out at the property to turn the building into flats, and there were workmen, in their hi-vis jackets and helmets, walking around doing their individual tasks. Roman walked away from the immediate area and then took a taxi to a large Do-It-Yourself store on the edge of the city. Here he bought a hi-vis jacket and a hard hat. He hoped that this would gain him access to the site in his guise as a building inspector. He needed to have a look around the inside of the building to check out its suitability. Once he had visited the site, he would then need to contact two people whose names he had written in a small pocket notebook that he kept alongside his wallet.

It was Friday evening, and Roman had been in Oxford for two days. He had conducted both meetings and was satisfied with the outcomes of both. The building site was closed until Monday, and Roman was inside the office building. He was familiar with the internal layout. In his guise as a building inspector, he had inspected all six floors and had secretly opened a ground floor window, but left it in a closed position, so that he could climb in at his leisure. He climbed the staircase to the top floor and walked over to the open lift shaft that was barriered off to prevent people from falling through the opening.

Here, Roman removed the barriers and placed scaffold planks across the open lift shaft. He placed an old swivel chair and desk on the other side of the shaft, which he had retrieved from the skip outside. There was no exit from this part of the building for someone sitting at the desk other than across the scaffold planks, which he placed atop the lift shaft opening.

The following morning, Mick was awakened by a knock at his front door. He went down in his dressing gown to open it. In the doorway, stood a young man in his early twenties.

"You're Mick, aren't you?" said the young man. "It's you who's got the office block on Cromwell Road, isn't it?"

Mick nodded. "Why? Is it on fire or something?" he asked.

"No," the man replied. "But I've just seen someone climbing through a window to get inside. There's a girl with him. They're new age hippies or something. They're notorious around here for squatting in places like yours. Once they're in, it's hard to get them out. They'll bring your job to a standstill."

"Wait there whilst I get dressed," replied Mick. "What were you doing round there anyway?"

"My brother's working there. He left his crowbar out in the car park. He asked me to pick it up for him before someone nicked it," replied the man, holding out a metal crowbar. "I've got to get back now anyway. If I were you, I would throw the squatter out before he turns it into an illegal rave or something."

"Thanks for the advice, mate, but don't worry," said Mick. "He'll be gone in an hour, even if I have to drag him out by his ears."

With that, he closed his front door and went upstairs to get dressed. Thirty minutes later, he had parked his car in the office car park and was heading towards the front doors. He unlocked and opened the entrance door, then walked into the building. He could see the open ground floor window that Roman had climbed through.

"I know you're in here!" shouted Mick as he opened the doors on the ground floor. "Come out and clear it off, and we'll say no more about it. If I have to look for you, it won't end well for you."

Nobody answered, and so Mick picked up a broken metal table leg and methodically searched every room on the ground floor. Once he had searched the ground floor, he walked up the stairs to the first floor and started searching again. He carried on until he reached the top floor. As he rounded the stairwell, he saw Roman sitting facing him from behind a desk. He recognised him immediately, and immediately he walked towards him to block Roman's exit if he tried to run.

"Well, I can honestly say that I never expected to see you again," smiled Mick. "Not alive anyway. What are you doing here?"

"I've got a proposition for you," said Roman.

"Go on," said Mick. "Not that you've got anything to bargain with, but I will hear you out."

"My proposition is this," said Roman. "You swear to leave me and my family alone, and I won't interfere with your life. I know that you're married with a kid, and I know you've done alright for yourself money-wise. We can shake on it, and both move on with our lives."

Mick burst out laughing. "You killed my cousin, and you want to shake my hand. Blimey, you've got some neck on you. You dropped me here, away from my family and friends, and you want to walk away? I don't think so. There are some new foundations being dug out there on Monday. You're going to be part of them. Part of the structure. Every time I walk past this building, I will tip my cap towards your grave. It's nothing personal, Son, but I'll sleep a lot better knowing that you're not around."

"I can take you back to your own time if you want," said Roman. "You and your family. You can pick up your life where you left off. You can still be rich."

"No thanks," said Mick, moving towards Roman. "I've made my bed and all that."

Mick raised the table leg that he was holding and walked towards Roman. He took a couple of steps onto the scaffold planks and disappeared down the lift shaft as the sawn-through planks gave way under his weight. It happened too fast for Mick to realise what had happened. He plummeted from the sixth floor and crashed onto the concrete ground floor, along with half the planks. He died instantly in a broken pile of bones and wood. Roman stood up, edged around the gap surrounding the lift shaft, and started to walk down the stairs. When he got to the ground floor, he was confronted by the young man who had told Mick about the squatter at his offices.

"Good riddance," said the man. "Payback for shoving my brother under a train," he looked at Mick's broken body. "Ricky was my half-brother, but he was still my big brother. He didn't deserve to die so young. I'm glad Mick's dead."

Someone else walked into the ground floor lobby.

"I came through the back door," said Mick's business partner. "It all went as planned I see," he said. Staring at Mick's body.

"I gave him a way out," said Roman. "He could have emptied his bank account and come away with me, but he just wanted revenge," he shook his head. "You are going to have to get rid of all the sawn-through planks from here and upstairs, and then put the barriers back around the exposed lift shaft, leaving a gap wide enough to walk through. This will stop the police and health and safety from nosing around too much. Shut the open window before you leave, and leave it to the workmen on Monday to find the body. Don't move the body in any way. It's got an accident written all over it."

With that, Roman exited the building through the rear doors and walked off towards the bus stop. Two hours later, he was home, dismantling the time frame. Once the frame and components were packed away in his garden shed, Roman sat down in front of his laptop and conducted an internet search for Mick's death.

The coroner ruled Mick's death an accident. Marriage records revealed that Mick's wife moved on with her life and remarried a year later. An internet search revealed that the flats were entirely owned by Mick's business partner, and he himself was now very rich. Roman couldn't find any information online about Ricky's half-brother.

Chapter 18
Randolph

Roman had followed Mick's trial in the newspapers, albeit old newspapers that he was reading online twenty odd years later. He had originally felt sorry for Mick. Mental illness was serious, no matter what the cause, and at the time, he hoped that Mick would get proper treatment for it whilst he was in rehab. Obviously, things never worked out for Mick, but in Roman's eyes, Mick had brought his demise on himself. He was given the chance to walk away. The amount of time that Roman was spending online was paying off in another way, though. He was elated to find one of Morgan's direct descendants alive in the twentieth century, but then disappointed to find that this relation, had died in an accident in 1940. Roman dug deeper and was able to piece the story together of a nine-year-old boy who had been hit by a car during the blackout and had died two days later in the hospital.

It transpired that this boy was the last relation from Morgan's direct bloodline, and Roman decided that he would ensure that this boy lived to be an old man. First thing was first, though. He booked himself onto an intense car driving course, which he passed, and then he brought a car. The car was twenty years old, but it was road legal. This was all done out of Tony Babbage's money.

Roman had traced the street on which the boy, Ryan, had died. It was in Banbury. He drove over there to see what the street looked like eighty-three years on. It was still there. He could almost imagine what it would have looked like during the war. Obviously, there were no plastic windows or doors or none of the ugly stone effect cladding or rendering. Very few road or street signs, no dropped kerbs or block-paved drives, and no cars in the driveways. *It would have looked quite quaint back in the day,* thought Roman.

He spied a small, wooded area about a quarter of a mile from the street. These trees were old and so should have been in the same place during the war. He decided to set his time frame up amongst them to give himself cover and quick access to and from the street if he needed to escape quickly. He also needed a more accurate way of landing in the past at the right time.

Roman decided to set up the frame in a particularly hard to access section of the woods. This would hopefully give him the invisibility he would need and deter people from nosing around and possibly disconnecting his power supply whilst he was in the past. He printed and then laminated a small sign saying, "Wildlife Observation Survey. Do Not Disturb," Which he positioned near to the frame in case someone did become inquisitive. He had purchased a small, silent suitcase generator and fitted it with a voltage divider that he had adjusted to control the voltage output. With this divider, he could micro-drop the volts and record what particular voltage took you back to what particular place in time. In theory, this should guarantee at least the week and hopefully the day that he would arrive in the past. It was unlikely that the generator's micro-power fluctuations would allow the divider to be more accurate than that.

Dressed in his suit and holding a small, heavy suitcase, he started the generator and stepped through the portal. On the other side of time, he could clearly see the street in question, he just didn't know the date. It looked like the forties, judging by the traffic, but he needed to be more accurate than that. He stopped someone in the street and was told it was May 1943. He went back through the portal, adjusted the divider, and then stepped back through. June 1942. He topped up the generator's petrol tank and stepped through it again.

May 1941. It took seventeen attempts and numerous petrol top-ups before he arrived on the correct day. He recorded the voltage required to get him to this same day and stepped through again. He didn't have a plan, so he would have to play it by ear. On the other side, as he walked down the street, he noticed a red and white striped roadworks tent on the path. He peered inside and saw two men digging a hole through the tarmac. He walked back to the time frame and stepped through it. An idea was formed in his mind.

Roman turned the generator off and covered it with fallen tree branches. He then got into his parked car and drove home. He sorted through the remainder of Tony's banknotes that he had stolen. He found a rare five-shilling note dated to 1938, and he found about one hundred pounds in notes dated between 1930 and 1940. He folded these up and put them all in his wallet. He then sorted through his grandfather's old coin collection and picked out various half-crowns, two-shilling pieces, and some random shillings, sixpences, and copper coins that were dated before 1940 and put them into his pocket. He then opened his laptop and typed, then printed off two forms. Roman then went into the garden shed and took out the empty 15 kg propane gas bottle from an old gas heater that was used to heat the shed. He looked around the shed for some paint and then painted the bottle with grey primer. He then returned to the wooded area.

Roman topped up the tank on the generator and then started it up. He checked the resonators and then calibrated the digital divider to the correct voltage. He then picked up the gas bottle and suitcase and stepped through the wooden frame. Once on the other side, he covered the gas bottle and suitcase with leaves and branches and then nailed a sign to a nearby tree. The sign read: "AIR MINISTRY EXERCISE, DO NOT ENTER." He brushed himself down and walked down the road to the workmen's tent. When he got there, he produced another piece of printed paper.

"Excuse me," said Roman politely. "I'm with the home guard, and I have a stop notice ordering you to stop working."

Both men stopped. They exited the tent. "What is a stop notice?" said one of the men. "And why have we got to stop? We are nearly down to the leak."

"It's from the council," said Roman. "The stop order is so that the home guard can set up an observation operation with a checkpoint on the path, right on this very spot. They will be checking identification papers and looking for spies. That kind of stuff."

"Spies…In Banbury," said the other man. "There's no spies in Banbury."

"It's just an exercise, just training. It's not real," said Roman, taking out some change from his pocket. "My commanding officer told me to give you both a ten bob note for the inconvenience, with an extra two-bob if you leave that tent up so the men don't get wet."

The men looked at the money and then at each other. They smiled and readily agreed. It didn't matter how long it took to fix the pipe; they just wouldn't tell that they had had to leave the job for half a day. They would just tell their supervisor that the repair had taken longer than anticipated. Jobs went over all the time. Nobody queried it. This way, the water board wouldn't dock their wages for being absent from work.

"Come back tomorrow," said Roman to the men as he gave them the money. "We'll leave a man with the tent all night to make sure it doesn't get nicked but take your tools with you."

The men picked up the tools and walked off down the road. As soon as they were out of sight, Roman hurried back to the woods, picked up the gas bottle, and took a small axe out of the suitcase. He concealed both items in a bin bag and hurried back to the tent. Once inside the tent, Roman tied the door flap closed. He took out the axe and chopped at the tarmac to make the original hole bigger. Once big enough to accommodate the gas bottle circumference, he tipped the bottle upside down and forced it six inches into the ground. Once it was vertical and solidly in place, he brushed in some of the loose chippings that surrounded it into the hole's edges to level up the path. He then stepped out of the tent and tied it closed from the outside. He walked back to the woods to kill some time before it got dark.

It was dusk, and Roman was at a public phone box two streets away from the 'bomb' in the path. He had just telephoned the police, who in turn had phoned the army, who in turn were sending out the bomb squad. Roman rushed back to remove the tent just as the police arrived and cordoned off both ends of the street from traffic. They then went door to door, evacuating the households to a safe distance away. Roman joined the crowd, on the lookout for a nine-year-old boy called Ryan. The boy was easy to spot. There were only three other boys in the street around his age, and his father was constantly calling him back as he tried to sneak off down the street to watch the soldiers.

Roman hurried to the woods and stepped through the portal. He needed to top the generator up whilst it was still running so that he wouldn't have to turn it off and recalibrate the divider. He did this successfully and then stepped back through to the other side, just as the bomb squad detonated a controlled explosion of the gas bottle, which was now surrounded by a wall of sandbags. The detonation didn't produce the massive explosion that the squad was expecting. One of the soldiers removed part of the sandbag wall and picked up the broken canister. He handed it to his commanding officer.

"Obviously a hoax, sir," he said.

"I'm not blind corporal," came the reply. The soldier walked over to a plain-clothed policeman and handed him the remains of the gas canister. "Someone's had us on," he said. "It's just a piece of metal tube, made to look like a bomb. I suppose it would have been kids. Find them, and do me a favour when you get them. Give them a bloody good hiding."

The policeman nodded, making a mental note to do just that.

The army packed the sandbags and their equipment away and drove off. The police gave the all clear and then the uniformed policemen drove off. The householders returned to their houses, but the plain clothes detective, Randolph, decided to hang around. No doubt the boys responsible would have been hiding and watching the commotion that they had caused. They were most likely laughing at him somewhere now. Well, he had a nose for sniffing out troublemakers, and he had been cautioned twice for his over-the-top treatment of people that he had taken into custody, but this was his patch, and he was taking it personally.

Randolph was a tall man and a bully. He was disliked by his colleagues and was despised by the local criminal fraternity. He was forty years old and married, but he had a mistress, Mabel, living in the next street from the one who had the bomb scare. His first encounter with Mabel was when he arrested her for soliciting. After going around her house to take a statement later that night, he dropped all the charges. In his mind, Mabel was everything that his wife was not. She was tall and busty, drank like a fish, and swore like a trooper. In Randolph's mind, she was not the type of girl to be seen in public with, but in private, she fulfilled his needs. Randolph was also a bitter man. He was regularly overstepped for promotions, and there were rumours around the police station that he was on the take.

Roman waited for the family to settle down, then walked over and knocked on Morgan's relative's door. The door was opened by Ryan's father. Roman noticed that he had only one hand.

"Hello!" said Roman. "I'm acting on behalf of Strand and Strand, and we need to have a chat. May I come in?"

"Give us a chance," said the man. "I thought we had until the end of the month to vacate the premises."

"That's not why I'm here," replied Roman. "I'm here about your inheritance. You've been left a tidy sum by a woman in Newcastle. Can we talk about it inside?"

The man looked puzzled and invited him inside. Ryan and the man's wife were standing in the kitchen when Morgan walked in.

"Please don't put us out tonight," pleaded the woman. "It wouldn't be fair on the boy."

Roman smiled. He asked if he could sit down and then proceeded to tell the family how a woman in Newcastle, living in rented accommodation and buried in a pauper's grave, had made a will. She had no family alive, so she left everything to this family. She didn't know this family personally, but a relative in this family had saved the life of someone dear to her many years ago. A small chest was discovered in a bank vault, and the contents have been brought over personally. There is an inventory that you will need to sign, then the contents are yours.

The man looked at the inventory sheet. He didn't understand it, and neither did his wife. He explained that he hadn't signed anything since losing his hand at Dunkirk.

Roman smiled and held out a pen. "Just put a mark on there with your other hand, and we'll get it over with." He was conscious of the time that the generator had left to run. Once signed, Roman opened his wallet.

"Right!" said Roman, looking at Ryan as he opened his wallet. "This ten-shilling note is for you." He passed Ryan the note. The boy just stared at it. It was the highest amount of money that he had ever had. "Keep it safe and spend it wisely."

"This one hundred pounds is for you two," said Roman to the man and woman. The woman sat down and started to cry. "Now, the contents of this chest are extremely valuable, and so I would suggest that you put it somewhere safe and don't tell anyone about it. Not yet, anyway. You'll be a target for robbery."

Roman opened the chest lid and revealed Eddie's seventeenth-century hoard of golden objects and gold coins.

"There is three pounds of gold in there. 3lb of gold melted down is worth two hundred pounds, which is easily enough to buy a terraced house like this one in today's market. Bear in mind, though, that you will get more money from a collector or a museum. If you're thinking of buying a house, don't hang around. House prices will skyrocket from next year."

With that, Roman stood up. "I think it would be a nice gesture for you to send some money up to the church in Newcastle for a gravestone for the deceased lady. I've written the details on the back of that paper." The couple agreed.

"I will leave you now," said Roman, smiling at the family. He put his thumb up to the boy.

"Don't spend it all at once."

With that, he said his goodbye, to the shocked but happy family and was let out of the front door. He hurried to the woods. Twice he thought that he was being followed, but both times when he looked around, he couldn't see anyone in the dark. He got to the portal and stepped through it. As he knelt to turn the generator off, a man stumbled through the frame from the other side. Randolph hit the ground after tripping on the bottom of the frame.

His outstretched hand hit a sharp tree branch, and the wood pierced his palm, going all the way through to the other side. Randolph's immediate reaction was to pull his hand back, and this released his hand from the wooden spike. However, the cut was severe and would need stitches.

Chapter 19
A Fish out of Water

Randolph sat up and looked around. He was confused. Had he been knocked unconscious when he fell over? He had stepped through a bush at night, and now the sun was high in the sky. He turned to the boy.

"What happened?" he said.

"It's complicated, but if you want to go back, step through the frame before I turn this generator off," replied Roman.

Randolph looked at the yellow portable generator and then at the various electrical instruments that surrounded the frame. "I need to sort my hand out," he said. "It won't stop bleeding."

Roman looked at Randolph's hand. "Who are you?" he asked.

"Randolph. Detective constable Randolph," he said. "Is this secret air ministry stuff? I saw the sign on the other side of the bushes."

"Not quite," said Roman. "It's complicated, though, and for your own sake, it might be better to go back through the frame and get your hand looked at."

"You are responsible for that bomb scare," said Randolph. "I've been watching you since you went into that house. I'd put money on it that you've got something to do with it, and I want you to come with me to answer some questions."

Roman looked at Randolph. "Look, detective constable Randolph, you've stumbled into something that doesn't concern you. You're trapped in 2023, and only I can send you back to your own time. I'm willing to drive you to the medical centre to get your hand stitched up, and then I will bring you back here to send you back to your own time. It'll be a shock for you to see how everything has moved on in the last eighty years, but just treat it as a wonderful daytrip and then go back."

"Who was that family that you just visited, at number twenty-three?" asked Randolph, thinking that the boy was lying to try to get himself off with the criminal charges that he was going to bring.

"Just distant relatives. They didn't believe that I was from the future, and so I left." said Roman. The last thing he wanted was for the police to go sniffing around the family and their newfound wealth.

"Come with me, and we'll get this cleared up," said Randolph. The boy was obviously trying to lie himself out of a criminal conviction, but he would take him in handcuffs if he had to.

"Follow me to my car," said Roman as he turned off the generator and started to walk away through the woods. Randolph followed him and made threats to Roman as he walked.

"Roman's car was parked up in a layby. The two of them walked over to it. Roman remotely unlocked the car doors. Get in, and I'll take you to the medical centre. Hurry up, and let's get back. I've got things to do."

Randolph was stunned. His mouth dropped open when he climbed inside the car, and Roman started it up. The dashboard lit up when the key was turned, and the music came on over the radio. Randolph became visibly worried.

"Relax!" said Roman. "The medical centre is ten minutes away, according to the satnav. The satnav started to speak out the directions, and Randolph thought about jumping from the moving car. He forced himself to remain calm.

"What year are we in?" he asked, trying to disguise the tremor in his voice.

"Twenty twenty-three," came the reply. "It's going to take some getting used to, I know," said Roman. "I've gone back hundreds of years recently, and I'm shocked every time that I do. Just take it all in. This is how your grandkids will be living eighty years into your future. Eighty years is a long time in the tech era."

"Was that a time machine back there?" asked Randolph, recalling a book he had once read by H G Wells.

"Yeah, sort of," came the reply. "You can only go backwards, though, and then back to the point that you started from. You cannot go forward."

Roman stopped the car in the medical centre car park. "There are not too many cars, so hopefully you won't have to wait too long," he said. He led Randolph up the steps and through the glass doors. They walked up to the reception, and Roman explained that his friend had fallen onto a sharp branch. The receptionist took Randolph's details.

"Are your tetanus jabs up to-date? Up," she asked.

"No," answered Roman. "He will definitely need one, as the branch was dirty."

"Okay, take a seat; they will call you in in a few minutes."

Randolph and Roman sat down. The man sitting next to Randolph was playing music through his mobile phone whilst also scrolling through some photos. Randolph was amazed, and when the mobile rang and the man answered and engaged in a conversation with the other person, Randolph forgot the pain in his hand; he was that spellbound.

Randolph's name was called, and Roman directed him to the treatment room. "Don't tell them where you're from; they will lock you up in the nut house," warned Roman.

Fifteen minutes later, Randolph appeared. His wound had been cleaned, sterilised, stitched closed, and then bandaged. He had also been given a blister pack of strong paracetamol to take home with him. Roman led the way back to the car, and they drove back to the layby.

"I will start the generator up, and you can go home," said Roman.

They walked to the clearing and Roman started up the generator, carefully aligned the resonators and calibrated the divider.

"Ready when you are," said Roman to Randolph.

"I'm not going," said Randolph. I don't trust that it won't send me back too far. You're going, though. He picked up the hammer from the ground that Roman had used to cut through the pavement tarmac. "You can go back and bring me something back that's personal to me, so I know it's set for the right time."

Roman looked at Randolph. "I will step, through it with you if you want. It's set up for the right time."

"No, you're going on your own. You're going to fetch me something from my house, thirteen Pevril Place, and bring it back here."

"Is your house far away?" replied Roman. "If I can't get there and back in under two hours, then we're both stuck."

Randolph thought about it for a few seconds. "You can pick something up from my bird's house," he said. "Go round to number six, Broadlands, and tell Mabel that you want the photo of me and her in the rowing boat. Tell her I will bring it back later. I'll know when you get back that it's safe for me to go back."

Roman stood up. "Don't touch any of that stuff." He said, pointing at the time frame. "It's booby-trapped. If you do, you risk immediate transportation to the moon. There is no food, water, or air there, and you will be dead within three minutes. You will be joining a handful of other dead people who touched it without my permission."

With that, he checked the petrol in the generator's tank and stepped through the door frame. On the other side, he jogged down to number six and knocked on the door. It was around six pm. The door was opened by a lady wearing a pinny with a woodbine cigarette in the corner of her mouth.

"You, Mabel?" asked Roman.

"Who wants to know?" replied Mabel.

"Randolph sent me to pick up the photo of you and him in the boat," said Roman.

"What's he wants it for?" said Mabel. "And why has he sent you round for it. Do you work with him? Are you a copper as well? You don't look very old."

"Yeah, I work with him. He's tied up at the moment, and that's why he's asked me to come round."

"You better come in then whilst I find it. I think I know where it is," said Mabel. She led the way into the living room. "I can't keep it on display in case anyone comes round and sees it. Folks around here are so small minded that they would put two and two together and make five, or go and tell his wife." She handed Roman the photograph. "What did you say he wants it for?"

"He's planning to leave his wife, and he wants to show your photo to the lads at work," lied Roman. "In fact, he asked me to ask if you would go round to his house and tell his wife that he's leaving her to move in with you and to pick up his shaving stuff and that."

"Did he?" said Mabel, smiling. "It's about bloody time. All this sneaking around does my nut in. He is totally spineless when it comes to his wife. He's been saying that he's going to leave her for months, and now he's finally grown a bloody backbone. Yeah, I'll go round. What is the number again? Thirteen?"

"Yeah, thirteen," replied Roman. "Anyway, I've got to shoot off; he's waiting for me." With that, he turned, walked out of the house, and started jogging back to the woods. He stepped through the portal to find Randolph sitting on a log.

"You got it?" He asked. Roman handed it over.

"Come on then," said Roman, "before the petrol runs out."

"I'm not ready to go back yet," said Randolph. "I'm not going back to be skint. I want to be rich, extremely rich when I go back, and so I want to take some stuff back with me. I want money—lots of it. I need that telephone that's plugged into your car dashboard. I want one of those screens that shows the news and the weather that was in the doctor's waiting room. I also want some boxes of these pain relief tablets. There is loads of stuff that I want. You can get it all in your car. When I'm satisfied is when we go back," he took the hammer out of his pocket. "I also want the plans for the time machine so that I can build my own."

Roman was stunned. This was a policeman saying this and threatening him. He casually walked over to the generator and turned it off.

"Leave this stuff here, but cover it with leaves," said Roman. He waited for a few minutes and then led Randolph to his car. "The electrical stuff might not work in your time," he said.

"I'll take the chance," said Randolph. "And don't try to trick me. It'll be worse for you if you do. I'm still a copper, you know, no matter how many years have passed."

Roman started the car, and the pair of them drove ten miles out of town. Roman pulled into a service station.

"The phones are in there," said Roman, stopping the car and pointing to a shop.

They both got out of the car. "Give me the car keys," said Randolph, tapping the front of his jacket, where he had concealed the hammer.

Roman locked the car remotely and handed the key to Randolph.

"I need to go to the toilet first," said Roman. "The toilets are in there," he started to walk towards them, and Randolph followed him inside. Roman went into an unoccupied cubicle and locked the door. "I'll be five minutes," he said to Randolph.

Randolph waited for thirty seconds and then realised that he needed to go to the toilet himself. He walked to the urinal. If the boy made a break for it, he wouldn't get far. He was holding the car key. He walked over to the urinal and stood there, whilst also trying to swivel his head to keep an eye on the cubicle door. Roman was watching through a gap between the cubicle door and its frame. As soon as Randolph started, Roman made a break for it. Instead of running to the car park, though, Roman ran into the adjacent disabled toilets and locked the door. Randolph came running out of the gents and, thinking that Roman must have a spare key to his car, headed for the car park.

He got there before Roman and waited for him to turn up to the car. Roman walked out of the building and watched him from a vantage point behind some giant bins. Randolph tried to unlock the car door with the key that he had in his hand. It wouldn't go into the lock. He tried the doors and the boot, but the key wouldn't open either. He looked at the key and read the words "Yale." It dawned on him that he had been given the wrong key. Roman edged closer and waited. Randolph tried the passenger door again, and this time it opened. Roman had unlocked the car door remotely at the same time that Randolph had lifted the handle.

With an audible sigh of relief, Randolph climbed into the passenger side, to wait for Roman to return. He could wait. He was good at waiting. He saw a heap of one-pound and two-pound coins in the console cup holder. He put these in his pocket. From his vantage point, Roman remotely locked and then deadlocked the car doors. Hearing the noise from the door locks, Randolph pulled on the door handle to open the door. The door opened, and the car alarm went off. The indicators were flashing, and the alarm siren was wailing loudly. People were stopping to look. Randolph jumped out of the car and walked away, trying to distance himself from the car in case he was accused of trying to steal it. As soon as Randolph was far enough away to stop him, Roman ran to the car and started the ignition. He pressed the door lock nib to lock himself inside.

His way was clear to leave the car park and he sped off, almost hitting Randolph, who was now running back to the car. Roman drove past Randolph and waved at him. He drove about fifty metres along the road and then stopped the car. Randolph started to jog over to it. He had almost reached the car when Roman sped off and stopped another fifty metres down the road. Randolph hesitated for a few seconds and then walked towards the car. He had almost reached it when Roman drove off again. This time, for good. Randolph shouted some obscenities towards the moving car, but Roman was out of earshot.

By walking and jogging, Randolph eventually reached the woods, where the time frame had been. He knew the area and had cut across some fields for part of the way. It had taken him three hours to get there, but everything had been packed away. There was nothing there except a piece of paper pinned to a tree with the words "Wot, no time machine," written on it and a picture of a man's face peering over the top of a wall. Randolph smiled to himself. Roman thought he had got one over on him, but he would have the last laugh. He took a piece of paper out of his pocket. It read MOT Test Certificate and was dated less than a week ago. It never had Roman's address on it, but it had the garage's address and the car registration number on it. Randolph didn't know what a test certificate was, but he was sure that he could trace Roman through it.

Randolph thumbed his way to the high street where the MOT garage was sited. He knew the town anyway, as he had lived there briefly as a child. It had changed massively over the years, but the street names hadn't changed. He decided to do some legwork first. This usually paid off to some extent. He walked out of the high street and into a side street, looking for a matching car. He had been walking around for an hour when he saw a car in somebody's driveway that looked like Roman's. He walked over to it and stood and checked the registration plate against the MOT certificate. The registrations didn't match, but they could have been switched. He tried the door and peered through the windows. He was about to walk away when the front door of the house opened, and a tall, thin man wearing a leather jacket, aged in his early twenties, came out. He was smoking a roll-up cigarette with a strange smell. He asked Randolph what he was up to.

"Just checking," said Randolph, with an air of authority. "Who are you?"

"Tarquin," came the reply. "Checking what? You police or something?"

"Yes, I am," said Randolph. "Do you know of any more of these autos in this area?"

Tarquin hurriedly threw away his cigarette. "Why do you want to know?" He asked.

"Police business," said Randolph. "Just answer the question."

"I'm assuming you've got a warrant card," said Tarquin.

Randolph took his wallet out and opened it to show the man his card. Tarquin looked at it and laughed. "You just been released from hospital?" he asked, thinking that the supposed policeman had recently been sectioned and then released back into the community. "Did they let you print it in there?"

"I have just been released," said Randoph, thinking that the man was talking about his bandaged hand. "Just answer the question. Are there any more of these in the area?"

Tarquin looked at Randolph and then showed him an embroidered patch of a human skull with a snake coming out of the eye socket that was sewn onto his sleeve. "You obviously know what this is," he said, trying to sound threatening.

Randolph gripped the boy's arm to look closely at the patch. He then put his finger in a gap between the patch and the leather jacket sleeve. With a sharp tug, he ripped the patch off and threw it on the ground. He let go of the man's arm, and Tarquin took a couple of steps backwards.

"You'll pay for that," said Tarquin loudly. "Nobody disrespects the badge and gets away with it."

"I'm not paying for anything," said Randolph. "Get your mother to sew it back on; she won't charge you."

"You saying that my mother charges? Nobody disrespects my mother and gets away with it," said Tarquin in a menacing tone. "I could make one phone call and have half a dozen blokes round here."

"Excellent!" replied Randolph. "I can spread them about the area."

"You reckon?" said Tarquin, looking Randolph up and down. He started to retreat closer to his front door, just in case. 'The Snake Eyes' don't take prisoners. "I've got a shank in there with your name on."

"I just ate," said Randolph. "It's all bone anyway. Make your phone call, and I'll be back in an hour." With that, he turned and walked off down the road. Tarquin went back inside his house. This was a test. The Snake Eyes had never actually been in a group fight before, but if they let this insult go and word got around, then their reputation would be in tatters. He made some phone calls and went into the kitchen to make a sandwich. He looked up at a shelf and spotted a jar of chilli powder. He took it down and put it in his pocket.

An hour later, three men were waiting outside for Randolph to arrive. One was holding a snooker cue, one carried a pair of home-made nunchucks (two pieces of wood connected with a metal chain), and Tarquin, who had met Randolph earlier, had a handful of chilli powder. On time, Randolph walked up to the group. The group watched him approach.

"I don't think it's nice you laughing," said the man holding the pool cue, narrowing his eyes. Randolph wasn't laughing.

"Tarquin doesn't like people laughing. He gets the crazy idea that you're laughing at him," carried on the man. Randolph still wasn't laughing.

"But if you were to apologise, like I know that you're going to, I might convince him that you really didn't mean it." He looked around at the other two men and winked. He had recently watched "A Fistful of Dollars," a 1960s spaghetti western, and had been secretly hoping that an opportunity would arise someday whereby he could use those lines.

Randolph stepped forward, and the men took a step back. Randolph took another step forward, and the men took another step backwards.

"Keep stepping backwards, and you'll be back inside the house," said Randolph.

Tarquin threw the chilli powder into Randolph's eyes. Randolph blinked a couple of times and then let out a cry of pain. Two other men took this as their cue to spring into action. Randolph received numerous blows with the pool cue across his legs and arms, whilst the other man rained numerous blows on top of Randolph's head with the nunchucks. Randolph dropped to the ground and curled up into a ball, trying to protect his head. Tarquin took this as his cue to put the boot in. Unfortunately, for him, he was still in his slippers, so he stopped almost immediately when the pain in his toes became unbearable. The blows eased and then stopped.

"Don't ever mess with the Snake Eyes," said the man with the pool cue.

"You cut off the legs, and the head comes looking for you," he paused for a moment to reflect on what he had just said.

"You cut off the tail and the head comes looking for you." They walked through the front door into Tarquin's house. Randolph then heard laughing and then arguing coming from inside.

"I distinctly remember you saying that you were going to film it," said one man, clearly irritated.

"How could I?" came the reply. "I had the nunchucks. You only had the chilli powder."

Randolph got up from the ground and started to walk away. He was bruised, but nothing seemed broken. He made a mental note to come back and sort Tarquin out when he was in his house alone. He walked around to the garage and caught the receptionist just as she was about to close.

"I need your help," he said. The receptionist looked at his bruised face. "How?" she asked.

"Police," said Randolph, taking the MOT test certificate out of his pocket. "Did you issue this certificate? We need to know if it's genuine."

The woman studied it. "Yes, it's one of ours," she said.

"We caught a man with around thirty certificates on him. I tried to arrest him, but he put up a fight, hence my face. We're trying to locate him. Have you got an address for the owner of this car?" said Randolph.

The woman opened the booking diary on the desk. "We haven't got an address. Just a name, Roman, and a landline telephone number. Do you want me to write it down for you?" she said. "He's local, with that number."

Randolph took the number and thanked her. He then wandered around the town, looking for a public telephone box. He managed to find two. But one contained a load of paperback books, and the other contained a defibrillator. He walked around some more and eventually found the town library. He went in and asked the librarian for help. She told him to pop over the road to the council offices, as there was a public payphone in there. Randolph walked over and called Roman's house. The telephone rang and Roman picked up.

"Hi!" said Randolph. "This is Adam from the garage. We just noticed that the MOT certificate we issued to you has the wrong registration number on it. Where your number plate starts with a 'B', the registration number on the MOT certificate starts with a 'G'. Can you pop by and pick up the new certificate up, later today, or alternatively, if you give me your address, I will pop it in the post first class, and you will get it tomorrow?"

Roman gave Adam his address, and Randolph wrote it down. Within an hour, Randolph was standing in the field behind Roman's back garden. He followed the boundary hedge around until he found a weak spot in the hedge, a gap that had been cut through recently. He forced his way through. He hurried to the garden shed and walked in through the unlocked door. From this vantage point, he could watch Roman's house and see when Roman left the house or went to bed. The shed observation point wasn't brilliant in that he wouldn't be able to see if Roman walked out of his front door and did his errands on foot, but if he went anywhere in his car, Randolph would see the car drive off the driveway.

Two hours passed, and Randolph was starting to get bored. He was toying with the idea of creeping over to the house for a closer look when he saw Roman unlock the car door and climb inside. A few seconds later, the car drove off. Randolph left the shed immediately and walked over to the house. He noticed that the top opener to the kitchen window was ajar, and if he could get his arm through this, he could release the catch to the side window and climb inside. He walked back down to the shed and came back with a wooden crate. He positioned the crate underneath the kitchen window and climbed onto it. From there, he opened the window and climbed into Roman's kitchen.

It was not Randolph's intention to wait for the boy and capture him. That would be too difficult to do in the long term. He was a fish out of water, and Roman was a clever lad. What he wanted was information that he could use to force the boy to do his bidding. He started to methodically search every room, quickly and quietly, leaving no trace that anyone had conducted a search. In under an hour, he had located Roman's mother's address, Roman's grandparents' identification details about where they were living during the 1940s and bank statements showing how much money Roman had in the bank.

He wrote all the details down on a piece of paper and replaced the original paperwork. Temptation got the better of him though when he found Roman's historic currency collection and stole the notes and coins dated to the 1930s and 1940s, as well as a wad of modern notes that he found in a coffee tin on the kitchen shelf. He smiled to himself. All in all, it had been a very productive day.

Chapter 20
Dream Big, Dream Bigger

Roman had had a busy day. He had met the official receiver at George's printing workshop and had agreed, a price to purchase the building. This would be an ideal place to set up a permanent time portal with a permanent electric power supply so that he wouldn't need to keep popping back every couple of hours to top up the generator or recharge the car batteries. From there, he could keep his original Robin Hood promise of robbing the rich and distributing the wealth amongst the poor. The first thing he intended to do when everything was sorted was to go back in time and stop his grandfather from ending up in an asylum, and the second thing would be to take some medicine in the form of a tuberculosis vaccine to Mary, the young girl he had met at the orphanage.

He had stopped for a pint and a sandwich in a pub on the high street when the meeting with the official receiver finished, but he had met some friends and was persuaded to stay out longer for a few more beers. He said his goodbyes to these friends at around 9.00 pm and walked home. Roman took a shortcut through the town. As he entered the market square, he could see an ambulance outside one of the pubs and a man being stretchered into the back of it. He asked another man, who was standing there, what was going on.

"A group of lads from a gang called the Snake Eyes were out celebrating something, and they kicked off with the doorman at the pub when he wouldn't let them in. One of the men had tried to throw some curry powder or something into the doorman's face, and he leathered four of them. The other two ran off. That's one of them being stretchered into the ambulance."

Roman wondered if this gang was the same gang that was in the year above him at school. The gang had the same name. They had once tried to bring the whole school out on strike for something or other, but none of the pupils did, and most of the Snake Eyes ended up getting suspended themselves. They were regarded as a bit of a joke by the rest of the school, although they had a different opinion of themselves as they sat on the playground smoking cannabis. Roman remembered one of the boys, a lad called Tarquin, bringing a replica samurai sword into school and then getting expelled for it. The lad that got stretchered into the ambulance did look a bit like Tarquin.

Roman arrived home and went straight into the kitchen. He poured himself a bowl of cornflakes and milk and walked into the lounge. It was dark, and he turned on the light. Randolph was sitting in the chair with his feet up on the coffee table.

"Hello, Roman," he said. "Don't bother with my supper; I've already eaten." He stood up. Roman was frozen to the spot. He wasn't sure what to do. He thought about running back into the kitchen and grabbing a knife, but Randolph was already at the lounge door, closing it.

"I should bash your head in," said Randolph. "But that won't solve the problem of getting me back home with all my nice stuff." He took the bowl out of Roman's hand and placed it on the arm of the settee.

"Nothing to say?" he said to the speechless Roman. "Cat got your tongue? Mouth not working? Maybe this will help."

He punched Roman in the face, sending him flying across the room.

"You see, there is a pecking order that needs to be followed. I'm the general, and you're the private," said Randolph, punching the now kneeling Roman in the face again and knocking him back onto the floor.

"We've got to establish the ground rules and the consequences of not following these rules," said Randolph, kicking Roman in the stomach.

"I hold all the aces, and so you better listen to what I'm about to say," said Randolph.

"Firstly, I know how much money you have in the bank. I want all of it, and I want it converted to 1940s money. Secondly, I want every electrical item in this house. If you want to keep the said items for sentimental reasons, you can get me replacements; I'm not bothered about which way you want to play that. Thirdly, I want the plans for the time machine and all the component parts. I saw some of the bits in your garden shed. Finally, remember this. I know where you live, and I know where your mother lives. Both houses and occupants can easily be destroyed in a fire. If you somehow trick me into going back without all my stuff, I will kill your grandparents. I also know where they live. Oh, and by the way, I found a letter stating that you will be buying the printing workshop on Victoria

Street. I also found a sketch plan of where you intend to build the time machine, or portal frame, as you call it, in relation to the building floor. This is good. We can pass all of my new stuff through it without it being seen by anyone. I want you to remember what I'm capable of and remember that I've got nothing to lose. I don't even exist in this time. So, with that, I will bid you au revoir for the time being, and I will meet you at the printer shop tomorrow morning."

Randolph opened the lounge door and walked into the kitchen. He turned and looked back at Roman.

"Don't try to cross me, Son," he said. "Your mother wouldn't like it." He laughed. "I'll be staying in a hotel tonight, courtesy of your coffee tin." He laughed again and walked out of the house.

Roman got up from the floor. He straightened his trousers and changed his blood-stained shirt for a clean one. He then picked up his car keys and went out to the car. Twenty minutes later, he was at his mother's. It was dark inside the house, and so Roman let himself in with his key. He silently walked into the kitchen and over to a key rack that was screwed to the wall. He searched the bundles of keys and picked out George's old front and rear door keys for the printing workshop. George was supposed to have surrendered all of the keys to the workshop when he went into administration.

However, he had kept a spare pair in case the new owners turned the place into a shop or storage facility, and then he could pop round during the night and help himself to their stock. Roman silently walked to the front door and left the house. He would drive down to the workshop tomorrow and try the door keys. He drove back home and went to bed.

Early the following morning, Roman was at the print workshop. He tried the front door key, but the lock had been changed. He climbed over the gate and tried the back door. The key unlocked it, and the door opened. He had brought with him the copper wiring and the rest of the electrical equipment needed to construct the portal. He was wiring the coils around the frame when Randolph stepped through the door.

"You trying to trick me, boy," said Randolph angrily. "I told you what would happen if you did."

"I'm just trying to get everything prepared. It's not easy to calibrate everything when you're rushing," replied Roman.

"One digit out and everything will go pear-shaped," he knelt over the two resonators. "One of them keeps flicking from seventy-six to seventy-seven," he said.

"I don't know why, though. It might be damp or something. If they don't stabilise at the same number, the amount of time spent in the past will go from a couple of hours to a couple of minutes."

"And I get trapped there without my stuff," snarled Randolph. "Nice try, but you're going to sort it out," he lashed out at Roman with the palm of his hand and knocked Roman onto his back. The resonator fell out of his hand, and the digital screen went blank.

"Well, that's the end of that, then," said Roman, standing up. "You can't go anywhere on just one."

"Fix it!" Shouted Randolph. "Or I'll do you here and now."

"I can't!" shouted Roman defiantly. "You fix it. You know as much as I do about digital electronics."

Randolph calmed down. "Okay. We'll get a new one. Where do they sell them?"

"You might get one in Oxford or London, but they're not really an off-the-shelf item. I can look them up online, but you'll need a pair. I wouldn't risk pairing the old one with a new one. He picked up his mobile phone and did an internet search. 'There's a place in Oxford; they've got three in stock. They are open until one o'clock this afternoon.'"

"You just tell me where to get them, and I will go and get them," said Randolph. "You will be staying here. I will take your car. If you try anything smart, I will take it out on your mother. I'm too close to being rich to let you take it away from me. The sooner we get done, the longer you live. I mean, the sooner you can get your life back."

Roman gave Randolph the car keys, the address of the shop, and some money, and watched Randolph hurry round to the car. As the car drove off, Roman picked up the broken resonator. He was troubled by Randolph's last sentence about the length of time that he would live. It suddenly dawned on him that Randolph was planning to dispose of him as soon as he had gotten everything he wanted. It made sense. If Randolph let Roman live, what would stop Roman from going back to an earlier time and disposing of Randolph before they had even met? He had to do something and do it quickly. It would be around two hours before Randolph got back.

He picked up the broken resonator and shook it. The screen came to life for a couple of seconds and then went blank again. He shook it more violently, and the screen came back. He scrolled through the digital display and stopped at number seventy-five. The digital display started jumping between seventy-five and seventy-eight, but he realised that this was the best that he was going to get. He set the other resonator to seventy-five and finished the construction of the time frame. He knew that he could go back in time now, but he would only be able to stay for three minutes at most before he was trapped there, as his own time would move on.

He decided to go back to 1944, a few days or weeks after his encounter with Roger. He wouldn't have the luxury of refining the date by going backwards and forwards in time to get the exact date due to the imminent return of Randolph. He reasoned that he might get there within a few days though and hopefully be able to get Roger to help him if he was still stationed in the printing workshop in 1944. He was set to go. The flickering resonator was a cause for concern, but he felt like he didn't have any other option. He took a deep breath and stepped through the frame. He was on the other side of the print room, and he was alone. Roger wasn't there. He quickly walked over to the workshop telephone and picked up the thin telephone directory next to it.

He thumbed through the pages, found Roger's home telephone number, and quickly phoned it. Roger's wife answered the phone. She explained that Roger had been seconded to the police and was on duty somewhere. She said that he usually phoned home in the evenings to check that she and the baby were okay and that she could take a message if Roman wanted her to. She went to look for a pen and returned a few seconds later, and Roman explained the situation. He stressed how important it was that Roger got the message. With that, he hung up the telephone and jumped back through the portal. Once on the other side, he disconnected both resonators and waited for Randolph to get back.

An hour later, Randolph appeared with the resonators, and Roman wired them up. The time frame was up and running. It was connected to a fully charged lorry battery, and Roman had programmed the date coordinates in. Roman was confident of getting the correct day but didn't know if it would be morning or night-time when they would appear in the past. He was anxious that Roger or someone else would be on the other side to help, especially since Randolph had now taken to wearing a butcher's knife in his trouser waistband, which he had stolen from Roman's house. The pair had driven to Oxford, and Roman had filled his car with electrical items that he had bought on his credit card. Randolph was happy. He kept singing and whistling the Ginger Rogers performance song, "We're in the money." He was finding it hard to contain his excitement, especially since he now had plans to make his own time machine in his pocket. Unbeknownst to him, Roman had not written down the correct digital coordinates, so if Randolph did try to go back in time. He would disappear in oblivion.

It was time to step through the time frame. Randolph was growing ever more suspicious of Roman and was starting to distrust him more as time grew closer. There was a pile of various electrical items stacked beside the frame. These included a digital television, digital radios, a microwave oven, a couple of laptops, and various other electronic items. They were all still in their packaging and still in the boxes. Randolph had started to gently throw the boxes through the frame, and he watched them disappear on the other side. When they had all gone, he called Roman over. Roman was apprehensive but slowly walked over. Randolph quickly grabbed Roman and twisted his arm behind his back. With his other hand, he took the knife out of his waistband.

"You're coming with me," he hissed. "Just in case there's an army of cavemen on the other side." They stepped through the frame together.

Randolph and Roman appeared through the portal door. Randolph still had Roman's arm twisted behind his back and the knife blade pressed against Roman's neck.

"It had better be 1944," Randolph threatened. "Your life depends on it."

Roman nodded but didn't say anything. A voice called out loudly from the shadows.

"Drop the weapon, George Woodford." said Roger Neeve, stepping forward.

For a brief second, Randolph looked confused. He started to protest that he wasn't George Woodford when a shot rang out and a small hole appeared in his forehead. His head jerked backwards, and his body followed. He lay motionless on the floor.

"Nice work!" said Mick to Steve.

"We aim above the mark, to hit the mark," grinned Steve, quoting Ralph Emerson. He walked over to Randolph's dead body.

"Who's he?" he said, pointing his pistol at Roman.

"He's one of us," replied Roger. "We used him as bait."

"Okay!" came the reply.

Steve was now standing over the dead body. He turned 180 degrees and fired his pistol into the brick wall. He then knelt beside the body and put the pistol in the dead man's hands.

"Can you deal with it from here," said Mick. "It was self-defence. You won't have any problems. We'll get our gear, pick up John from London, and get back. We will be back in France this time tomorrow."

"Yes, no problem," said Roger. "I'll sort it. Have a good trip." He shook both men's hands. "Bon Voyage."

The men disappeared through the door that they had come in through. Roger watched their car start up and drive away. "You can come out now, George," he said. George stood up from behind a wooden crate that he had been hiding behind.

Roger took a small ink pad out of his pocket. "Press your thumb and forefinger into the ink pad and put your prints onto this paper pad." He said to George. "This is evidence that you died here today. The SAS guys will be debriefed when they get back, and they will back up my story. I will tell Brass that I came back to the workshop later in my car. I'll say I put your body in the boot, tied some heavy iron printing machinery around your body, and then dropped you off the bridge into the river. This will tie up any loose ends if you pardon the pun."

Roman looked at the body and then at George. "Give me a hand to throw this stuff back through." Roger came over to Roman.

"You okay?" he asked, looking at Roman's bruised face.

"I am now, thanks to you. He was going to kill me," he said, looking at Randolph's body. "You obviously got my message. Who were the other two guys?"

"SAS," said Roger, "Who is he?"

"He's from this time. A bent copper," said Roman. "He wanted all this stuff and more. He wanted to be a millionaire." He bent down and took his time frame drawings out of Randolph's pocket and put them into his own. "All the digital electronic stuff will be fried, and so it will never work. The time frame does that to high-end electronics. But I will leave you with the microwave cooker, the electronic alarm clock, the kettle, and all the other stuff. That will all work. You might need to change the plugs on them, though. You can patent it all. It will make you rich. Also, take this money," said Roman, taking a large bundle of notes out of Randolph's pocket. "He made me give it to him. It's all dated around this time or earlier. I can't spend it on myself, so take it and treat the wife to something nice. It's not a bribe or anything; it's just that you can use it and I can't. Please accept it with all my thanks. You saved my life."

George had thrown the rest of the packages back through the portal doorway. Roman figured that he could return these items to the shops that he had bought them from for a refund or replacement. The three men stood there and said their goodbyes. Roman and George both shook Roger's hand.

"Until next time!" said George to Roger.

"There won't be a next time," interrupted Roman as he and George stepped into the twenty-first century.

Back in their own time, outside of the printing workshop, George tried to start a conversation with Roman.

"We should go into partnership. We'd be millionaires. We can rule this town. The whole of Oxfordshire, probably. We can live like kings. I've got a proposition for you. I've got a few ideas. I'll contact Tony and Morgan, and—"

Roman interrupted him. "Tony, Eddie, Morgan, and Clem are all dead," said Roman. "They were all involved in the death of my father. I want you to stay away from my mother, and if you contact her again, the same thing will happen to you. Just go away and get on with your life and forget everything that's happened. After a few months, you'll think that you dreamt it all anyway."

With that, they parted company. George smiled to himself. "If the boy thought that this was the end, then he was mistaken. He was connected, and he wanted a share of what was rightly his. He had earned it. He had nearly been killed. It was only his honed survival instincts that had kept him alive. He should be the one dipping in and out of the past. He should be the one sending his enemies back in time. Well, he was back, and he was back with a vengeance."

Chapter 21
George Climbs the Ladder

A few days after returning to the present, George was locked in thought. There was a massive rift between him and Roman, and this needed to be settled, or at least have the appearance of being settled, if he was to gain the boy's trust. They would have to bury the hatchet. He had seen Roman take the time machine plans off Randolph's dead body, and so he knew that there was a set of plans out there for the taking. He had also noticed how calmly Roman had taken the money from Randolph's corpse. Roman never batted an eyelid. *I expect that he will have nightmares every night,* thought George. George needed three things.

Money, power, and the time machine. He knew that his friends wouldn't believe him if he told them about the machine, and if they did, they would take it for themselves. He needed someone who would work under him to do his bidding. The trouble was that he was currently *below* the bottom rung of the criminal ladder, and there weren't many people below him. He decided that he absolutely needed to start climbing the rungs.

There were a couple of drug addicts that George knew who would shoplift in shops and sell the stolen goods for cash to buy drugs. George decided to put his orders in. He had been round Roman's mums to pick up his possessions at a time when he knew she wouldn't be in. Whilst there, he stole her rental money from the tin in the pantry, before locking up and replacing her spare key under a brick in the front garden. He drove the drug addicts to a designer clothes shop just outside of Oxford and told them what he wanted and the sizes that he wanted the clothes to be. One of the addicts, the decoy, had been challenged and had run out of the shop. The other walked out a few minutes later with the stolen property.

George paid him and dropped him off in Oxford on the way back to his bedsit. "Clothes maketh the man," said George to himself as he convinced himself that he had reached that little bit higher to the bottom rung.

Ruth had phoned Roman the day after George had picked up his clothes. She told him that George had used the spare key to get in and had stolen her rent money. Roman arranged for a locksmith to go round and change the locks in case George had made a copy of the key. He also paid the rent payment for his mum. Once again, he offered to let her live with him, but once again, she refused. Roman put it down to her pride. Roman knew that George wouldn't let things lie. He was greedy, lazy, and untrustworthy. Now, after travelling backwards through time, he wouldn't be satisfied until he could time travel whenever and wherever he wanted, especially as now, he could see the potential in taking modern stuff back to the past to flog or claim to have invented.

He knew that George would need help in whatever he decided as his next move, and he knew that he would have to watch George closely so that he could intervene before any of George's schemes went too far.

After trailing George for a few days, it became apparent that George was once again mixing with the local criminal fraternity. These were different people from Tony's old entourage, but they vaguely knew George and knew which side of the law he stood on. George met the two addicts daily and told them what they needed to steal and how much he would pay for the stolen items. He then took the stolen goods down to the pub and sold them. This didn't bring him much money, but to the criminals in the pub, it proved that he did have at least some connections, and so they accepted him into the fold. George kept quiet about the time machine, but he would need help if he was going to abduct Roman and force him to build him a time machine, and these people had ready access to muscle, and they wouldn't think twice about using torture to get what they wanted.

Over the next few weeks, George became a runner and then an enforcer for the drug gang. He was working his way up the criminal ladder faster than he could ever have imagined. Roman watched this ascendance from a distance. George's friends didn't know Roman, and this made it easier for him to observe the group, so long as George wasn't amongst them. He identified the main men, Moss and his brother, Nobby, and he also got to know the group's habits. They all tended to meet at the pub lounge on a Thursday night for a pub meal and then drink in the bar afterwards. Roman dusted off his black wig and thick-rimmed spectacles, put on his hoodie, and then travelled to the pub. He sat in the corner of the bar in a position where he could observe George and the rest of his group.

Around an hour after the meal, George stood up and made his way to the toilet. As soon as he was out of sight, Roman walked towards the group. He made it seem as if he was going to walk straight past them when he suddenly stopped at George's empty chair and reached underneath the seat. He produced the mobile phone that he had been concealing in his hand and placed it on the table. He then carried on past the group and walked out of the exit door and into the car park. The phone looked identical to George's phone, complete with a cannabis leaf motif on the front. It was easily identifiable as George's phone. A text message came through almost immediately. It said:

"Try to get them to talk about the drug deals."

Nobby, who was seated next to George's seat, read the message out of curiosity. When he read it, he showed it to Moss. The boss had just finished reading it and put it back down on the table as George made his way back to his seat.

"You dropped your phone, mate," said Nobby.

For a couple of seconds, George looked confused. "It's not mine," he said, pulling his mobile phone out of his pocket. "It does look like mine, though."

"Why do you have two phones, George?" said a man sitting opposite. "You got a bit on the side?" The group started laughing.

"It's not mine," repeated George. "Where did it come from?"

"It was under your seat. Someone walked by and picked it up and put it on the table," said Nobby. "Perhaps it's not yours then. A bit of a coincidence, though, having the same phone with the same leaf on the front."

George shrugged. "Stranger things have happened," he said.

The meeting ended early, and nobody went to the bar area afterwards. George got into his car, and drove home. He would have liked to have kept the phone as a spare, but 'Moss the Boss' had claimed it. Moss was sitting in his car scrolling through the call and message history on the phone. There was no history except for the one solitary message. He put the phone in his pocket and decided to keep it fully charged at home in case any other messages came through. He also decided to ask around to see if anyone knew of George's background.

George was now somebody. In the grand scheme of things, he was still at the lower levels, but at least he wasn't at the bottom. He now had runners doing his bidding and commanded at least some respect. He had decided to keep an eye on

Roman's movements so that he could formulate his plan of attack, but unfortunately, Roman never seemed to be anywhere that George thought he should be at the times George thought he should be. He had gone around to Roman's cottage on various occasions to observe Roman's routines but had failed to find him on every occasion. What he didn't know was that on these occasions, he himself was being observed by Roman, who was formulating his own plan of attack. Roman knew that George would make his move imminently.

It was Thursday night, and George and the rest of the gang were eating their meals in the pub. Moss, still harbouring suspicions about George, didn't speak as freely around George as he used to, but he listened to George's conversations and carefully observed his actions. Midway through the meal, a voice came from George's pocket.

"Get them to talk about the money," it said. Everyone at the table heard it, including George, who looked around the room innocently.

"It came from your pocket, George," said Moss, pointing at George's coat pocket.

George put his hand into his pocket and pulled out a small wireless Bluetooth speaker. It was black in colour and wasn't much bigger than a fifty pence piece. He looked at it carefully. He didn't know what it was or to whom it belonged, but he started to feel the suspicion being directed at him from the other people sitting around the table.

"It's not mine," he said. "What is it?" He studied it more closely. He shook it, but no other sound came from it. He put it on the table, and Moss picked it up. He looked it over and then put it in his pocket. "I'll get someone to have a look at it," he said.

The meeting finished early again, and the group began leaving the pub and going their separate ways. Moss had a quiet word with Nobby, and Nobby stayed behind. When George headed for his car, Nobby headed to his. Roman, watching from behind his parked car, realised at once that Nobby was going to follow George's car in his own car. As George pulled out of the pub car park, with Nobby a few seconds behind, George's mobile phone rang. The number was withheld.

"George Woodford?" said the posh voice.

"Yes," said George.

"Hi, it's Kevin at the front desk at the police station on Kimble Street. Have you lost your wallet by any chance? Only a black leather wallet has been handed in, and it says G Woodford in gold lettering across the front. There are no cards or identification in there, but it contains around five hundred pounds in cash. We were wondering if it's yours, and if so, can you swing by and pick it up? Bring some identification. I'm at the front desk until 10:00 pm."

George replied that he had lost a wallet matching that description with that amount of money in it, and he asked how the police had obtained his mobile phone number. He was told that it was on file for some reason, but he wasn't a policeman, so he didn't know why. George said that he would swing by immediately and made a mental note to swap this phone for a burner phone. Nobby was still following George at a discreet distance and was surprised to see George swing into the police station car park and then enter the station through the front door. He sat across the road and observed George take a credit-sized card out of his wallet before stepping through the station door. He phoned his brother to explain the situation.

"He's parked up at the police station and walked in through the main entrance." He said. "He took a card out of his wallet first. I don't know what it was. Yes, it could have been a warrant card, but he was too far away for me to see. He's been in there for about five minutes. Hang on, he's coming out now. He's alone. He looks angry about something. I will keep following him and phone you again later." Nobby followed George home and then parked up around the corner to phone Moss again.

"He's home. He's locked his car up, so I think that's him for the night. What do you think?"

"He's either fuzz or a grass," replied Moss. "We don't know how much he's blabbed but we better calm it down around him. Change the routine and cool it for a bit. We'll need to move the stuff, though. I think the best bet will be to discredit him before anyone gets lifted; that way, his testimonial won't hold water."

"Yeah, I agree," said Nobby. "Leave it with me."

George sat in his room. He had been angry with the woman at the front desk in the police station at first, and it was only afterwards, that he realised he had been set up for a joke by some of the other lads that he had been out with that night. They had obviously planted the black thing in his pocket, and they had called him to tell him to pick up the wallet from the police station. It all made sense now. The police wouldn't have his mobile phone number, no more than they would hand over five hundred pounds without doing checks first. The posh voice gave it away too. Nobody spoke with that accent anymore. It was like something from a Pathe News film.

He thought about who had made the call and arrived at the conclusion that it was Rick. Definitely. Rick fancied himself as a comedian and was always having a sly dig at him. I bet the others were all listening in to the call and laughing their heads off. At one point during the conversation, it did sound like someone had sniggered. Well, he would repay the compliment when he saw Rick next Thursday at the pub. He smiled to himself as he plotted his revenge.

Work was unusually quiet, and so George decided to concentrate his energy on kidnapping and torturing Roman into building him a time machine. He had acquired a stun gun as part payment of a drug debt, and he had bought a roll of curtain wire and a clown mask. He wasn't quite ready to carry out the kidnapping, though, as he still hadn't discovered Roman's lifestyle routine, so he stuffed these under his car's back seat. He drove past Roman's house just as Roman was pulling into his drive. George parked down the road and observed Roman carrying electrical items from his car.

These looked like the component parts of the time machine. It looked to George like Roman was going to store them in his garden shed or set up the time machine in his back garden. Either way, they would be easy for him to steal if he entered the garden through the rear garden hedge. He would wait until it was dark and then come back.

It was dark, damp, foggy, and George had squeezed through a gap in Roman's rear garden hedge. As he thought, the time machine was set up in Roman's garden. George walked around it. It looked complete and identical to the machine that he had been through. The copper wires around the frame buzzed slightly in the damp air as the electric current from the car battery flowed through them. George thought about stepping through the door frame but thought better of it. Until he had tortured Roman into telling him how the machine worked, he didn't want to risk being stuck in the past again. He wondered if Roman had travelled back in time and was there now. He hoped so.

He disconnected the live wire from the battery terminal, and the machine went silent. He laughed out loud. Either way, Roman was done for in the past or he wasn't, but he had the machine anyway. He started to dismantle it and carried the parts back to his parked car in a field gateway just down the road from Roman's house.

George didn't want to bring the items through Roman's front garden in case Roman *was* home and spotted him. It was safer all around to carry the parts through the field behind Roman's house and get to his car that way. It would take longer between journeys, but it would be safer.

Nobby had followed George in his car and watched from a safe distance as George parked up and climbed over the field gate. He waited for fifteen minutes and observed George appear with a wooden doorframe at the gate and lift it over to his car. He then opened up the hatchback door and slid the frame in across the seats. He then climbed back over the gate again and disappeared. Fifteen minutes later, George reappeared with the car battery. It was heavy, and George was using both hands to carry it. He opened the passenger door and placed it on the seat, then closed the door and climbed back over the gate. Nobby couldn't see what George was carrying from where he was parked, so he decided to walk down to George's car and take a look. He reckoned he had around fifteen minutes before George got back to his car again.

As he walked towards the car, the interior light came on for a couple of seconds and then went off again. He stopped and pressed his back into a hedge. It was almost as if someone had briefly opened a door and then closed it again, but he couldn't see anyone at the car, and he hadn't seen George climb back over the gate. He carried on walking towards the car, all the time, keeping a lookout for George returning across the field. He opened the passenger door, which was nearest to him, to find a car battery on the seat. There was a box on the driver's seat as well. He walked around the car and opened the driver's door.

The box on the seat was gift-wrapped, but the top hadn't been closed. On the attached tag was written: "To Moss the Boss. Congratulations. From a friend." Nobby flipped open the lid and jumped backwards in shock. Inside the box was a ticking alarm clock, wired to three tubes that were each wrapped in brown paper. Each tube had 'TNT' stencilled on it. Nobby closed the box lid and the car door. He ran towards his own car and drove off at speed.

George arrived at his car a few minutes later, carrying the last of the machine component parts. He was putting them on the back seat when he realised that the interior light was already on before he opened the rear door. He closed that door and walked around the car to try the other doors. He immediately discovered that the driver's door had been left ajar. He looked around the car and then inside the car. Nothing was amiss. He reasoned that he must have left it open; the time machine parts were all still there, and so he climbed into the driver's seat and started the car. He drove back home and unloaded the contents into his bedsit.

Nobby phoned Moss as soon as he was out of the area. He explained how he had followed George to an empty field where George had stored some stuff. Other than the doorframe and the car battery, he didn't know what the other stuff was. He explained the gift of dynamite wired to an alarm clock, hidden in a gift box addressed to Moss. At this point, Moss interjected.

"Dynamite?" he asked loudly. "George was taking things to another level!" They had to work fast. They couldn't kill him if he was an undercover cop. They would be first on the list of suspects. They had never killed anyone before anyway and were bound to make a mistake somewhere down the line that would lead to prison time. No, they had to think things out rationally. George had obviously gone rogue. Moss had read about undercover cops who had been undercover for so long that they had convinced themselves that they were actual criminals. What was George trying to do? Take over the drug empire that they had built up? Moss needed time to think. What was the copper-wired doorframe all about? Did George actually think that he could replace Moss's front door with an exploding doorframe? His wife and kids were home every day. It can't be done covertly. What if the exploding doorframe was for Nobby's house? Nobby lived alone. It was all falling into place now. George was going to assassinate the pair of them and take over their drug empire.

It was Thursday morning, and George was walking back from the corner shop with his newspaper. He did this every day, around the same time. He passed some children playing with a football in their front garden as he headed back to his bedsit. A few seconds later, a football overtook him and rolled to a stop.

"Hey mister!" said a blonde-headed boy, aged around twelve years old. "Kick the ball back, please."

George reached the ball and positioned his body as if he was going to hoof it back to the boys, but at the last minute, he side-footed the football into the path of an oncoming car. The car ran over the ball and burst it with an audible "pop." George laughed at the boys' shocked faces.

"You did that on purpose, you tosser," shouted the blonde-headed boy to George. One of the younger boys knew George's Christian name from hearing someone greet him outside of the paper shop and started shouting 'Georgy Porgy pudding and pie' after him. Various insults were then shouted at George by the other two boys as well. George stopped and turned around to the boys.

"Take this as a valuable lesson learned," shouted George in reply. "Life is cruel." With that, he laughed, turned around, and carried on down the road for another fifty metres, until he reached the front entrance door of the house containing his bedsit. He walked inside. The boys whose football George had popped all watched George enter the house with angry interest.

"I think it's time for Operation Insect Farm," said Alan, the blonde-headed boy, to the others. They nodded in agreement. "Go inside and get some plastic bags, and we'll go hunting." The boys did go hunting for about an hour, but all they found was a few woodlice, a couple of spiders, and a centipede. It wasn't nearly enough to post through George's letterbox and get a reaction. They decided to change tack.

"I know where there's a dead rat," said Alan. "The cat killed it. It's half-eaten, but we can push that through his letterbox."

"My hamster died a few weeks ago," said another boy. "We put it in a shoebox and buried it in the garden. I could dig that up."

"My sister's got a pet rabbit," said another boy. "I could kill that."

"I'm not sure about that," said Alan. "Your sister will know that it's gone, won't she?"

"Yes, but she did have two," replied the boy. "But she cuddled the other one too much and strangled it. I could strangle this one and leave the cage open. She will think that it's been nicked, or it's escaped, Mum will buy her another one."

"Okay," said Alan. "Chris," he said to the youngest boy in the group. "You just dig up some worms."

"I know where there's a dead deer," replied Chris. "It's a baby deer. I saw it on the side of the road when Mum took me to school yesterday. I could fetch that."

"Wouldn't it be too heavy?" said Alan, thoughtfully.

"I will bring half of it then," said Chris. "I know where Dad keeps his saw."

The boys disappeared and reappeared two hours later. The dead animals were put into one plastic bag, which was then doubled and triple-bagged to stop the juices from dripping out. The half deer filled most of the bag, and this smelled the worst, not least because Chris had vomited a couple of times over the deer when he was sawing it in half. Alan squashed everything down and then tore out a couple of pages from an old 'Sooty and Sweep' comic. He wiped the blood off his hands on the pages, then screwed the paper up and threw that into the bag as well. The boys put in a few earthworms for good measure and then headed to George's place.

Alan and Ian, the second oldest boy, walked into the front reception and walked up to the man sitting there reading a newspaper.

"Is Uncle George in?" said Alan to the landlord. "Mum sent his shopping round."

"He's out," said the landlord. "He's usually back around teatime."

"Can we leave his shopping outside of his front door?" said Alan. "My arm's aching."

"No, it will get nicked if you just leave it there," replied the landlord. "Bring it upstairs, and I will unlock his door, and you can leave it in his room."

The two boys followed the landlord up the stairs and stopped outside George's room.

"Just put it down there," said the landlord as he unlocked the door and pushed it open.

As the door swung open, the other boy shouted. "What's that?" pointing to something on the carpet behind the landlord's back.

"What's what?" said the landlord, looking at where the boy was pointing.

The boy walked over to a spot on the carpet and stamped his foot down on the floor. "It was just an ant," said the boy.

The landlord turned back towards the flat door just as Alan was walking out.

"All done," said Alan to the landlord as he pulled the entrance door closed. During the distraction, he had emptied the contents of the bag onto the carpet beside George's bed. With any luck, George would get into bed in the dark and put his bare feet on the animal bodies. The boys said their thank-yous and walked out of the building.

Thursday night arrived, and George was in a good mood at the pub meeting. Moss and Nobby couldn't make the meeting until later, but they had told everyone there to wait for them at the pub as they would be back with a small cash dividend for each group member, the proceeds of a large successful drug sale, and on top of that, the meal would be paid for by the two brothers also. The group was told to eat, drink, and make merry until they arrived. George and the group didn't need telling twice. George had brought the doorframe and the rest of the electrical components with him in his car.

Midway through the meal, he intended to set up the time machine in the car park and invite Rick through it. Rick would disappear. George might not be able to bring him back, but that was part of the plan. The ultimate joke. The others would think that George and Rick had concocted the joke between themselves, and Rick would reappear later. George would calmly pack the 'props' away afterwards. He laughed to himself as he thought about Rick wandering around in the 1940s.

George left the meal and went out to his car. Roman sat in his car at the other end of the car park and watched as George set up the time portal. Unbeknownst to George, the machine would never work. Most of the electrical parts had been removed from the electrical components, leaving only the basic digital clocks still working. When George walked back into the pub to collect the others, Roman ran over and removed all the electrical parts and cut the copper wire from around the door frame. He had just gotten back to his car when George and the others exited the pub. They walked over to the frame, and George let out an angry bellow. All the copper and metal parts had been stolen. Someone was obviously out to make a couple of quid for the scrap value of the metal. He swore and kicked the doorframe. The frame toppled over.

George was over the drink-drive limit when he got into his car at the end of the night. He was still angry. As he put his key into the ignition, two uniformed policemen walked up to his car door and tapped on the window. They asked him to step out of the car. As one policeman breathalysed George, the other searched his car. He discreetly called for backup when he found the stun gun, the clown mask, and the roll of curtain wire under the back seat.

On top of the back seat, but under a coat, was a paper folder with a ream of printed papers inside. The papers detailed the comings and goings of a young male bank employee. The police officer flicked through the pages and then showed them to the arresting officer.

"He was getting set to kidnap a bank cashier," said the policeman. "There's the boy's home address and photos of him and his house. Even a method of cutting off the boys' fingers if the bank didn't cough up with the dough. There's even a typed letter demanding twenty thousand pounds from the bank. We'll charge him with drink driving now and let the CPS decide on the charges of stun gun possession and the conspiracy to kidnap."

George started to protest. He genuinely had never seen the paper folder before, and he didn't know how it had gotten into his car. He realised that he was between a rock and a hard place. The gun, wire, and mask were going to be used in an abduction. But not that one. He didn't know anything about that one. But on the other hand, he couldn't admit to the real one either. He shut his mouth and told the policemen that he needed to speak to a solicitor. At the station, George's car was given a more thorough search. Underneath the spare wheel were the clock and dynamite combination. The station was evacuated whilst the army bomb squad came over to diffuse the bomb. It was revealed to be a hoax, with the three tubes actually being cardboard confectionary tubes filled with foam. However, this was deemed as being part of the kidnapping plot, and so the fake bomb was admitted as evidence.

Moss and Nobby pulled up outside the house that contained George's bedsit. Moss opened the rear car door, and a beautiful lady stepped out. Over her shoulder, she had a large handbag, and in her hands, she had a bottle of champagne and a bunch of flowers. She walked through the front door and walked over to a man sitting on a chair, attempting a crossword puzzle.

"Excuse me!" she said to the man. "Can you do me a favour and unlock George Woodford's front door? He's my boyfriend."

The man looked at the woman. *George was definitely punching above his weight with this one,* he thought. "I'm not supposed to let anyone into someone's room," he said. "Without authorisation from the rent payer."

"Oh, it's a birthday surprise," she said. "I'm going to sprinkle these rose petals on the bed and pour out two glasses of bubbly. When he opens the door and walks in, he will get his birthday surprise. Me. Waiting for him. Naked on the bed. What more can a girl do." She giggled.

The man looked at the girl and then at the flowers and champagne. Nothing like this had ever happened to *him* in all of his sixty years on this planet. He led the woman upstairs and opened George's door with the spare key. The woman stepped inside the room, turned around to the man, and blew him a kiss. "Don't let on when he gets back," she said as the man exited the room.

As soon as the door closed, the woman put on a pair of rubber gloves and slid the floor mat to one side to reveal the bare floorboards. She looked for the floorboard that was eighteen inches long and wasn't nailed down. She lifted the board up by prying a spoon handle under one side and easing it up. The board came out, revealing a wad of cash, a wristwatch, and a few small packets of cocaine. There was also a small bag of cannabis in there. She walked over to her handbag and took out a plastic bag with a kilogramme of cocaine inside it.

She carefully wrapped this bag in a newspaper that was displaying that day's date. This would scupper George's defence if he said the drugs had been in the room before he moved in. She placed the bag into the void. She then took out some small electronic weighing scales and placed them into the hole as well. She also finished up by stuffing a handful of one-gramme plastic bags into the hole. She then replaced the floorboard and put the mat back over it.

She had been conscious of a horrible smell in the room from the moment that she had walked in. She wondered what George had been smoking to leave such an unpleasant smell. How could he even sleep in this room? She wanted to go outside for some fresh air, and she was about to walk out of the room when she noticed the head and half body of the deer beside the bed. She slowly walked over and retched when she saw the half-eaten rat, the maggot-infested hamster, and the dead rabbit. All with worms crawling over them. She opened the door and looked outside. Nobody was about and so after closing the door behind her, she ran to the secondary exit door that led down another staircase, which terminated at the house's back door. The door was locked, but the key was in the lock. She opened it and ran around to Moss's car. She climbed in and blurted out in a panic.

"He's been eating dead animals," she said, trying to get the words out without panicking. "There's a dead deer beside his bed. He's eaten half of it. There's a dead rat as well. I swear, I can see the bite marks on it. He's eaten its insides and then puked up on the floor. There are dead mice and rabbits as well. He's a psychopath!"

Moss shuddered. This was more serious than he thought. George had always seemed so normal.

"He's one sick man," said Nobby. "Did he cook the animals first?"

"No," replied the girl. "He's eaten them raw. He's eaten the back half of the deer, organs an' all."

"Has he been eating the rabbit?" said Nobby.

"No," replied the girl. "He hasn't touched that. Well. Not in that way anyway."

Moss shook his head. "We gotta get rid. ASAP," he said. "If he's capable of that, he's capable of anything."

Nobby made a phone call to the group, saying that they were on their way. He then phoned a police contact that he knew and advised him of George's address and what they might find there if they got round there sharpish.

At the police station, things were going from bad to worse for George. The police had executed a search warrant on George's bedsit and had found the kilo of cocaine, the plastic bags, and the electronic scales. This was a massive find, and the press were invited along to take photos of the drugs and drug paraphernalia. The press was more concerned with the half-eaten animals, though.

"You can see his teeth marks where he's been gnawing on the rat," said the landlord to the press reporter. "The carpet's ruined."

"And I had him down as an animal lover," said the landlord's wife. "It just goes to show, you never know. Now I think back, it was strange how he looked at my cat. It was almost as if he *desired* it."

"We discovered earlier that the back door had been left unlocked," said the landlord. "That's where the bins are. I expect that's where he's been getting the rats from. God knows how long he's been killing and eating animals in this room."

"He makes my skin crawl," interjected the landlady, visibly shuddering.

"The dead rabbit looks like a domestic rabbit," said the policeman, gently moving it with his shoe. "It doesn't look wild. I'll put a call out to see if anyone has had their pet rabbit nicked recently. I reckon he's been prowling around in people's gardens, scavenging for food."

"Look at the pages of the comic next to it," said the landlord. "He's been reading stuff about puppets. You don't think he was going to turn the rabbit into a glove puppet, do you?"

"It certainly looks that way," replied the policeman.

Upon hearing this, the landlady gave out a small scream and said that she was feeling faint. She left the room. George was re-interviewed by the police about the contents of his flat. The policeman who interviewed him was slightly worried for his own safety. George looked normal, but…He wondered if he could have George fitted with a muzzle for the duration of the interview, or would that violate George's human rights? He had rearranged the furniture slightly in the interview room so that it was easier for him to hit the panic button on the wall if George lunged for his throat. He tightened his shirt collar to make it harder for George to get to his neck.

George was refused bail and was told by his solicitor that he had been caught bang to rights and so should enter a guilty plea for a reduced prison sentence. George flatly refused to do this at first, but the evidence mounting against him was so strong that a not guilty verdict seemed highly unlikely. George especially protested his innocence about the kilo of cocaine and the story that had made the front page of the local newspaper, claiming that he had been killing and eating uncooked wild animals in his bedroom. The headlines to the story were: "The Wolf-man's Lair: Where the Deer Hunter meets the Pied Piper." The newspaper had claimed that George was the man who single-handedly turned more meat eaters into vegetarians than any amount of campaigning or crusading that the vegetarians did. George had also seen the photo of his bedroom in a newspaper.

He thought that it was obviously staged. It was more than likely the work of the police trying to fit him up. His bedroom looked nothing like that when he left the house. Another headline made the paper the following day. "George Woodford ate my hedgehog." A previous girlfriend of George had come forward and alleged that George had once eaten a hedgehog that was living at the bottom of her garden. She claimed that whilst George was living with her, she had gone to work, leaving George at home. When she returned that evening, the hedgehog was gone, and George had a plaster on his thumb. He had obviously pricked it on the hedgehog's spines. She hadn't confronted George about it at the time, "because George had a temper."

George eventually pleaded guilty and was sentenced to sixteen years in prison. He was never entirely sure of who had set him up, but he strongly suspected Roman of being involved somewhere down the line.

Chapter 22
All's Well That Ends Well

Roman was sitting at the kitchen table when there was a knock at the front door. He opened the door to find Alan Bates, Eddie Monkton's business rival, standing there. He was holding a leather briefcase. Roman invited him into the house. They both walked into the kitchen, and Alan put the briefcase on the table. Roman pulled out a chair from the table's edge and gestured for Alan to sit down. Alan opened the briefcase to reveal bundles of twenty-pound notes, all arranged neatly inside.

"It's all there if you want to count it," said Alan, taking bundles out and stacking them on the table. "Two hundred thousand. As agreed,"

Roman let him stack the notes into separate piles and then stood up and collected two bottles of beer from the fridge. He opened them both and poured them into two glasses, then gave Alan one and took a sip out of the other.

"Come on then," said Alan. "I want to hear it from the horses' mouth."

"Well," said Roman. "Tony is dead, as you know. Tony was always going to die. He and Clem killed my father. They were dead men walking even before I came to you with this proposition. I had a plan in motion to take away everything that Tony loved, and it was working. I set Clem up so that Tony would kill him. Which he did. I then contacted Clem's family and told them that Tony was responsible for Clem's death. Clem's two cousins had come over from Jamaica to kill Tony, but Tony killed himself before they had a chance to."

"What on purpose?" said Alan.

"No, he wanted to kill me but ended up killing himself and Nick. They drowned when they smashed a hole through the workhouse basement wall and let the pond water flood in. They were electrocuted first, which rendered them unconscious, and then they drowned. It's a long story, and I won't bore you with the details. Suffice to say, at that time, Tony, Clem, and Nick were dead."

"What about Morgan?" said Alan. "I haven't seen him around for a while."

"He's dead as well," said Roman. "I grew to like him at the end. He actually saved my life when Eddie was going to kill me. I took care of his family financially, though. It was the least that I could do."

"How did he die?" said Alan.

"He died by poisoning." said Roman, thinking back to the glass of water that he had given Morgan whilst Morgan was recovering in bed from the tick bite. "I put a couple of drops of poison into a glass of water. He died a couple of days later. His family thought that he died from the tick bite."

"What about Eddie?" asked Alan. "I hope he suffered."

"No, it was quick," replied Roman, thinking back to the trap he set in the time frame. "I had stretched a length of fishing line across a door frame, around nine inches up from the ground. You couldn't see it and you couldn't avoid it if you didn't know that it was there. He caught his foot on it, on the way through the door frame and disconnected an electrical wire that was also connected to the fishing line. It's fair to say that he's gone forever. Floating around the universe with the angels."

"And Eddie's brother? He needs to be gone as well," said Alan.

"He's dead. He was executed in London," said Roman.

"What about that idiot that used to go with your mum? Is he out of the picture?" Said Alan.

"Yeah, he's doing time for a potential kidnap, of a bank employee." said Roman. "Unluckily for George, the bank employee was the nephew of a gangster in Manchester called Gino Turtelli. Gino has put a price on George's head. George won't see the year out."

"And what about Nick's cousin, Mick?" said Alan.

"Mick was a little trickier to pin down. But he's dead now as well," said Roman, thinking of Mick's broken body at the bottom of the lift shaft. "That's everyone gone that could stop your takeover of the businesses, and best of all, there are no ties back to you."

"Or you," replied Alan, finishing his beer. "Have you got the central heating on full? It's getting very hot in here. I'm starting to sweat."

"There's a couple of loose ends that I need to tidy up first," said Roman, ignoring Alan's question about the central heating being on. "For instance, I knew that you would never walk away from here and leave two hundred grand sitting on my table, no matter how well our deal turned out for you. I also know that there are two men in the car outside, waiting for you to leave the house and then come in to do me and get the money back."

Alan looked at Roman suspiciously. "Look, no offence. Give me the money back. You can keep twenty grand. That's a tidy sum. I swear I will leave here and drive away, and our paths will never cross again. You have my word on that."

Roman looked at Alan and smiled. "It's too late for that," he said. "The reason you're hot is because you've ingested poisoned beer. You couldn't even lift that empty briefcase, let alone walk out of here. You won't even be able to talk or breathe in a few minutes."

Alan tried to jump up from his chair but fell backwards onto the kitchen floor. He tried to reach into his jackets inside pocket to retrieve a revolver that he had hidden in there. He managed to grip the gun handle but dropped the pistol onto the floor. His legs went into spasms, and he writhed and gasped as he clutched at his throat, trying to force air into his lungs.

"As soon as you stop moving, I'm going to send your body back in time." said Roman, picking up the revolver from the floor. "Someone will eventually find you, but no one will know who you were. You should get a Christian burial, though, so that's a small comfort. I'm going to do the same with your two henchmen as well. Then I'm going to drive your car to the coast and drive my car back. As you can see, I've been planning this for a while."

Alan stopped moving, and Roman dragged him into the dining room. He had cleared the room of furniture. He had positioned a wooden doorframe just inside the room, tightly against the existing doorframe, so that whoever went into the room would have to pass through both door frames. He carried a wooden chair into the centre of the room and managed to lift Alan onto the chair. Alan had his back to the door, and upon looking through the doorway, it looked like Alan was asleep in the chair. Roman lifted the closed, empty briefcase and positioned it at the side of Alan's lifeless body. He then took the bundles of money off the table and placed them all in a kitchen cupboard. Roman then took a vial of red liquid, which looked suspiciously like blood, and poured a puddle onto the kitchen floor. He then laid down next to the blood and waited. He didn't have long to wait.

The front door quietly opened, and two men walked silently into the kitchen. One man gasped when he saw Roman's face-down body stretched out on the kitchen floor with a pool of blood coming from a supposed head wound.

"He's already done him," said one man to the other, looking around the room for Alan. He looked through the open dining room door and noticed Alan sitting on a chair with his back to the men. The other man took out a metal bar from inside his jacket. Without speaking, they silently walked up to Alan's back, and the man with the bar raised it above his head. He brought it down on Alan's head, hard. Alan's head tipped forward, but his body remained where it was seated. The man landed another blow, this time across the back of Alan's head, and Alan slid off the chair and onto the floor.

"Is he dead?" said the other man.

"He looks it," replied the other. "He looks like he was already dead."

"Get the case and let's get gone," said the other man. "Put the bar into the boys' hand, it will look like they both killed each other."

They both turned around to see a grinning Roman kneeling in the doorway. He was holding a red electrical wire a few inches away from the car battery terminal and pointing Alan's revolver at them with his other hand.

"Blimey," he said to the two men. "Talk about honour amongst thieves. Throw me your car keys." One of the men took the car keys out of his pocket and threw them behind Roman onto the kitchen floor.

"You two really are a nasty pair, aren't you?" carried on Roman. "I was going to press this wire onto here, and you two would go back in time to start a new life with your empty briefcase. I've now decided to remove this wire as well. This will send you somewhere where nobody wants to go."

The men took a couple of steps towards Roman and then disappeared. In fact, all three men had gone, and so had Roman's kitchen chair. Roman swore under his breath, Alan must have been touching the chair with his dead body still. He had totally forgotten that the chair would go as well, and he would now have to buy a replacement. Still, he had plenty of money in his cupboard to buy a completely new set of chairs and a table. He wiped the beetroot juice from the floor, then went outside and drove Alan's car away. Three hours later, he was back in his own kitchen with his own car parked in his driveway. He picked up a screwdriver and began dismantling someone's laptop to replace the battery and add more memory to their hard drive. He enjoyed his job.

Tomorrow, he would set up the time frame and take some medicine for the young girl at the orphanage. If it wasn't possible to get the medicine to her, he would arrange for the girl's release and bring her back with him to the twenty-first century. He wasn't sure what he was going to do from there, but he was sure that there was no way that he was going to leave her in the orphanage to die. Trying to arrange the release of his grandfather from the asylum would be trickier. This might not happen at all, especially with the mental state that the grandfather was in. Still, one person out of two was a positive result. He carried on unscrewing the hard drive casing on the laptop. To the outside world, he was just a mild-mannered computer repairman.